AF390633

———————

Mondrala Press wishes to thank all its friends, fans, patrons, and investors for making this book possible, and especially:

Ms. Randa Dumanian
Mr. and Mrs. Karol and Dagmara Maziukiewicz
de domo Sowul

without whose enthusiasm and open hearts this book could never have happened.

———————

Thank you for reading with me!

My micro-publisher, Mondrala Press, publishes English translations of great Polish books—books with a track record of international critical and commercial success but which, for political reasons, have never been published in English. And now, finally, they are!

I have grown up reading these books and I have been telling my American friends about them all my life. And my American friends have always asked: "When will you translate them so we can read them, too?"

And now, finally, I am doing it and I am delighted that I can finally share these books with you.

To see my newest titles, or to subscribe to my news, or just to say "Hi!" please visit:

WWW.MONDRALA.COM
THE GREATEST BOOKS YOU HAVE NEVER HEARD OF

Thank you for reading with me!

My micro-publisher, Mondrala Press, publishes English translations of great Polish books—books with a track record of international critical and commercial success but which, for political reasons, have never been published in English. And now, finally, they are!

I have grown up reading these books and I have been telling my American friends about them all my life. And my American friends have always asked: "When will you translate them so we can read them, too?"

And now, finally, I am doing it and I am delighted that I can finally share these books with you.

To see my newest titles, or to subscribe to my news, or just to say "Hi!" please visit:

WWW.MONDRALA.COM
THE GREATEST BOOKS YOU HAVE NEVER HEARD OF

MR WHEELS AND

THE TEMPLAR TREASURE

BY

ZBIG NIENACKI

TRANSLATED BY

TOM PINCH

©1966 The Estate of Zbigniew Tomasz Nienacki
©This English translation Ringel&Esch, SARL-S, 2024
Originally published in Polish in 1966 as *Pan Samochodzik i templariusze*.

Mondrala Press is an imprint of
Ringel & Esch, S.A.R.L.-S
www.mondrala.com

All rights reserved. No part of this book may be reproduced in any form whatsoever without permission in writing from the publisher, except for brief quotations in reviews.

ISBN epub and kindle: 978-2-919820-84-9
ISBN Paperback: 978-2-919820-85-6
ISBN Hardcover: 978-2-919820-86-3

Edited by Mondrala Press
Cover Design by Mondrala Press

TABLE OF CONTENTS

On Mr. Wheels

The discovery of an ancient document in Scotland reveals that the legendary treasure was buried in one of the Teutonic castles in Poland. It sets off a race between several groups of professional treasure hunters, some much less savory than others. Puzzles and mysteries galore, plus break-ins, robberies, and car chases, all in clean good old fun.

This is the first book in a Polish smash-hit series, wildly popular behind the Iron Curtain, which has spawned 160 (and counting!) fan fiction novels, comic books, radio plays, TV series, and cinematic releases, including most recently, a Netflix production (2023).

Unlike the English Sherlock Holmes or the French Inspector Maigret, the Polish Mr. Wheels does not track down serial killers or cannibals; he tracks down thieves, forgers, and smugglers of... art. All his mysteries come with fascinating historical and artistic background, plenty of action, a dose of humor, and opponents who are gentlemen criminals.

Zbigniew Nienacki was the pen name of Zbigniew Nowicki (1929-1994), a Polish novelist and dramatist from Łódź ("Wooj"). His budding career as a film script writer was interrupted in 1950, when, as a scholarship student at a Moscow film school, he committed an act described as "demonstrating anti-Stalin attitude" which resulted in expulsion and deportation. After his return to Poland, Nowicki cooperated fully with the Communist regime, was an active member of the Polish communist party, wrote articles criticizing the Solidarity movement, and wrote 26 novels, five plays, and six film scripts. He has won numerous awards and decorations, including the highest civilian order granted by the Polish government: *Polonia Restituta* in 1982.

An Important Note:
On the Spelling of Polish names

In this book, I use a phonetic spelling of Polish names.

Some of you may be familiar with the Polish script and may be surprised that I write "Helmno" instead of "Chełmno" or "Wooj" instead of "Łódź."

I do this because I have discovered that people unfamiliar with Polish script cannot pronounce these names, and because they cannot pronounce them, they cannot keep them straight. One of my readers put it best: "I can't keep track of who is who because they all have long names, and most start with an S."

Now, phonetic transcription of foreign names is a matter of course. Translators of Tolstoy write *Trubetskoy*, not *Трубецкой*. Translators of Chinese write *Li Bai*, not 李白. So, why not write *Helmno* instead of *Chełmno*? No spelling convention should ever stand in the way of a good book, right? As a translator and editor, I have the duty to make my books readable and fun, and I find that this phonetic spelling helps my British and American readers.

But for those of you who are familiar with the Polish script and would prefer to see it in this book, contact me via www.mondrala.com. We are preparing an edition of this book with Polish spelling.

An Important Note:
Old Prussians Versus New Prussians

Once upon a time, on the shores of the Baltic Sea, lived a pagan nation called the Prussians (the "Old Prussians"). Then, a Catholic religious order arrived from Palestine and exterminated them. In their place, the order brought German settlers. Over time, those settlers came to call themselves "Prussians," and their country became the "Kingdom of Prussia." This "new" Prussia went on to become a great military power and existed until the end of World War 2, when, by the decision of the victorious allies, it was dissolved and its territory divided between Poland and Russia.

When we speak of "Prussians" in this book, we mean the "Old Prussians."

From Your Translator:
The Knights Templar and The Teutonic Knights

You've probably bought this book because of the Knights Templar in the title. That order of warrior monks has played a huge role in the history of Western Europe, and its shocking destruction by Philip the Fair of France in 1307-1314 made a permanent mark on Western civilization. Every decade brings a dozen new books about the Templars, new films, podcasts, and documentaries, as well as numerous theories connecting the Templars with the Masons and the Rosicrucians, astrology, witchcraft, magic, Mary Magdalene, devil worship, gemology, aliens, and so forth.

But the Knights Templars had a brother institution—the Teutonic Knights—also an order of warrior-monks, also born in Palestine during the Crusades, and also as important. That order went on to play an equally important role in another part of the world: in Eastern Europe. While the Templars became Western Europe's richest bankers, the Teutonic Knights went a step further: they created an independent state. In the process, they eradicated whole nations—The Prussians, the Yotvingians, and the Kurs—and came very close to destroying several others, including Poland and Lithuania.

To see just how important the Teutonic state was in Eastern Europe, just look at the map below. It shows the present-day borders of Europe and, superimposed on them, the borders of the Teutonic State at the height of its power in AD 1410. It is no exaggeration to say that the destruction of the Teutonic Order in the battle of Grunwald on 15 July 1410 by the combined Polish and Lithuanian army was one of the watershed events in East European history.

The relations between the Knights Templar and the Teutonic Knights were close, if not always friendly; plans to unite the two institutions were floated several times. And the Teutonic decision to become an independent state was perhaps in part motivated by the destruction of the Templars in France: the Teutons saw how vulnerable a religious order was to its king and decided to have no king over them.

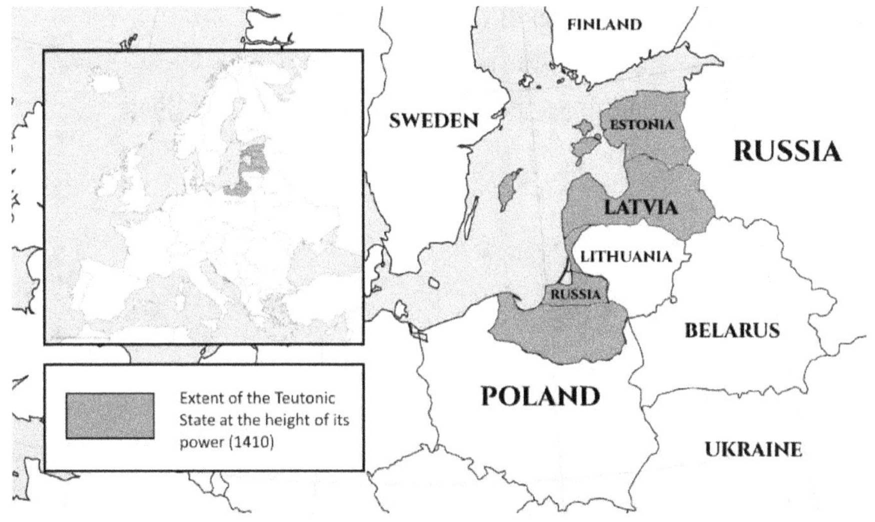

The Teutonic State in Eastern Europe circa 1410
The Teutonic State, a church organization with no ethnic basis of any sort, became a dominant power in Eastern Europe.

This book tells a tale of the legendary Templar treasure. This treasure was the reason why the King of France destroyed the Templars: he preferred to spend the money himself. Alas, he never found the treasure, and a persistent rumor has it that the treasure remains hidden and waiting to be discovered.

The departure point of this book is this: when the Knights Templar realized that the King of France was going to rob them, they sent a portion of their treasure to their Teutonic cousins in Poland for safekeeping.

And the rest, as they say, is history.

A Map of the "Land of Lakes"
of North-Eastern Poland
Showing Important Places Mentioned in this Book

Map of the North-East corner of Poland
showing the national boundary and the most important locations mentioned in this book

Two important notes:

1. The Village and Lake of **Milkokuk** (featured in the first part of this novel) is really the Village of Vilkokuk (Wilkokuk in Polish) and we know its location precisely.

2. The Village of **Kortumovo** is completely imaginary, and we place it on our map on the basis of various clues (such as driving distances) given in this book.

CHAPTER ONE: THE TREASURE

Is the Templar treasure in Poland? A mysterious document. The Society of Treasure Hunters. Captain Petersen and his proposal. The grand master of the Order of the Temple hides the order's treasures. A secret clue for Jacques de Molay.

At the end of June, at high noon, my doorbell peeled like there was no tomorrow. Reluctantly, I got up from my desk at which I had been poring over the history of the Templar Order. I opened the door and saw the friendly faces of my three Boy Scout friends: William Tell, Squirrel, and Hawkeye.

"Mr. Wheels! Mr. Wheels!" they called out. "A new adventure is in the works, right?"

Their faces expressed great excitement. They didn't even ask if I had time to talk. They packed right into the room and colonized my chairs.

"And what do you think? What do you think, Mr. Thomas?" William Tell asked, waving a newspaper.

I made an equivocal face.

"I haven't read today's press yet..."

"Then read it! An adventure! A new expedition in search of the golden fleece!" they called past each other. And they shoved into my hands the newspaper they had brought.

"But I have work to do...." I tried to object.

They raised an uproar:

"Mr. Thomas, what's happened to you? Don't you want to look for adventures? Are you happy to rest on your laurels? Enough with all those triumphs? Or are you afraid of a new challenge? We are not going to give up on the Templar treasure because of you, are we?"

"What's that?" I must have blushed. "Templar treasure? How do you know about that?"

"What do you mean: how do we know? From the *newspaper* you're holding in your hand!"

I glanced at the newspaper. Immediately, a title in bold type caught my eye:

IS THE TEMPLAR TREASURE IN POLAND?

I flushed hot and cold. Then, as I read the content of the published article, a feeling of anger rose in me.

"What a fool! What a bonehead! Oh, that I could lay my hands on him!" I shouted, slapping the unfolded newspaper. "Why did he write this?!"

The boys were very surprised.

"You suppose this is a fake story? You think that there is no Templar treasure in Poland?"

I went to the kitchen and had a drink of cold water. That calmed me down a bit. I said:

"I do not know if there are any Templar treasures in Poland. But millions of people read this newspaper. Of these millions, a few—perhaps a few dozen—will now decide to recover this priceless treasure. And such a search for treasure will begin that it gives me a shiver just to think about it. They will start drilling holes in all the old castles and digging up every square foot of their courtyards. They won't find the treasure, of course, because it may not be here at all—for all we know—but they will certainly make the search more difficult for those who want to take this matter seriously. That is why this article made me so angry."

"So you doubt this treasure is in Poland?" asked Tell.

"Oh, no. I don't think that," I replied wryly. "But this is an extremely complicated story."

Suddenly, Hawkeye stood up, came closer, and, for a moment, hovered around my desk, inspecting the books and journals spread out on the desk.

"Mr. Thomas," he said finally with grave seriousness. "Why are you trying to fool us? Us? The people who helped you find the Dunin collection? What does all this mean?" He pointed to the desk. "You've been reading about the Templars! And from the pile of notes I see here, you have been reading about them for some time."

Saying this, he ran his finger over the papers and triumphantly pointed to my notebook full of notes.

"In a word, you have been interested in the matter of the Templar treasure for some time, and you certainly know a lot about it. It seems clear, that you are preparing a new expedition. So let us be of a different opinion about the author of this newspaper article. Thanks to him, *we* learned about the treasure and thanks to him, we now learned that *you* intend to search for it without your associates."

"That's very disrespectful of you," Tell was deeply insulted.

I spread my hands helplessly:

"Alright. Well. You have caught me red-handed. Yes, that's right. I have been preparing for a new expedition to look for the Templar treasure. And I have not told you about it because I was afraid that you would want to take part in it. And I could not agree to that."

"And why? It's obvious that we have to take part in the expedition," Squirrel said indignantly.

I shook my head.

"No, boys. I like you very much, and I owe a lot to your vigilance and loyalty. But this expedition will be arduous and may even be dangerous. When we were looking for the Dunin collection, you were at a Boy Scout camp nearby and helped me by the way of your holiday. Now you're on holiday again, you will again go to camp, perhaps in some other part of the country. And besides, you need to rest before the new school year."

"Mr. Wheels! We beg you, spare us lofty speeches," groaned William Tell.

"Mr. Thomas," said Hawkeye. "We have anticipated all your objections. Here are our parents' written permissions. They entrust us to your care."

And all three took out of their pockets their parents' signed permissions to take part in my "expedition."

"Our parents will call you about it," said Squirrel.

"No, boys. This is impossible. You do not know the history associated with these treasures and do not realize the difficulties that lie before me. Plus, this expedition will probably end in a big fat nothing. You will have wasted your vacation."

I didn't want to look at their distraught faces and reached for the newspaper they had brought. This time, the last few sentences of the article—sentences that I had not noticed in my first cursory reading, jumped out at me.

"Dear God!" I jumped up from my seat. "I should have left already. This morning! They will beat me to it! And—shoot!—my car is in the shop!"

Fingers trembling with excitement, I dialed my phone.

"Mr. Roolka? I beg you, hurry up with the inspection of my car," I said tearfully into the phone. "I must have it today. Immediately! What?... Not until tomorrow morning? There is no way to do it faster?"

In despair, I hung up.

"What a nice start," I sighed. "Right out of the gate, I lose twelve hours. And, no, I'm not the only one who has read this article. Others are surely already on their way to Milkokuk".

The thoughts that now rushed through my head were not among the most cheerful. The boys were also gloomily silent, offended by my refusal. Finally, Hawkeye spoke up:

"If it weren't for us, perhaps your expedition would have been delayed not by a few hours but by a few days. You would probably have sat here hunched over your desk all day, and you may not even have read today's newspaper at all. We brought it to you, and that's how you found out that it was time to leave."

He was right. I looked at them gratefully.

"It's true. Very well, then, I will not move from the house at all and will finish with these materials first. So I am very grateful to you and thank you for your help. And while it is very sad, I cannot take you with me."

At that moment, my phone rang. William Tell's father was on the line.

"Are you really going on that expedition?" he asked. "When my son read that story in the newspaper, he immediately decided that you would definitely take part in the search for the Templar treasure. He forced me to give him my permission to go with you. Not only that, I had to call Squirrel's and Hawkeye's parents and persuade them to give their permission as well. Admittedly, the boys were due to leave for the Boy Scout camp the day after tomorrow, but under your supervision..."

"I don't really wish to take them because it will be a very tiring trip," I interrupted the doctor's speech.

"Tiring? Perhaps," agreed the doctor. "But you do realize that since that story with that collection, Dunin or whatever, the boys have improved in their studies? This year, they all had A's in history, they organized an anthropology circle at school, and the school principal is delighted with them. So, when my son said that you were going on a new expedition, I did not hesitate. After all, the boys are already quite grown up and very independent..."

"When I just..." I started.

"Ah, I see," said the doctor. "Do you think they will be in your way?"

"In my way?" I became indignant. "No! They helped me a lot with the Dunin collection. And now..."

"Oh, yes?" the doctor was very pleased. "In that case, I would very much like you to tell me how to equip our boys. They have a three-person tent, mattresses, sleeping bags, backpacks, a spirit stove. What else should they take with them? And when do you plan to leave?"

"Tomorrow morning," I groaned. "They should be here at daybreak."

I could not hear what else the doctor said because his words were drowned out by the tribal yell of the boys. They let out loud war whoops and gave each other powerful body slams. Then, they began to dance around my desk. I had to end the phone call quickly.

"Since everyone is against me, I have to give in," I said. "Let's go together then. Tomorrow at dawn, we start our search of the Templar treasure."

And now there was a complete silence. The faces of the boys became suddenly serious. This was perhaps the best indication of their suitability as my fellow explorers. The moment I made the decision to take them along, they realized they stood before an extraordinary adventure. They were going to face challenges and perhaps dangers that no one could foresee. They had to be vigilant, serious, and responsible.

"Do I bring my crossbow?" William Tell asked quietly.

I nodded. Hawkeye said:

"The newspaper article annoyed you but did not surprise you. This means that you already knew about this treasure business. And therefore you probably know more about this story than is written in the newspaper. If we are to be of any help to you, we also should know more than we can read in the newspaper."

The others joined in:

"Yeah. Like, who were The Knights Templar?"

"And—what would be a good place to start?"

"It's a very long story," I said. "It will take a couple of hours and we do have to leave tomorrow morning. But it will be a long drive because we will go all the way to Milkokuk, so I will have plenty of time to tell you about it on the way. Right now, I have to pack and pick up the car from the shop. You, too, should prepare for the expedition. I don't think I need to enumerate what scouts going on a dangerous expedition should bring with them."

"Well, don't leave us like this! Tell us *something* so that we know what to pack!" said Hawkeye.

"We're all ears!" exclaimed the boys.

"Very well," I said and began:

"As you know, I wrote a couple of books about some successful treasure hunts in Poland. Some of these books must have found their way abroad because one day recently, I received a letter from Paris. It was written by a certain Mr. Chabrol, president of the Society of Treasure Hunters. The headquarters of this Society is in Paris."

"The Society of Treasure Hunters?" Hawkeye burst out laughing.

"Well, the name sounds a little silly, yes, but I assure you that it is a very serious society. Entry and membership fees are staggering. And the members are professional treasure hunters—yes, there really are such people. You would think they are some metal-detector guys, but they aren't. They do a great deal of preparatory research, employ lots of people, use aerial photography, machines, sensors, and all that jazz.

Quite a few do deep-sea dives for Spanish galleons. One of the Society's members, a Dane named Petersen, made a fortune extracting gold from Spanish galleons sunk off Cape Engano near Santo Domingo.

"Well, the president of this Society, Mr. Chabrol, offered me membership in his organization. I respectfully declined since I cannot afford the fees, and, at any rate, treasure hunting is not my profession since I don't make any profit from it. And if I do sometimes search for lost treasure, I do it for the art and for the adventure. The treasures I find go to museums while I, at most, write a new book."

"We have seen the Dunin collection in the museum. It looks very impressive, and the kids were really having fun with all the ancient weaponry," Tell testified with all seriousness.

"Last winter," I continued my story, "Mr. Chabrol approached me again. This time, he asked if I would be willing, for appropriate remuneration, to take part in an expedition led by Captain Petersen to search in Poland for the treasure of the Knights Templar. He made a big mystery of it all and said that I would only learn details of the mission once I had signed the contract and the appropriate non-disclosure agreements. My contract, he said, would be directly with Captain Petersen who was just then diving for Spanish galleons in the Matanzas Bay in Cuba. By the way, there had been eleven of these galleons. They carried a hundred thousand ounces of gold."

"Oh God!" groaned Squirrel in astonishment.

"I gave Mr. Chabrol a very polite no, once again reminding him that I do not search for treasure for profit. And if I ever found the Templar treasure, I would hand it over to the Ministry of Culture and not to Captain Petersen, so there really could be no question of cooperation. I also expressed my belief that the Templar treasure was most likely to be found in France, where the headquarters of the order had once been. And that, it seemed to me, was the end of the matter.

"So imagine my great astonishment when, a month ago, a large article on the Templar treasure appeared in a French magazine. It suggested that according to some documents discovered in a library of a Scottish castle, only some of the treasure was buried in France, and the remainder was deposited by the last Grand Master of the Templar Order, Jacob de Molay, with the Grand Master of the Teutonic

Knights, Siegfried von Feuchtwangen, who was, at that time, based in Venice. Now, that same Siegfried soon moved the capital of the Teutonic Knights to Malbork in Poland and may have brought the Templar treasure with him. It is, therefore, possible that the treasure, or at least some part of it, was hidden not in France but in one of the Teutonic castles on Polish territory."

Malbork Castle
a 13th-century castle complex located in the town of Malbork, Poland. It is the former capital of the Teutonic State, the largest surviving castle in the world measured by land area, and a UNESCO World Heritage Site.

"But why would the Grand Master of the Templar Order hand his treasure to the Teutonic Knights?" asked Hawkeye.

"It is a long story. You will understand why when I tell you the history of the order tomorrow. For now, it is enough to say that Jacob de Molay expected that the King of France, Philip the Fair, was going to try to rob the order. Soon, it proved the king had an even more radical idea in mind: he dissolved the order and burnt its knights at the stake, along with their Grand Master de Molay. Yet, the king failed in his main objective: he never found the monastic treasure. Anticipating imminent danger, Jacques de Molay had hidden the monastic treasure and sent the rest to another order of knights. In trust, of course, as a deposit, not as a gift."

Jacques de Molay (burnt at the stake in Paris on 18 March 1314)
was the 23rd and last grand master of the Knights Templar, leading the order until its
dissolution in 1312.

"And after this French article, you became interested in the Templar treasure," Tell summed up.

"Yes. I set about studying the history of the Templar Order and the history of their brother order, the Teutonic Knights. But I have barely begun and—there you have it! An article in the Polish press! It says nothing new. It only repeats the French publication. But the author really angered me: didn't he realize that by running the story, he would spark a general treasure hunt? That thousands of amateurs, shovel in hand, would now descend on all our Teutonic castles? Just listen to the final sentences of his article!"

I grabbed the newspaper and read aloud:

```
It is difficult to say whether the treasure of
the Templar Order is located in any of the
```

Teutonic castles in Poland. Yet, this author
was allowed to see an old document with very
mysterious content. It bore the seal of the
Templar Order and is in the possession of a
certain schoolteacher who lives in the Seyna
district on Lake Milkokuk. He owns a rich
collection of memorabilia and antiquities,
which he has assembled during his travels in
Northeastern Poland. But will the document help
solve the mystery of the hidden treasure? So
far, our only clue is the sentence engraved on
an iron crucifix which the Grand Master of the
Teutonic Knights, Siegfried von Feuchtwangen,
sent to Jacob de Molay shortly before the
latter's death. The sentence read: "Your
treasure is where your heart is." Whoever
understands the meaning of those words might
perhaps find the treasure.

The boys' eyes lit up.

"So there is a *clue* to the treasure? 'Your treasure is where your heart is?' Mr. Wheels! Have you figured it out?"

I waved my hand dismissively.

"At the moment, the document in the possession of the schoolteacher on Lake Milkokuk seems more important—and it seems more important to make sure that it does not fall into the wrong hands. Do you understand? Perhaps Captain Petersen is already here? Perhaps someone has already pointed out this newspaper article to him? Is Petersen perhaps racing for Lake Milkokuk as we speak? He and five dozen other amateur treasure hunters? And we?" I took my head in my hands for pity. "And we sit here and carry on a polite chat. Do you now understand my anger and my despair?"

The boys were silent. Now, they understood why I was angry at the author of the article. They probably also shared my feelings of helplessness.

"Maybe that document will turn out unimportant?" suggested Squirrel.

"Let's hope so," I sighed. "But for now, let's be honest, we are handicapped from the start."

And here, my conversation with the boys ended. The three

scouts said goodbye and went to their respective homes to prepare for the trip. I, too, began packing my things and then dropped in on the mechanic. I wanted to make sure that my car would be ready to go the following morning.

The following morning, William Tell, Hawkeye, and Squirrel, dressed in their scout uniforms and laden with huge backpacks, appeared in front of my house. Tell carried his crossbow on his shoulder. In front of the house stood my trusty car.

It was because of that bizarre contraption that the boys had nicknamed me Mr. Wheels. The vehicle, despite the fact that I had given it a nice shiny chrome job, still aroused mainly derision, chuckles, and pity, for there was no way to change the shape given to it by its inventor. The car resembled a slimy maggot with bulging headlight eyes, and, really, when it came right down to it, it looked like a dugout on wheels. Only insiders knew that it had a Ferrari 410 engine and was one of the fastest cars in the world. And it could not only drive fast but also— zoom on the water along with the fastest of speedboats.

We loaded our luggage and took our seats. The morning was bright and sunny, and the day promised to be beautiful. It was the end of June. The weather service predicted a gorgeous July. So, we set out with the knowledge that many beautiful days awaited us. We did not ask ourselves whether we would actually find the Templar treasure; we were going to have fun. As soon as we set off, our moods improved.

Ferrari America was a series of top-end Ferrari models built in the 1950s and 1960s. They were large grand touring cars with the largest V12 engines and often had custom bodywork.

Two of the series, the 410 and the 400, were called *Superamerica*. Each body was custom made
and the engine was a 5-liter engine with 335 horsepower at 6,000 rpm.

Out of town, on the highway leading toward the northeastern corner of
the country, we sang our favorite song:

In the valleys and mountains,
Among the forests and lakes
He looked for his adventure.
But he found it not!

He sailed the seas,
He traveled the world,
But he found it not!

And he dreamed to see
Whether at night
His adventure may come to him
Stealing upon him like a druid with a golden sickle.

Adventure, where are you?
Reveal yourself!

Adventure, where are you?
What is your name?

CHAPTER TWO: NOT FOR US, O LORD, NOT FOR US

Monks with swords. "Not for us, O Lord, not for us." Masters of secret ciphers. Philip the Fair and his get-rich-quick scheme. The fall of the Templars. The death of the Grand Master. The mysterious Yotvingians.

After leaving Warsaw, we took the road to Bialystok. It was broad, well-surfaced, and empty, and I was able to put the pedal to the metal and, at the same time, to talk to my friends about the adventure awaiting us. I had to initiate them into the history of the two military orders—the Knight Templars and the Knights Teutonic, for they would have to know it in order to be able to help me.

"The story goes back to the 12th century," I said. "As a result of the Crusades about which you learned in school, the so-called Kingdom of Jerusalem was established in Palestine, presumably to defend the Sepulchre of Christ, but mainly because the Crusaders had conquered the land and now wanted to keep it. But, the Kingdom of Jerusalem faced a huge problem: a shortage of men. You see, the Crusaders were volunteer knights. They usually committed for a limited time, usually only for a single campaign, and then they returned home. Because of the superiority of European arms, they usually won battles and conquered lands but did not stick around to defend what they had captured.

"And when the Muslims counterattacked, sometimes there was no one there to oppose them, to defend the walls. And during one such attack, the monks of the Hospital of Saint John in Jerusalem—this hospital was a religious institution looking after the sick and wounded—stepped up. The Muslim attack was repulsed, but the monks, just in case, no longer parted with their swords; they became both monks and knights. And so, the world's first knightly order came into being, the order of the Hospitallers of St. John.

"That order has a long and complicated history, but it still exists and is even recognized by some countries as a state. It owns land and operates embassies. It is more fun and games than anything else today, but some rich people still pay hundreds of thousands of dollars to join the order to be able to call themselves 'a Knight of Saint John of Malta.'

The Coat of Arms of the Knights of Malta
The Sovereign Military Order of Malta, commonly known as the Knights of Malta, is
a Catholic lay religious order, traditionally of a military, chivalric, and noble nature. Though it
possesses no territory today, the order is often considered
a sovereign entity under international law.

"But back when the order was formed, it was run by poor monks who ran a hospital and who later took on the role of escorting pilgrims from the coast where they arrived to various holy places in Palestine. Palestine was a rough country, and it was at war, it was dangerous, and pilgrims were prepared to pay for security. And security proved to be a good business.

"And where there is a need, someone will provide the service. In 1118, a group of entrepreneurs established another knightly order of a similar nature. King Baldwin II of Jerusalem assigned to this new order a building near the ruins of the old Jewish temple. The new order took its name from the Temple and called itself 'Knights Templar.' Business was good; the order attracted new members in significant numbers, and it soon began to receive numerous privileges and estates from Pope Innocent II and his successors. By now all of Christian Europe contributed sums of money to the defense of the Holy Land, and a large portion of the money found its way to the Templars.

"Now, in addition to the usual monastic vows, that is, the vows of obedience, chastity, and poverty, the Templar knights also had to accept the obligation to fight the enemies of the church. The management of the order quickly figured out that it benefited their image to be hard to join. Thus, they required that any man who wanted to join them had to have been born in the knightly estate, from a lawful union, may not have been enslaved or have committed a felony; also, he had to be physically perfect—not crippled on the body, meaning chiefly in those days, not having been castrated as often happened in the East. Only such men could join the order as religious brothers—or Knights of the Temple—and don the white cloak with a red cross. The monastic ensign was black and white with a red stylized cross, and written on it was the motto: *Non nobis, Domine, non nobis, sed nomini Tuo da gloriam*, which means: "Not for us, Lord, not for us, but for the glory of Your Name.'

The **Baucent** (*bauceant, baussant*, etc.)
was the name of the war flag (*vexillum belli*) used by the Knights Templar
in the 12th and 13th centuries.

"Were Poles also allowed to join knightly orders?" asked Tell.

"Naturally. The knightly orders were supposed to be supranational. Few people know this, but even the Teutonic Knights, who in time became Poland's deadliest enemy, counted Polish knights among their number as late as the end of the 14th century. Nevertheless, as always happens, nations tend to hang together, and the Order of the Knights of St. John became dominated by the Italians and the Spanish, the Order of the Knights Templar by the French, and the Order of the Teutonic Knights by the Germans.

"Because, you see, one more order was created during the siege of Acre. Members—today, we would say, 'employees'—of the German Hospital of Acre founded their own military order under the name of the Blessed Virgin Mary. We call them the Teutonic Knights. At first, the knights of this order operated as a branch of the Knights of St. John; later, of the Knights Templar, from whom they adopted their garb: the white cloak, except that the cross on their cloaks was not red, but black. In time, they grew in strength during the reign of their fourth Grand Master, Herman von Salza, 1210-1239.

"But the Order of the Knights Templar grew even faster. Generous charitable gifts flowed to those who fought in the Holy Land, as well as privileges granted by popes, kings, and princes. In the 13th century, the Templars thrived greatly in the Middle East, setting up branches of their order and building local chapter houses—which were really defense fortifications. They also acquired estates in Europe—in Italy and Iberia, in Britain and Ireland, in Germany and France, in Bohemia and Austria, and even here, in Poland, when Prince Henry of Sandomesh brought the Templars in 1156, after returning from a Crusade.

"But the Templars became rich not only through endowments but also by transporting pilgrims to Palestine and handing their money. They became a kind of travel agency with banking operations attached. The business proved immensely profitable. By the 13th century, the Order of the Temple accumulated enormous wealth, which it spent only in part on fighting the Muslims in the Holy Land. They used the rest of their income to invest in the West, to acquire more productive assets, and to lend money on interest, often to various heads of state. Imagine an international organization, having its people and offices in every country of Christian Europe. A rich organization with numerous and talented international staff, with enormous influence and useful contacts everywhere, and even its own spy network.

"With their money and contacts, secret information, networks of intrigue and conspiracy, they learned to influence the course of political events in individual countries. And secret operations required secret means, so the Knights Templar became masters of ciphers which they used for communications. And because their castles were full of secret passages, hiding places, trapdoors, and clever mechanisms for opening and closing underground passages, they soon gained a reputation for mystery and inscrutability.

"Their riches, influence, and power soon became objects of envy of the other orders, above all the Knights of St. John, who tried to compete with them. But the Knights of the Blessed Virgin Mary—or Teutonic Knights as we call them—quickly gave up any idea of competing for influence in Western Europe. They were too far behind to achieve anything there. Instead, they turned their attention to Eastern Europe and began to build a state in what was then Prussia and now is northeastern Poland.

"But the fiercest and, at the same time, the most cunning opponent of the Templars proved to be King Philip the Fair of France, who had long feared the power of the order and long dreamed of seizing its wealth. There are reports that he communicated with the future Pope Clement V before the latter even became Pope and promised him support in his election on the condition that the Pope would then help him crack down on the Templars. Public opinion worked in the king's favor, too. The public has grown unsympathetic to the idea of knightly orders, their power, and influence, especially after the Holy Land was lost. Many thought that the Holy Land was lost precisely because the knightly orders—instead of fighting the Muslims—engaged in building up their power in Europe. Their political influence and frequent disregard for the authority of kings and princes, and even for the supremacy of the Pope, made them many enemies. And their penchant for secrecy and mystery fed rumors. Some began to whisper that the Templars no longer worshipped Christ but money, or perhaps even the devil, indulging in the foul and forbidden practices of black magic.

"And so, after carefully preparing the ground, King Philip the Fair ordered the imprisonment of the Templars on the night of October 12, 1307. An investigation was launched into the charges that the order engaged in heresy and 'impure and ungodly practices.' The investigators subjected the monks to elaborate and cruel tortures, and while they secured all kinds of confessions about devil worship, they failed to extract the most important thing: the location of the order's treasure. Philip's troops, who entered Templar castles, found them stripped of all riches.

King Philip the Fair of France (1268-1314)
He solved his financial problems by liquidating his creditors—the Templars.

"The Grand Master of the Order, Jacques de Molay, was burned at the stake on charges of heresy. However, the grand master's closest associate, Peter of Bologna, managed to escape from a Parisian prison and made his way to Scotland, carrying with him, as legend has it, 'the will of Jacques de Molay'—the secret of the location of the Order's treasure. In Scotland, Peter of Bologna founded a secret organization whose purpose was to take revenge on those who had destroyed the Order."

"And why didn't Peter of Bologna bring the treasures out of hiding?" asked Hawkeye. "After all, he probably needed the money for his new secret organization!"

"A very smart question," I nodded. "There are two hypotheses on this matter. According to one, Peter of Bologna managed, with the help of his emissaries, to recover the treasure of the order and used it to expand his organization and gain political influence. Therefore, the treasure of the Knights Templar cannot be discovered, because it is long gone, used by Peter of Bologna for his purposes. But according to another hypothesis, Peter of Bologna never managed to decipher the 'testament of Jacques de Molay,' and never learned the location of the treasure. And if so, then the Templar treasure still exists today and is probably hidden in some castle in France.

"But now we have a third hypothesis based on some document found in Scotland. According to this hypothesis, Peter of Bologna did indeed manage to recover the Templar treasure hidden in a French castle and used it to expand his organization. But it was not the entire Templar treasure. Another part of it, in the form of precious metalwork, had been deposited with the Teutonic Knights. The French article claimed that a copy of a letter, dating to 1330 and addressed to the Grand Master of the Teutonic Knights, Werner von Orseln, had been discovered. The letter is unsigned, but it seems to have been written by Peter of Bologna himself or one of his closest associates. Its author asks Werner von Orseln to return the Templar treasure. The author of the letter refers to a secret agreement between Jaques de Molay and the then Grand Master of the Teutonic Knights, Siegfried von Feuchtwangen. Under this agreement, the Order of the Teutonic Knights was obliged to return the deposit to any person who possessed the secret password. And the password was, yes, you guessed it, 'Your treasure is where your heart is.'"

"And Werner von Orseln returned the treasure?" the boys asked.

"No one knows. He was murdered that year, probably within a few months of receiving the letter."

"What? The Grand Master of the Teutonic Knights—assassinated?"

"Yes. He was murdered at the entrance to the church at Malbork Castle."

"Wow! Tell us about it, Mr. Thomas! We beg you!" cried the boys. But I did not want to continue my story.

"I've grown hoarse from all this talking," I said. "When we get to Bialystok, we will have lunch and coffee. We will then have the time for the story of the assassination of the Grand Master. Now watch the landscape, boys, it will be a useful lesson in geography for you. And think about that strange password: 'Your treasure is where your heart is.' This is probably the key to the whole riddle."

"Oh, you said it was just a password," Tell reminded me. "Like 'violets are blue,' or 'the eagle has landed,' or something."

"Maybe, maybe not. A story has been preserved that at the time of his arrest, Grand Master Jacques de Molay wore a Venetian-made iron crucifix. The arms of this cross bore a Latin inscription: *Thesaurus tuus ubi est cor tuum.* 'Your treasure is where your heart is.' And the Venetian archive of the Teutonic order preserves a record of a crucifix of iron being made on the orders of Siegfried von Feuchtwangen. Now, listen to this. According to that document, the inscription was a quotation from the Gospel of Matthew 'Your treasure is where your heart is.' Unless you think that crucifixes with that inscription were a fashion statement in 1307, it is probably the same crucifix that was later found on Jacques de Molay. Struck by this coincidence, some have supposed that the inscription on the cross contained a clue, understood by Molay, as to where the Templar treasure was hidden. Two years later, Feuchtwangen moved the headquarters of the Teutonic Order from Venice to Malbork. And so some think that maybe the treasure is hidden in Malbork."

"So why aren't we going to Malbork?" asked Squirrel.

"Have you been to Malbork Castle? It's a massive place with thousands of nooks and crannies. Anyway, it has been rebuilt and remodeled many times. To look for treasure there would be like looking for a needle in a haystack. We need some clue. And maybe this teacher in Seyna has it?"

"'Your treasure is where your heart is,'" repeated Hawkeye. "Maybe it's just a pious quote?"

"Well, yes, maybe. Perhaps it really says nothing about the treasure, or someone would have cracked the code long ago. Quite a few clever people have tried to puzzle this out. In any case, one thing seems certain: after receiving this crucifix, Jacques de Molay calmed down and never asked Feuchtwangen for any further explanations. Also..."

"Also?" the boys asked.

"Well, the sentence is not a literal quote from Saint Matthew. Chapter IV of the Gospel of Matthew reports the words of Jesus that go something like this:

Do not store up for yourselves treasures on earth, where moths and vermin will destroy and where thieves can break in and steal. But store up for yourselves treasure in heaven, where moths and vermin do not destroy and where thieves do not break in and steal.

And then comes the clincher:

For where your treasure is, there your heart will be also.

Now, that sentence is seemingly the same, and yet it is not the same. If you think about it, the two sentences have actually opposite meanings. And it is difficult to suppose that the Grand Master of the Teutonic Order got a Bible quote wrong. So, he must have done it on purpose. Is it possible that, by means of a slightly altered pious formula, he gave de Molay a clue as to where the treasure was hidden?"

I shrugged. My car began to pull violently to the right. I gripped the steering wheel hard and reduced speed by downshifting gears, then brought the car to a stop. We had caught a flat tire. I had a spare wheel with me, so it only took about a quarter of an hour to replace it. But I was afraid to set off on a long-distance trip full of surprises without a spare tire. I decided to give the punctured tire to a vulcanizer in Bialystok.

"And what rotten luck! Rotten luck is haunting me again," I said angrily.

But it was no use being angry. By the time we found a tire shop in Bialystok, where they repaired the tire, two hours had gone by. While waiting for the repair, we ate lunch and did not hit the road again until three in the afternoon. Between Grayevo and Rye-grood I pointed out to the boys the famous Kuwas—the land of marshes. The vast area, covering more than ten thousand acres, was covered with clumps of frail vegetation, dwarf bushes, pools of standing water, rushes, and stretches of grass yielding underfoot and threatening to suck in anyone who dared to set his foot there.

"We are going through a stretch of country that the Teutonic Knights called the Wilderness," I told the boys. "After they exterminated the original inhabitants of this land, the pagan Yotvingians, the Teutonic Knights left the land intentionally uninhabited and overgrown. They meant it to remain impassable as their first line of defense against the Poles and the Lithuanians. Only beyond this wilderness, on the isthmuses of the great Masurian lakes, they built strong castles—their second line of defense. It was not until the end of the 13th century that Polish peasants—settlers from the region around Warsaw—started moving into the area, giving it a Polish character. Of the former owners of these lands, the Yotvingians—only a few buried ruins remain in the forest. Some Yotvingian place names also remain, sounding a little foreign to our ears."

"The Wilderness"
The Land of a Thousand Lakes, the Suvalki region, formerly known as "The Wilderness."

Beyond Augustov, we drove along a paved road to Pshevensh, through the isthmus between Lake Bialy and Lake Studjenichny. And now the Augustov Forest began—a lush, dark-green wood stretching on both sides of the road. Time and again, we overtook passenger cars loaded with backpacks, tents, and tourist equipment. The vacation season had already started, with tourists flocking to Lake Vigry, the Augustov Lakes, and the Suvalki Lake District—the forests, lakes, and canals of this beautiful part of the country. It was already evening when we reached Ghiby, a small village on Lake Gyeret. I knew a little about these parts. I had once stayed at the Journalist Association's camping center some three miles from here, on Lake Pomozhe. I had even made a trip to the small forest lake of Milkokuk at the time. I now presumed that the author of the fateful newspaper article had made the same trip and, while at Milkokuk, met a certain teacher with a collection of local curiosities and antiquities.

At Ghiby, I had to turn onto a forest track bypassing Lake Pomerania. After seven miles through the forests, we would enter the isthmus separating Lake Zelva and Lake Milkokuk. A little farther on lay the village of Milkokuk. We were going to look for our schoolteacher there.

Dusk was falling slowly, as it does this far north in the summer. The boys, tired with the journey, fell asleep in the back seat of the car. I drove carefully along the bumpy forest road and had no inkling that just a quarter mile ahead, just around the bend, the first of a series of great adventures awaited us.

CHAPTER THREE: THE FAIR-HAIRED BEAUTY

The fair-haired beauty. "Are you perhaps Mr. Malinovski?" Captain Petersen in full swing. The English interpreter. Does one help his enemies? My vehicle rescues a Lincoln. Who is following us? Treachery.

It was dusk, and we were driving through a tall pine forest. Overhead, we could see the sky reddened by the setting sun. Down below, it was already dark. Time and again the road turned suddenly to the left, then again to the right, sometimes climbing up a small hill, then descending gentle inclines or into a ravine carved by the rains. And just around the next bend, at the bottom of a shallow ravine through which ran a forest stream, I saw the back of a large caravan. Just ahead of it, a huge Lincoln Continental sat stuck in the muddy stream bed with all four wheels deep in the water. The car had a low-set chassis, was heavy, and sank into the water up to its axles.

The Lincoln Continental
was a series of mid-sized and full-sized luxury cars produced between 1939 and 2020
by Lincoln, a division of the American automaker Ford Motor Company.

The trailer and car blocked my way, so I had to stop. I got out of the car and saw sitting by the roadside... an extremely beautiful girl. A little further away, on the bank of the stream, two men stood studying the water. One of them—short, stocky, with lush gray hair—was dressed in a checkered, collared shirt and tattered pants. The other, much younger, wore an elegant, well-tailored, light-colored suit and white shirt. Carefully combed black hair testified that he remembered to maintain a refined figure in every situation.

"Good evening," I said to the girl.

She vaguely nodded at me. She was smoking a cigarette, and her face expressed boredom. For a brief moment, it seemed that the bizarre shape of my vehicle, as well as my unexpected appearance on the forest road, aroused a flash of interest in her eyes. But it lasted an extremely short time. After a while, she looked up at the sky and continued smoking as if she didn't care at all about the Lincoln stuck in the stream. She was dressed in tight pants and a sleeveless sweater. She had blond, long hair and the face of a Hollywood star. Her whole demeanor seemed to say: "I know I'm very beautiful. I'm used to being admired for my beauty. I am beautiful, I am rich, nothing can surprise me, and I am not surprised by anything."

I confess that her attitude annoyed me.

"You should not smoke in the forest," I said to her, "because you could cause a fire."

She shrugged her shoulders and did not even deign to look at me. Meanwhile, the elegant young man approached us in a hurry.

"This lady is a foreigner and does not understand Polish," he explained and, at the same time, threw me a rather critical look. At the sight of my car, an ironic smile appeared on his lips.

"In that case," I said, "perhaps you will be kind enough to point out to this lady that one should not smoke cigarettes in the forest."

"Are you the forester here?" the young man suddenly beamed. "That's great! We need horses to pull our car out of the mud!"

"I am not a forester," I said.

The young man shrugged his shoulders. He stopped being polite and said contemptuously:

"So why are you meddling in what is none of your business?"

"Oh, sorry. This is a state forest, and I am a citizen of this state, so in a sense, this forest is also under my care."

The young man looked at me ironically, the way one looks at some harmless freak. Then he shrugged his shoulders again and turned his back on me. But just at this moment, the gray-haired man in a checkered shirt approached. He grabbed the button of my leather jacket and asked in English:

"Are you Mr. Malinovski?"

I speak English and understood his question, but I did not want to reveal my knowledge of the language. These foreigners met on the road to Milkokuk did not inspire my confidence. So, I just shrugged my shoulders, just the way the girl did when I addressed her in Polish. The young man rushed in to translate:

"This gentleman asked you if you are perhaps Mr. Malinovski?"

"Er?" I made a puzzled face. "Of course, I am not Malinovski."

The young man turned to the gray-haired man and said in English:

"He says he is not Malinovski."

The foreigner turned red with anger, clenched his fists, and angrily waved them in the air, repeating in English:

"Ah, that Malinovski, Malinovski! Wait till I lay my hands on him! I'll skin him alive!"

At this, the girl spoke up, trying to calm down the gray-haired man.

"Are you angry again? Papa, give this matter a rest. We have more important problems. After all, we have to get to that god-forsaken place somehow."

I said to the young man:

"You're blocking my way, and I am in a hurry."

"So are we. But you can see for yourself what happened. Why don't you take another road?"

"There is no other road. All around are forests and swamps."

"In that case, you must wait until we get our car out of the mud."

Meanwhile, the scouts woke up and, one by one, crawled out of my vehicle. It looked rather funny because first, the shaggy head of William Tell emerged from the car. Then, the entire boy followed. Then, another head popped out. That was Squirrel. He took a while to scramble out. And again, a third head appeared, sporting the long nose of Hawkeye. The others marveled at the sight, even the young girl lost the expression of indifference. When the third boy stood on the forest road, the girl laughed and said in English:

"How many more does he have in that hearse? I think he's carrying the whole class!"

I said to the scouts:

"Our path is blocked. Go look around and see if there is any other crossing somewhere nearby."

The boys ran off, and the beautiful girl turned to the elegant young man:

"Tell this man that we want to hire him. Let him go to the village and bring some horses here."

The young man repeated her offer in Polish.

"Thank you. Alas, I am not for hire," I replied.

He relayed my answer to her.

"Tell him that we will pay well," she added.

"Tell her that I am a rich man. I will buy her caravan from her. I will pay well," I said after he translated her words.

I was talking nonsense, of course. I had no money of any sort. I was a modestly paid museum employee, a scholar with a bit of literary ambition. On several occasions, I have been entrusted with the task of finding valuable museum collections lost during the war, and I later described those adventures in books. I also enjoyed solving historical puzzles, but this did not bring me any additional income. It only consumed my free time and filled my vacations. These people, on the other hand, were probably very wealthy. But I was angered by their imperious proposal. I don't like conceited rich people.

"Don't be silly!" cried the young man. "You do not have a penny to your soul. Just look at that thing you drive. And do you know who these people are? They are very rich people. Anyway, you are behaving very rudely. They are guests in our country. They are paying with hard currency, which our country needs. I am assigned to facilitate their tour because they don't know the language. They need to get to this hole, Milkokuk. Every Polish citizen should help them."

I pretended to be abashed.

"But what are they looking for here, in this wilderness?"

"Oh, foreigners have the strangest fancies," he explained. "But now that you know who you are dealing with, please notify the peasants of the nearest village. Have them bring horses. We'll pay them well."

Meanwhile, the boys returned. It turned out that just to the right, there was a suitable ford and enough space left between the trees for the vehicle to pass.

"That's great," I said. "I will go to Milkokuk and notify the farmers there. I'm sure they will help you."

"What's that? Are you going to Milkokuk?" asked the young man, surprised.

He wanted to say something else, but I had already jumped into my vehicle—and long with me, my friends. I reversed the car, then turned into the woods and, illuminating my way with my headlights, dodged among the tree trunks. The vehicle did a great job of fording the stream. Soon, we were back on the forest road well in front of the Lincoln debacle.

But the girl stood there expecting me—and, along with her, the young man. He said to me:

"Miss Petersen asks you if you would be willing to use a rope to pull their car out of the mud?"

"Miss Petersen?" I chuckled. And the scouts, sitting in the back, hissed with anger. That I had not immediately guessed who the stocky man in the checkered shirt was! Why, it was Captain Petersen, the treasure hunter. Of course! He'd come looking for the Templar treasure! He had learned from the newspaper about a mysterious document in the possession of a schoolteacher from Milkokuk and, like me, rushed to see it. I thought:

Well, well, here is my chance to get ahead of my opponents. Let them wallow in the mud, and in the meantime, I will get to Milkokuk.

But I felt bad at the thought of handling the matter in this way. After all, Petersen had no idea that I was his opponent and would take my behavior as rudeness and would think that all Poles were rude to their guests. So, I had to either tell Petersen that he was my rival and leave for Milkokuk or help him without telling him who I was.

"Very well. I will try to help you," I said after a moment's hesitation. And I started to reverse my vehicle towards the Lincoln.

"What are you doing?!" whispered the scouts behind my back. "You're helping your enemies?"

I was upset:

"I have always played fair. Without fairness, there is no real adventure. If Petersen needs my help, I must give it to him."

"And will he help you if you find yourself in a similar situation?" William Tell asked.

"I don't know," I said. "I don't know, and I don't care. But I know that I must not do otherwise."

After a second, a thought popped into my head:

"You take your flashlights and march to Milkokuk. It's about three miles from here. Find the schoolteacher and tell him not to show the Templar document to anyone under any circumstances until my arrival. Do you understand? And in the meantime, I will try to pull the Petersens out of the mud."

It was almost completely dark by now. The boys slipped out of the car unnoticed by the others and disappeared into the night. And I reversed to the edge of the stream. Miss Petersen turned on the headlights of the Lincoln. We had light, and our rescue could proceed.

The young man—who it turned out was Petersen's translator—patted me on the back.

"Glad you wised up. You'll make a pretty penny doing this."

Then he leaned in and whispered into my ear:

"These people are loaded. Plus, it will be patriotic of you because they will leave hard currency in our country."

Miss Petersen took the leadership role in the rescue operation. She disconnected the trailer from the Lincoln to make it easier for me to pull the car out of the mud. Then she took a rope out of the trunk. She rolled up her pants, stepped into the water, and attached the rope to a hook on the front of her vehicle.

"Please attach the other end to the back of your car," she commanded in English, and I involuntarily followed her orders.

Only then did I remember that I was not supposed to know English. So, I immediately began to follow all her orders backward, which made her very angry. She called upon the support of the young man who, with his hands in his pockets, stood to one side and observed us getting dirty. Petersen smoked a pipe and occasionally muttered something under his breath.

Miss Petersen impressed me. Well, alright, I like slender blondes, what can I do, how boringly traditional of me. I sometimes feel bad about it, but more importantly, her superior indifference and boredom turned out to be only a mask, and she proved to be very enterprising. I watched with pleasure as she stepped into the water again and again to adjust the knot on the rope, which she had tied expertly, like a seasoned sailor. I reflected that as her father's daughter, she probably was one.

"And what is the young lady's name?" I turned to the young man. He passed on my question. She laughed.

"Karen. My name is Karen. Do you like my name?"

I said I liked it very much. There was once a Karen whose books I read.

"My name is Thomas," I said.

"Thomas?" she repeated. And she laughed. I asked the young man:

"What is she laughing at?"

She replied that she liked me because I have such a quirky, funny car. My car and I made an entertaining team. But the young man translated her words quite differently.

"She says you are ridiculous."

Ridiculous? I thought. *You just wait, little man, I'll give you 'ridiculous.'*

He didn't even notice when I looped the rope around his legs. I hooked the other end of the rope to the back of my car. Then, I got into the vehicle and slowly started forward. The rope, which had been lying loosely so far, began to strain. Then, I quickly let go of the clutch and added gas. The vehicle jerked, and the elegant fellow pulled by the rope flew up and fell flat in the mud. I stopped.

He cursed while crawling out of the mud. Miss Petersen shouted at me that I shouldn't have started so suddenly.

I got out of the car, pretending to be full of remorse, and re-tied the rope.

"Dear God, look at my new suit!" groaned the young man.

When he appeared in the beams of the headlights, Miss Petersen burst into loud laughter. Streams of dirty water ran down his bright suit. He had a large patch of black mud on his forehead.

"You have made me look like a fool! I know you now," he raged at me.

Miss Petersen led him aside and wiped the mud off his clothes with a handkerchief. She was quietly explaining something to him at the same time, but I couldn't hear her words.

I re-tied the rope and double-checked it, but I was in no hurry to pull out the Lincoln. I tried to calculate whether the scouts had had enough time to reach Milkokuk and whether they had found the schoolteacher's house. So, time and time again, I found some new excuse to slow the operation. Now, the rope that was poorly tied, now something under the hood of my vehicle needed attention. Miss Karen was getting impatient, and her anger was conveyed to me in Polish by the young man in a soiled suit.

"Sir, can't you hurry up? Miss Petersen says your car is probably not up to snuff."

"Oh?" I said and unhooked the rope, pretending to feel offended. An apology ensued, and I continued to stall for time. Finally, out of the blue, I asked:

"Why are you in such a hurry?"

At this, all three became flustered. Miss Petersen rushed to respond.

"We are traveling around Poland as tourists. We are not in a hurry at all, we just don't want to spend the night in the forest. And you, what are you doing here?"

"I live nearby," I lied.

"Oh?" asked the young man. "Your car, if this contraption can be called a car, has a Wooj registration."

"What, what are you saying?" Mr. Petersen turned to his translator.

Wanting to avoid awkward questions, I looked at my watch and got into the vehicle. It was eleven o'clock, the scouts had certainly reached Milkokuk by now. This time, I started the vehicle slowly. The rope tightened, I added gas and the Lincoln, inch by inch, climbed out of the mud. My engine howled like mad, but in a few more seconds, the Lincoln's front wheels found firm ground. Then Miss Petersen, sitting behind the wheel of her machine, also added gas. After a moment, their car cleared the stream. But their camper remained on the other side.

"I'll haul it," I offered.

The Lincoln drove forward a bit to get out of the way, and I backed up across the stream all the way to the trailer. Miss Petersen crossed the stream to help me tie the trailer to the vehicle. Suddenly, she shouted in fright.

"Look! Someone is hiding there! Oh, there, behind the trees!" she called out, pointing to the forest to the right side of the road.

"Maybe it's some kind of animal?" Petersen said.

"No! It was a face! A human face. Someone is watching us," she said, clearly flustered by her discovery.

"Mr. Kozlovski," she turned to the elegant young man, "come with me. We will find out who is following us. You, Papa," she called out to her father, "also come with us. You are very strong."

But Mr. Petersen showed no interest.

"Come on, Karen," he said, "What do you care who's out there creeping around in the woods? I have no intention of getting clubbed over the head."

Karen stomped her foot.

"Oh, you cowards! Cowards!" she shouted. "If you don't want to come with me, I'll go alone."

The young man smiled maliciously at me.

"Perhaps you will be the brave man to provide masculine protection? You are probably not afraid of the dark?"

Karen looked at me expectantly. I saw her beautiful green eyes and thought that, for her sake, I would roam the forest all night among wild animals and robbers lurking behind tree trunks, clubs in hand.

Shoulder to shoulder, we plunged into the woods to the right side of the road. The lights of our car headlights disappeared behind the trees. Complete darkness surrounded us. Only after some time, when our eyes became accustomed to the dark, did we begin to distinguish tree trunks. We stumbled over roots protruding from the ground, bumped into bushes, and our feet got caught in the undergrowth.

"Quiet!" hissed Miss Petersen and squeezed my shoulder.

We stopped, holding our breath. At one point I thought I heard the hum of an engine from the direction where we had left our cars. But soon, there was silence again. And there was silence all around us. Suddenly, Miss Petersen said:

"Well, we can go back now."

She let go of my arm and marched toward the road. I followed her with a growing sense of unease. A dozen more steps and the suspicion turned into certainty.

The Petersen's car was no longer on the forest path. Only their trailer and my vehicle remained. The air had been let out of my front tires. I looked at Karen. She smiled apologetically.

"Mr. Thomas," she said in English. "Did you take me for a fool? Do you think I would let you swipe that document from right under my nose?"

"You fooled me!" I staggered in my best English.

"Yes?" she feigned amazement. "And did you not try to deceive me? I immediately guessed that you understood English perfectly. You are a poor actor, Mr. Thomas. Chabrol wrote to you to Wooj. When Kozlovski told me that your car had a Wooj registration, I immediately guessed who you were. I was not born yesterday."

I was furious. I was livid. The scouts had been right to warn me against helping the Petersens. They repaid my courtesy with treachery.

"Don't be angry, Mr. Thomas," Miss Petersen unexpectedly stroked my cheek. "We only let the air out of two front wheels. We did not puncture them. I will now help you, and within an hour, you will be able to move on. All I needed was an hour."

"Oh, yes, I will move on, Ma'am. But you and your camper will stay here."

Karen smiled her most charming smile.

"There is not a snowflake's chance in hell that you would do a thing like that! Leave a damsel in distress to fend for herself? In a dark wood? All alone? No, Mr Thomas. One knows a real man by the fact that he not only knows how to win but also knows how to save his face in defeat."

I laughed.

A malicious thought came to my mind.

"Defeat? Why are you talking about defeat? Haven't you noticed that my three young friends have disappeared?"

"Oh?" she became concerned. "I thought they were sleeping in your car."

"No, Miss Karen. They are in Milkokuk by now. Perhaps they already have the document we both seek in their hands. And in any case, they will certainly thwart your father."

She pursed her lips. She was no longer smiling. I gave her a triumphant look. But Miss Karen knew how to lose. After a while, she said:

"You impress me, Mr. Thomas. I am happy to have an opponent like you. It makes our expedition all the more interesting."

CHAPTER FOUR: THE LADY IN BLACK

A crook in Paris. Who is Kozlovski? War or Peace? What happened to the scouts. A mysterious lady in black. Where is the schoolteacher? Let us cooperate.

It took me almost an hour to pump air into my tires. Anyway, I wasn't in much of a hurry. Petersen and Kozlovski had already reached Milkokuk. And if the scouts hadn't proven clever, my rushing now wouldn't change a thing. Miss Petersen tried to put me in a better mood. She smiled charmingly, and when I got tired of pumping, she brought some lemonade from the trailer.

"I would very much like you to understand my father," she explained. "He is furious because right off the bat, he had been tricked by a certain Malinovski."

"Is that why he keeps asking about this Malinovski?"

"Yes. And it all happened because of me. While in London, I learned about the discovery of a document that suggested that a part of the Templar treasure was in Poland. It was a letter from Peter of Bologna to the Grand Master of the Teutonic Knights, Werner von Orseln. With the permission of my father—he was diving in the Matanzas Bay in Cuba at the time—I bought this document for a rather large sum of money. I confess that buying that paper really made me want to undertake the search for the Templar treasure. I have never had a taste for extracting gold from old wrecks. That's an activity for sweaty, muscular men. But to search for the treasure of the Knights Templar, well, that's different. I thought I would be able to test my intelligence. Because, in this case, you need brains, scholarship, and knowledge of history. And I'm currently studying history in London. So, I persuaded my father to undertake an expedition to Poland after he finished in Matanzas Bay. But we needed to find someone who would know something about the Teutonic castles in Poland. The president of the Society of Treasure Hunters, Mr. Chabrol, took it upon himself to find the right man."

"He wrote to me about it, but I refused."

"And a great pity, that. But how about entering into a partnership with us now?"

"No. It is impossible," I said. "I do not do this for profit."

"Whatever you think is best," she shrugged her shoulders. "Mr. Chabrol finally found another man. It was someone from Poland who had only come to Paris for a short visit. He introduced himself as Malinovski. He extracted some information from Chabrol—about the treasure and about us. He promised to sign a contract with Mr. Chabrol to work with us, but he never did. He kept wriggling out with various excuses. And in the meantime, he wrote a letter to my father in Cuba and informed him that he had already made an agreement with Chabrol, but he still needed additional information about the treasure and four hundred dollars to start the search in Poland.

"My father, whom Chabrol informed that he had found the right man for the search, was fooled by Malinovski's letter. He sent him information and four hundred dollars. And then all trace of Malinovski disappeared. And, oh my god, had that been the end of it! But the rascal then sold this information to some journalist, and that's why an article appeared in the press. Then it turned out that Mr. Chabrol had not yet signed the contract with Malinovski, did not have a copy of his passport, did not know who he was or where to look for him.

"Basically, the man turned out to be a crook. My father became very angry, but at the same time, his pride awoke in him. He decided that despite the setback, he would not give up his search. He must find this treasure. Because, you see, our expedition here is not really financially worthwhile. According to Polish law, the finder of the treasure is only entitled to a finder's fee of ten percent of the total value of the treasure, with the rest going to the state. My father agreed to this, he signed an agreement with the ministry: ten percent for us and ninety percent for the state, with the understanding that the state would cover part of our expenses related to the search if the search proved fruitful. But, as I say, in this case, we no longer care about the money. I suspect that my father did not come here to look for treasure at all but only to find Malinovski and put him in jail."

"So, the state has given you a treasure-hunting contract," I wondered. "You do it legally with the approval of the authorities. This, of course, changes the nature of things somewhat."

"So why don't you work with us then?"

I shook my head.

"I always work alone."

"Look, we will send Kozlovski away, and we will take you on."

"Who is this Kozlovski?"

"A friendly, helpful fellow. Speaks perfect French and English. Handsome," she laughed.

"And who is he by profession?"

"He says he works at a Polish travel agency. We met him in Warsaw while we were looking for an interpreter for the entire period of our stay in Poland. He offered his services and even took a leave of absence from work."

"I don't blame him. To be a translator for you..."

We drank another glass of lemonade. It was already midnight. I attached the trailer to my vehicle and slowly set off in the direction of Milkokuk. We soon passed a forester's lodge standing at the edge of the forest, then—next to a wooden bridge over the river connecting Lake Zelva and Lake Milkokuk—we saw Petersen's Lincoln. Neither Petersen nor Kozlovski were anywhere to be seen—they obviously preferred to remain out of sight. I didn't look for them too hard—the memory of the trick they played on me awoke old anger in me.

These people can forget about me ever working with them, I thought.

I unhooked the trailer and said goodbye to Miss Karen.

"Would you tell me where you are going?" she asked.

"Oh, I don't know. The world is a huge place."

"Don't you want to stay in touch? Come on, let's make peace."

I remained silent.

"Oh, come. What's it going to be? War or peace?" she asked.

I remained silent for a while, then gave her a wide grin.

"War, Ma'am," I said slowly.

I got into my vehicle and drove toward the village. The most important thing right now was to find out what my three friends had managed to achieve in the matter of the mysterious document. I really hoped they had beaten the Petersens to the punch—exactly because the Petersens had tricked me.

I must have driven about half a mile when I saw the red flashlight of William Tell signalling for me to pull over. Soon, I saw all three boys sitting at the roadside.

"You've taken your sweet time, Mr. Thomas!" said Hawkeye. "We waited and waited and waited, and then Petersen arrived. Why?"

"Oh, I will explain it later," I waved my hand in embarrassment. Now I want to know: what about the document?"

They spread their hands in a gesture of helplessness.

"Nothing doing."

"What? Petersen's got it?" I shouted.

"Nah. The schoolteacher is away. He went away on a sightseeing trip with a group of schoolboys. His house is locked up. And if you ask the neighbors, he does not even know about the article in the press or that crowds have beat a path to his door."

"What? What crowds?"

"Well, we exaggerate a little," laughed Hawkeye. "But a couple in a blue *Skoda* has been camping nearby for two days. They were the first to inquire about the teacher and his whereabouts.

"He, too, inquired where the teacher was. Then, near the teacher's house, we met a rather suspicious young lady. Very clever, too. She immediately unmasked us."

"What?"

And Squirrel told the story.

"We knocked on the door of the cottage, and out of the dark came this lady. She asked: 'And you, boys, are here about the mysterious document, too?' We did not know what to say. Then she said: 'I don't think you should bother. You'd better look for accommodation for tonight.' And she explained that the schoolteacher was on a trip that was expected to last a few days."

"She seems like a very nice person," Tell said. "She was concerned about us hanging around after dark. She was asking: 'Have you boys eaten?'

"And: 'Where will you sleep?' She also asked who had brought us here."

Skoda
The Škoda was a rear-engined, rear-wheel drive compact car produced by
Czechoslovakian automaker AZNP.
The make is owned by Volkswagen today.

"Then a man on a *Yunak* arrived."

Yunak
Yunak (Junak) was a brand of Polish motorcycles, produced in Poland between World War II
and 1989. The name means "brave young man."

"And you, of course, told her," I said with heavy sarcasm. I did not like the direction the story was taking.

"No," stammered Tell.

Hawkeye said grimly:

"We nearly gave away that we were with you. She is very clever and asks such trick questions that a person doesn't even notice how she arrives at the truth. For example, she asked me: 'How long does it take to go through the forest on foot?' So, I told her, 'I don't know because we came by car.' 'Oh? Whose car?' That, of course, we didn't say. Fortunately. Then this fellow Petersen arrived, she got into a conversation with him and we managed to slip away. That is why we are waiting for you here and not in the village. Walking here, we stopped by one of the cottages to get a drink of water. I mean, we did not really stop for a drink of water. We wanted to do a little investigation. And in that cottage that we learned about all these unusual tourists, who had come to Milkokuk since yesterday. Until now, tourists have rarely come here. And then all of a sudden, so many. I think they are all amateur treasure hunters."

"Phew, I don't think I like to be in a crowd," muttered Squirrel.

And now, I told them about my adventure with Petersen and the joke they played on me. The boys were outraged.

"You deserve what you got, Mr. Thomas. You wanted to be a gentleman."

"Petersen is a viper!" exclaimed Hawkeye.

"And Karen?" I wondered.

"She makes eyes at you, and you get all giddy," Hawkeye said firmly.

I grunted with embarrassment. It was true. But it didn't seem to me to be a proper topic of conversation with underage boys.

"Ok, now we sleep!" I commanded. "It's high time for you to pitch your tent!"

Then we heard a woman's voice in the dark:

"Sure enough! They should have been in bed a long time ago. I'm very surprised that you let three young people bushwhack through the night."

"That's her," whispered Tell. "The one who met us near the teacher's house."

The conversation with the boys took place near my car, which, with its lights off, stood at the edge of the village. I had no idea how long the strange woman had stood in the dark, unnoticed by us, listening. Perhaps she had heard our entire conversation.

"It's not polite to eavesdrop," I said to the approaching figure.

"You spoke so loudly you could be heard a mile away," she laughed.

She was a tall girl with dark, short-cropped hair. She wore black pants and a black, thick sweater. She was barely visible in the dark.

"All the treasure hunters have set up camp on the shore of the lake," she said with gentle mockery in her voice. "They want to be as close to the teacher's house as possible. The road to the lake is just beyond those trees," she pointed out the direction.

Unnecessarily, as it turned out, because we had just spotted the powerful lights of the Petersen Lincoln on the road leading to the lake. He, too, planned to spend the night there.

"I know a better place to camp," I said.

"Have you been here before?"

I pretended not to have heard the question.

"Get in, boys, let's go," I said.

And then we saw a new set of car headlights. Another car of some sort came out of the woods heading for Milkokuk. After a while, a *Varshava* passed us, heading into the village.

"More treasure hunters," sighed the Lady in Black. "I better go back to the village to tell these people of the teacher's absence."

"And who are you?" I asked. "A tour guide for treasure hunters? In Templar pay?"

"Perhaps," she nodded. Suddenly, she changed her mind.

"Which way are you going? Perhaps I will ride with you. I'm tired of giving information. Especially since the Templars aren't paying me."

William Tell interjected:

A 1972 Varshava (Warszawa)

The Varshava (Warszawa) was the first newly designed car built in Poland after World War II.
Varshavas were popular as taxis because of their sturdiness and ruggedness. However, they
were underpowered for their weight and had high fuel consumption. 254,471 Warszawas were
made between 1951 and 1973.

"It won't be wise at all if we camp far from the teacher's cabin. What if the teacher unexpectedly returns from a trip in the middle of the night?"

He pulled me aside and, in a whisper, began to explain that the three of them should set up their tent in the vicinity of the teacher's house and that it made absolutely no sense for all of us to operate from one and the same place. We should divide tasks and responsibilities; that way, we could be more effective. They would watch the teacher's house and wait for his return while I should watch our competitors, primarily the Petersens. This was not a bad plan, so I accepted Tell's proposal. We divided the sleeping bags, blankets, and food.

"If something happens, look for me at Lake Pomerania. It's a mile and a half away. From the forester's lodge, you go along the road to the right until you reach a small cove on the lake. I will camp there," I told the boys in farewell.

The Lady in Black asked:

"In that case, I'll go with Mr. Wheels."

"I am not Mr. Wheels to you," I said indignantly.

"I am very sorry if this violates a tabu. But it is a nice nickname."

"Yes, I like it, but only from my friends."

"Do you think we will not become friends? I became very fond of your boys."

"Very well, Madam, please condescend to accept a ride," I ended the conversation.

We drove along a forest road to Lake Pomerania. During the entire trip—not a long one, anyway—we exchanged hardly a dozen sentences: the region is very beautiful, rich in forests and lakes, great place to spend the summer, blah blah. I confess that my companion intrigued me, and I would have been glad to find out who she was and what she was doing in these parts, but I didn't want to seem too nosey.

The moon broke through the clouds, and it became a little brighter. The road approached the lake—I saw a huge expanse of water, rippling gently in the breeze as if from the touch of the moonlight. A narrow bay cut deep inland here, overgrown with reeds near the shore.

"We're here," I said, turning onto a gentle, grassy slope descending to the lake. A very nice, level meadow lay between the forest and the lake. I intended to spend the night there.

"And you? Where will you go? I don't think there is a house within two miles from here."

"I'll be fine. See you tomorrow."

She jumped out of the vehicle and ran across the meadow and down to the water. For a brief moment, she disappeared from sight in the shoreline reeds. Then, on the vast expanse of the lake, in the long beam of moonlight, I saw the oblong shape of a kayak gliding toward the opposite shore. So that was her mystery: she had hidden a kayak in the reeds.

She rowed fast, working the paddle evenly: she was an experienced rower. I remembered that I, too, had hidden my kayak in those reeds several times. The place was perfect for the purpose because the reeds were very dense. I had made my nicest trips in the area from this beach.

I followed the kayak with my eyes until it disappeared from sight and dissolved into the darkness that covered the other shore. I didn't want to pitch my tent anymore. I washed up in the cool water of the lake and lowered the seats in the car. Despite being tired and sleepy, I couldn't fall asleep.

It was only the first day of our expedition, and how many impressions we have had! I was angry at the memory of the mean trick of the Petersens. I thought of Karen's green eyes. She was driven by the desire to experience an interesting adventure and to test her abilities. And this aroused my sympathy. But Petersen? Kozlovski? And the tourists who suddenly came to the lake? Who will they turn out to be? Perhaps one of them will prove my fiercest opponent? Finally, there was this Lady in Black. Was she really mysterious, or did it only seem that way to me? Maybe her information about the schoolteacher, which she so generously lavishes on everyone, was simply a clever ploy aimed at making us wait with folded hands for his return while someone else has made off with the document?

There were a lot of questions on my mind, and I couldn't find an answer to any of them.

CHAPTER FIVE: OF THUGS AND HAMSTERS

The uses of imagination. What use is an objective observer? Of thugs and hamsters. Traveling over the map with one's finger. The goat market.

"Oh God, what kind of a student is this supposed to be? Sleeping till high noon?"

This exclamation woke me up after the night spent in my vehicle on the lake. I raised my head from my pillow, and through the window, I saw the Lady in Black, who stood knocking on my roof. In daylight, the black-dressed person did not look like a "lady" but rather like a young person of Miss Petersen's age. She was also very pretty but in a different way. Her eyes were cheerful, with a bit of an ironic gleam. I noticed sympathetic dimples on her face. In a word, she was a likable girl.

"Where did you find this ugly thing?" she wondered, circumambulating my car and studying it carefully. "It's neither a dog nor a hog. I can't believe that this thing drives. I would never have believed it if I hadn't ridden in it yesterday."

I was used to comments of this kind at the sight of my car. I yawned, rolled over onto the other side, and pulled the blanket over my head. I was sleepy.

"Hey, mister!" the Lady in Black knocked on the window. "Do you know what time it is? Twelve o'clock! Noon! Have you come here to sleep or to look for treasure? Mr. Wheels, it's time to get up!"

I raised my head again.

"Kindly refrain from calling me Mr Wheels."

"So, we're not friends yet?"

"I don't know you. I don't know anything about you."

"Let me introduce myself then. My name is Anna, but you can call me Anka. I am a journalist. Right now, I'm staying at the journalist center on the other side of the lake."

"Oh!" I began to crawl out of bed. "So you probably know that fool, that idiot, that bonehead, that .... well, I no longer know what to call him—that fellow who published that article about the Templar treasure? And who hinted of a mysterious document at the teacher's house in Milkokuk?"

She laughed.

"I do not personally know the gentleman you name. As for me, I'm going to write an article about the crazies who come here looking for treasures after reading an article in the press. May I interview you?"

I jumped out of the car as I was in my pajamas.

"You want to smear me in the newspaper, yes?"

"Nah. I consider you a very friendly and totally harmless nut," she said. "Also, your three friends are pretty cool."

"It is best if you direct your investigative passions at the Petersens and Mr. Kozlovski."

"Who is Mr. Kozlovski?"

"That fellow who came with the Petersens. I assure you that he is a very sober-minded man, not a madman of any kind."

"I prefer madmen," she stated firmly. "Aren't you hungry? You look like the kind of person who, when hungry, is inclined to be contrary. Shall I make you breakfast?"

I waved my hand dismissively. I took my shaving utensils, soap, and a towel from the vehicle. From a distance of twenty paces—because that was how much distance separated my vehicle and the shore—I watched Anka through my shaving mirror as she carefully inspected my belongings. Then, from among them, she pulled out a box of eggs, bread, butter, a spirit stove, and a frying pan and began to fry scrambled eggs with bacon. Their delicious smell reached my nostrils, and I suddenly felt ravenously hungry. If it weren't for her threat to slander me in her newspaper, the girl would have been a perfectly agreeable person.

"Could you open a can of condensed milk?" she called out to me. I nodded my head. My breakfast promised to be excellent.

"I'll take you into our partnership," I said, sitting down to eat. "The boys and I will search for treasure, and you will be entrusted with the function of the expedition cook."

She shrugged her shoulders:

"Treasure? I am a sensible girl."

"Yes, yes, it can see," I said. "But don't you think that it would be much more sensible to relax on a deck chair or go kayaking on the lake than to hang around Milkokuk and watch madmen dash about? And what will happen to your sanity if, against all reason, one of us manages to find the legendary Templar treasure? A huge, heavy chest of jewels worth several hundred million dollars?"

"Oh, is it that valuable?"

"Yes, Ma'am," I said with satisfaction, "I can see that the sum has appealed to your rationality."

"In that case, I will also search for treasure," she said cheerfully.

"Or perhaps you have already guessed where it is?"

"I was hoping you might tell me."

"Oh, I know absolutely nothing," I laughed. "Perhaps the Petersens know more. They claim to have some old Scottish document. Maybe you should go investigate that?"

We finished eating. I was washing the dishes, and the girl sat nearby on the grass.

"Er... You suggested that I might join your company."

"Oh, I changed my mind. I think you may not be a suitable partner."

"Oh? What happened? The breakfast was not to your liking?"

"On the contrary. The breakfast was superb. But—you are far too rational. This is not a challenge for rational people. You have to have a lot of fantasy and imagination."

"Imagination is needed to imagine where the treasure might be. And fantasy is useful in fantasizing that one has found it," she said mischievously.

"Ma'am, you are mistaken. Imagination and fantasy are needed to grasp the mindset of the people of the past and guess where they might have hidden the treasure. For example, imagine that you are the Grand Master of the Teutonic Knights, Siegfried von Feuchtwangen."

"No way. I can't imagine anything like that."

"Very well. I'm going to perform a certain psychological test on you. Please tell me how you understand the phrase, 'Your treasure is where your heart is'?"

"Oh, that's simple. This phrase should be understood like this: if you have fallen in love with someone, you have just found your greatest treasure."

I waved my hand dismissively.

"Then you get married and have three children. But can you really imagine the iron-clad Siegfried von Feuchtwangen as some kind of a love-bird? He was the Grand Master of the Knights of the Blessed Virgin Mary, an order famous for the cruelty and ruthlessness with which it conquered territory and carried out ethnic cleansing. And yet, this iron man had these words engraved on a crucifix. And, considering that the words are an intentional misquotation of the Gospel of Matthew and were inscribed on a crucifix he sent to Jacques to Molay, another iron man, we are entitled to think that they contain a clue to the hiding place of the treasure. You do know who de Molay was?"

She took offense:

"Oh, I do read my own newspaper, you know."

The dishes were washed and wiped dry. I put the seats in the car upright and rolled up the blanket under which I had slept.

"Now I'm going to visit my friends," I said. "Are you coming along?"

Without a word, still pretending to be offended, the Lady in Black took a seat in the car, and we drove to Milkokuk.

The day was bright, with clear and sunny skies, just like the day before. Only on the horizon did the sky seem a tad hazy. Looking at the haze, I felt sure that clouds would form towards evening and a storm would follow. For the time being, however, the birds sang loudly and cheerfully, and beams of sunshine shone in the forest.

The village of Milkokuk emerged around the bend—a dozen wooden, straw-roofed homesteads. A little to the side stood a lone cottage—the school teacher's house. In front of it stood the school— also wooden, tiny, surrounded by a low hedge. In the orchard adjacent to the teacher's house, under a vast, ancient apple tree, camped my three friends. When we arrived, they had just finished their morning meal. Hawkeye was washing dishes in a zinc tub borrowed from the neighbors. I was mistaken, however, in assuming that, like me, the three boys had overslept. It turned out that they had been busy with "intelligence work" since early morning, which is why their breakfast was delayed.

"They will lose weight under your care," the journalist said.

"Oh, we had more important things on our mind than breakfast!" William Tell answered her.

"Well, well," I said. "Time for your report."

Our journalist sighed with feigned regret.

"I wanted to join the team of Mr. Wheels, but he does not want to accept me. Why don't you stand up for me?"

I said with indignation:

"Did you fellows know that this lady is from the newspaper? She is going to give it all away."

"Really? Will you mention us?" the boys did not seem indignant. On the contrary, they seemed flattered.

I hastened to explain:

"Ask her how she intends to describe us. She thinks we are harmless madmen. She thinks only crazy people can engage in a search for Templar treasure. All of Poland will laugh at us. You will be the laughingstock of your classmates."

"Then we must be very careful with this lady!" cried Squirrel.

"Oh, yes," confirmed Tell. "And never peep a word to her."

Our friend laughed. She was amused by the indignation of the scouts. In the end, however, she stomped her foot:

"Quiet, boys! Now for your report. I want to know what has been going on here."

I interjected:

"Oh, no! You won't hear anything from us. We don't give any information to the press."

"That's right," nodded the scouts. "Whose side are you on? Ours or theirs? Please take a stand."

"I am on no side," she replied. "I am only an observer. An objective observer, do you understand?"

I didn't quite know how to behave in front of such an objective and rational person. The matter required careful thought and deliberation.

"Why don't we go somewhere off to the side and talk," suggested Tell. But Anka protested, making an offended face again:

"Oh, I am very sorry. It seems to me that I am a trustworthy person. You can be sure that I will not pass to your competition anything I hear from you. I will keep it for myself and—my newspaper."

Squirrel was the first to relent:

"I would like to be a journalist," he said. "And it seems to me that we should help the press."

"A journalist?" laughed Tell. "Last summer, you wanted to become an anthropologist."

"I have changed my mind," announced Squirrel angrily.

They started an argument about whether one should change one's views on one's choice of profession so quickly. I interrupted this dispute and asked them to report on what they had learned in the village, never mind the presence of a journalist.

"Late at night," began Hawkeye's story, "three thugs arrived in a *Varshava*."

"We saw a *Varshava* on the road to Milkokuk," I reminded the journalist.

"We call them thugs because they speak uncouth language and behave abominably. They started banging on the teacher's house, banging on the closed doors and shutters with their fists. We approached them and told them that the teacher had gone on a trip for several days. That angered them, they cursed; they called us loopy and snotty. They smelled of beer. Finally, they gave up banging on the shutters and went to spend the night at the lake. They must have made quite a racket there since, at dawn, the Petersens and Kozlovski dismantled their camp by the lake and showed up in the village. When they ascertained that the teacher had not yet returned, they asked a boy passing through the village about the objective of the teacher's excursion. We spoke with the boy later and learned that while he did not know exactly in which direction the teacher had gone, he had heard that the purpose of the trip was to visit the site of an 1863 battle somewhere near Suvalki. After hearing this, the Petersens left the village and disappeared around a bend in the road toward Ghiby. Probably, they went in search of the battlefield."

"We should do it, too," I stated.

"Then Hamster arrived on a *Yunak*."

"Who?"

"A young man dressed in a leather biker outfit. He has a face like a hamster. He knocked on the teacher's door and, after making sure that the teacher wasn't home, looked around and—began to pry the shutter open with a knife! He didn't notice us because we were sitting in the bushes."

"That is some suspicious type!" I called out.

"Definitely. But he gave up on breaking the shutter, put the knife in his pocket, and left—also in the direction of Ghiby. Then a blue *Skoda* arrived and in it—some middle-aged couple. They confirmed that the teacher was still not back and left."

"Also towards Ghiby?"

"No. Toward Lake Zelva. He started fishing there, and she sunbathed on a blanket."

At that very moment, we saw a cloud of dust on the road. From the direction of Lake Milkokuk came lumbering a pearl-grey *Varshava*. But the car did not turn to the teacher's house, but to the left, towards the forest and the forester's lodge. It disappeared around the bend of the road to Ghiby.

"They slept in, and now they probably went to get some beer," said Anka.

I was of a different opinion.

"They're all rushing to find the schoolteacher. And they are right. Sitting here waiting for him to return is an unnecessary waste of time. This document he has, or says he has, may not be worth anything, so it seems logical to eliminate it as soon as possible. We, too, should set out to find him."

"Well, yes, but where do we find him?" Tell shrugged his shoulders.

In the crate of books I had in my car, I had a guidebook to the Suvalki region. I now flipped through its many pages containing completely useless information about geological formations and types of agriculture until I finally came upon:

A BRIEF HISTORY
OF THE
SUVALKI REGION

I read aloud:

"Numerous battles were fought in the area during the 1863-1864 uprising, and the rebel's greatest victory was the capture of Rye-grood. The insurgents were led by Generals Ghyoogood, Dembinski, and Sherakovski.

"The preparations for and the outbreak of the 1863 uprising in the region had been led by a Polish officer formerly in Russian service, Karol Yastshembski, and the emissaries of the National Committee in Paris, Honjinski and Vaver-Ramontovski. The latter was a veteran of the 1831 uprising and an officer of the famed Fourth Regiment. He fought several successful engagements in the Augustov Forest: two in April 1863, between Lipsk and Yastshembna and between Balinka and the Black Ford, and two in May at Kadish and at Black Hancha. Traces of these battles can still be fond as well as many graves and monuments, some raised surreptitiously by the local population after the fall of the uprising."

"There you have it," I sighed. "'Traces of *many* battles.'"

But then I remembered that I also had a map that marked nature reserves, monuments, battlefields, and similar noteworthy sites.

After reviewing the map, I concluded:

"The most important localities commemorating the battles of 1863 are the village of Grushki, where the Vaver regiment defeated the Russians. Further on is the charming village of Goat Market, where there are graves of insurgents. Slightly further lies the village of Uprising, whose name commemorates the fact that the site once served as the insurgents' camp."

"So?" muttered Squirrel.

I wondered aloud:

"The teacher went on foot, right?"

"Yes," said the boys.

"So, he didn't have to head along paved roads but was free to walk along forest paths. Had I been in his shoes, I would have set off through the woods toward the village of Grushki. From there I would have gone to Goat Market, and only from there to Uprising. In this way, I would have made a circle and returned to Milkokuk. Of course, he could have done the opposite: first gone to Uprising, then Goat Market, and finally to Grushki. When did the teacher set out?”

“Two days ago,” replied the scouts.

“In that case, whichever way he had gone, he should be in Goat Market today.”

“Bravo, bravo!” Anka clapped her hands. “Elementary, Watson! Elementary!”

I paid no attention to her jibes.

“We are going to Goat Market, then. And that means now, my dear friends.”

“Goat Market? What a name for a town!” groaned Hawkeye. I looked at the guidebook.

“Goat Market,” I read, “is a charming forest enclave within a nature reserve of two hundred and eighty acres. The wilderness contains the graves of insurgents and the habitat of red elk. Access is difficult, especially during the rains when the area becomes waterlogged. One can get there by making a turn onto a forest track at a signpost on the Augustov-Lipsk highway. Or by leaving one’s car on the highway and walking through the forest. Goat Market is located about a mile and a half from the highway.”

“Well, well, well! Let’s rrrrrrumble, people! Let’s shop goat!” rejoiced Squirrel. “I’ve never been to a *charming forest enclave!* There are most likely very tall trees there. I would gladly climb to the very top of the tallest of them.”

“The place is a nature reserve,” Tell reminded him, “You will have to behave like a cultured and educated person, not like a monkey jumping from tree to tree. It is forbidden to frighten game, to light bonfires, and in general to disturb the appearance of the forest in any way.”

“Hey, how about spotting a moose in the wild?” daydreamed Hawkeye.

In short, we were all keen to see Goat Market. A sensible comment from Anka poured cold water on everything:

"And what happens if your calculations turn out to be wrong? Some truck gave them a ride, and the teacher will show up back in the village today? And the mysterious document will not get into your hands but into the hands of that married couple who most reasonably decided to wait here and are now relaxing at Lake Zelva?"

I nodded.

"This young lady is right. One of us must stay here. Our calculations may prove wrong."

It was obvious that I had to drive the car. Only the scouts, or at any rate one of them, were in the reckoning.

My friends made very sad faces: they were all anxious to visit a *charming forest enclave*. And then the journalist said:

"I'll tell you what. I'll stay here. You will find that I can be relied on. I guarantee that the mysterious document will be waiting here for you when you come back."

It was a very generous offer. We thanked her from the bottom of our hearts.

CHAPTER SIX: MASON'S MARKS

The attack of yellow jackets. A trek through the wilderness. A cry for help. The secret signs of the Knights Templar. A tale of old castles. A meeting in the forest.

We had an early dinner in Augustov, and at five in the afternoon, we set off for Goat Market. Despite the evening hour, the air was stifling, and the heat unrelieved by even the faintest breeze. The sky grew hazy as if someone had spilled milk all over it. A major storm was brewing.

We drove through the vast Augustov Forest. After twelve miles, we saw a signpost with the inscription *Goat Market*. All around us stretched a dense forest with not a trace of human occupation—neither a house nor a forester's lodge. It was a real wilderness full of... yellow jackets: of large, vicious insects that attacked us as soon as we hit the forest path. Perhaps the swarming season was underway, and the swampy area of the Goat Market was their favorite place to swarm. We were surrounded by billions of these monsters, half a finger in size, with yellow-gold bellies and large, painful stings. They filled the car with loud buzzing, smashing against the windows and against our noses. As if enraged by the heat, they thudded about in the car, colliding with each other and our faces.

It seemed fun at first until one hit me in the right eye, and another stung me on my neck. We closed the windows, but even so, many monsters remained inside, and it became terribly stuffy. The buzzing increased, the boys flailed about with a newspaper. I struggled to catch air through my open mouth.

Meanwhile, we arrived at a crossroads in the forest and a second signpost with the inscription *Goat Market*. But its arrow... pointed straight up to heaven.

"Someone's playing stupid jokes," I said. "Let's turn back, or we'll get lost and be devoured by these rabid insects. We will reach Goat Market on foot."

The flies seemed to quiet down for a while, but then, one by one, they emerged from some nooks of the car and began their wild dance from window to window, perching on our arms, necks, and faces while we sweated like mad. I bet the smell of our sweat probably irritated them even more. Wherever they sat, they stung.

Finally, we got out onto the highway. A yellowish cloud of large flies swirled above our car. I hit the gas, and the monsters stayed behind. We opened the windows and breathed in the outside air with relief. About a mile on, I turned the car into a forest clearing and left it there, obscured by bushes and trees and invisible from the road. But the yellow jackets were also rampant here—the entire forest seemed to tremble with their incessant buzzing. So, we took our rain ponchos from the car and, covering our heads with the hoods, plunged into the forest.

We tore through the bushes, our feet sinking into the fluffy moss covering the peaty soil. We trudged through huge clearings full of waist-high ferns. And everywhere, we were accompanied by constant buzzing and repeated attacks of the yellow beasts. We had already stopped fending them off and only huddled under our jackets, tightly covering our faces. Only once, having lifted my hood a bit, I looked up into the sky above the treetops. And I became frightened—for the sky was crimson as if reflecting the glare of a huge conflagration.

I glanced at the compass on my watch strap. We were walking in the right direction, but Goat Market was still nowhere to be seen. Besides, I had no idea what Goat Market looked like. Was it a settlement or merely a clearing in the forest? Or was it perhaps just a few graves scattered among the trees? In the thick forest, we could quite easily miss such graves, even at a distance of a dozen steps.

"Let's rest," gasped William Tell. He was carrying his huge crossbow on his shoulder and, not surprisingly, was the most tired.

I commanded a short rest. We sat down in a clearing overgrown with ferns.

"Phew!" I gasped, exhausted by the muggy heat. "I am not surprised that the ancient Yotvingians were able to resist the onslaught of the Teutonic Knights for so many years. A knight clapped in steel was worth little in this thicket."

"Please tell us about the Yotvingians, Mr. Wheels!"

"Now? I'm barely alive!" I gasped.

And just at that moment, a loud thunderclap resounded directly overhead.

"Get up, boys!" I commanded. "Goat Market can't be far, and we really should find the teacher before this storm breaks loose!"

Reluctantly, they rose from the ground. The air was so humid it felt as if someone had sucked out all oxygen from it. The approaching thunderstorm seemed to drive the flies mad. They attacked us again with redoubled fury, and we felt constant thuds on our heads and arms covered with the rain ponchos. Our eyes were flooded with sweat, every step seemed something beyond our strength. Whenever we stopped to catch our breath, all we heard was the mad buzzing of insects.

And the forest around us kept closing in with an ever more impenetrable thicket of tangled bushes and low-hanging branches. The sky turned from purple to brown and then black.

A thunder roared again, and its rumble rolled over the forest. It gradually quieted down, and then we heard a cry:

"Help! Help! Help!"

It was a woman's voice calling out in English. It was Miss Petersen!

The voice came from somewhere to the right. I jumped in that direction, and the boys ran after me.

Like a noble knight on a mission, I felt no heat and paid no attention to the enraged insects. I ran, tearing through the bushes, breaking branches, and ripping off leaves. I was not at all surprised to learn that Miss Petersen was here. Looking for the school teacher like us, she must have followed the same clues as we did. But why was she calling for help?

A small clearing opened before me. Miss Karen stood in its middle, surrounded by three men. Just as I ran out of the woods, one of them snatched her bag and ripped it off her shoulder.

Both she and they heard our approach at the same time. The three men looked at each other uncertainly. Miss Petersen ran toward me.

"Help, Mr. Thomas! Help! They are trying to rob me!"

Our scouts emerged behind me. William Tell immediately loaded his crossbow and aimed it menacingly at the men. I shouted:

"What do you want from this young lady?"

The men did not immediately answer. They looked closely first at me and then at the three scouts. It seemed to me that they were assessing our strength and theirs. It was obvious that they were stronger.

"I know them!" exclaimed Hawkeye suddenly. "They are these thugs from Warsaw. They came last night in a *Varshava*."

And he rattled off their license plate number. And this, I think, saved us from a fight in which we would probably have taken a good thrashing. The realization that we knew their license plate number stopped them on the dime.

One of the thugs, a thin and tall fellow, shrugged his shoulders.

"This lady can't speak Polish. We don't know why she got scared. We thought she got lost in the forest and wanted to lead her back to safety."

"And the bag?" I pointed with my finger.

"Bag?" the skinny fellow looked at the object he held in his hands. "Oh yes, the bag. Well, we are gentlemen, aren't we? W just wanted to help her carry it."

The second fellow came to his aid. And soon, so did the third, too. They took turns saying:

"She doesn't know Polish. She saw three men in the middle of the forest and started to scream. But none of us had the least thought of harming her."

They put the bag on the grass. The tall, skinny fellow looked up at the sky and said:

"Fellas, it's about to dump. Let's split.".

Meanwhile, Miss Petersen told her story in a voice still stifled by fear:

"They surrounded me in the forest. They snatched my bag. I defended myself and started calling for help."

Squirrel whispered in my ear:

"These three clowns tried to break into the teacher's house last night."

And at that instant, it thundered again: very, very close and very, very loud. We were all stunned by the noise for a moment. The thunder reverberated through the forest for several seconds.

"Now, let's move it," ordered the lean fellow.

And he was the first to disappear into the forest on the other side of the clearing. The other two ran after him. And now all there was left in the middle of the clearing was—Miss Petersen's bag. The scouts picked it up and handed it to Karen.

And then the storm broke in earnest. Leaves rustled, first quietly, then louder. A powerful gust of wind hit the treetops overhead, suddenly, it became dark all around, dry grasses and leaves swirled in the air. The black sky was ripped by a golden zigzag of lightning, and the thunderclap followed almost instantly. Then one more, then a third, then a fourth. First heavy raindrops, fat like grapeshot, hit us in our faces.

I knew we wouldn't have enough time to return to the car before all hell broke loose.

"Break two branches, guys. Let's put up a lean-to," I ordered.

A lean-to? That was easier said than done. We had four rain ponchos with us. In theory, you can make a very good lean-to with two. But have you ever tried to build a lean-to with blasting wind and pouring rain?

Still, we managed to cross two branches and hang our rain ponchos from them before it really began to pour. We climbed underneath, taking cover from the rain. There was no time for more refined construction. A torrential downpour began, and sitting under the lean-to we had the impression that someone had opened up at us with a fire hose. In the lean-to, it was cramped and dark. We couldn't even make out each other's faces. But we were mostly screened from the rain.

"Where is your father? Where is Kozlovski?" I asked Miss Karen.

"My father stayed in Ghiby. In that resort for journalists. He rented a motorboat."

"He is waiting for the teacher to return?" I guessed.

"Yes. And Mr. Kozlovski and I came here. But some good-for-nothings had messed with the signposts. We got lost in the forest, and at the last crossroads, we decided to split: Kozlovski would go left, and I would go right. And that's how I ended up in the clearing where these unsavory types attacked me.”

“They probably screwed up the signposts,” I guessed. “They, too, are looking for the Templar treasure. This is what I feared when I saw the article in the newspaper. I guessed that it might encourage all sorts to search for it. I expect this is not the last we hear of them.”

“I don’t think so,” she said. “I think they have already given up. In this kind of business, you need not just enthusiasm but, above all, some knowledge. Brute force won’t do anything here. They must have already come to the same conclusion because they decided to rob me. They thought that I had money in my bag and in this way, they would compensate themselves for the hardship of driving all the way here. They had to realize that after this, they could never return to Milkokuk again.”

“I, too, will probably give up the search,” I said unexpectedly, surprising even myself.

“You?” she wondered. “You must be joking.”

“No, I am not. I have no idea how to go about this business. In the past, with this kind of search, I have always had some sort of a plan of action, some single, if only modest, point of attack. But this time, I have nothing. Absolutely nothing.”

“But you have already started, isn’t that an ‘attack’?” she laughed.

“We have a saying in Polish: ‘all bad things have nice beginnings.’ Do you have a saying like that in Denmark? My nice beginning has been to sit with you in this improvised lean-to.”

“A very pleasant adventure,” she said agreeably.

“Well, yes. Only it doesn’t advance us one step forward. Let us assume that the Templar treasure has been hidden in one of the Teutonic castles. The thing is—which one? Do you know how many Teutonic castles we have in Poland?”

“No.”

“I would say, at a guess, a hundred.”

“Well, I am very much counting on this mysterious document in the possession of the schoolteacher.”

“There is no reason to think that the document contains any clue to the location of the treasure. It seems to me that I am wasting my time here. Look, there are very few private archives in Poland. I find it hard to believe that a humble schoolteacher from a village with a ridiculous name found an ancient document. Where? At the local library?"

"So why aren't you looking in Teutonic castles?"

"Well, I don't know which castle to go to."

We broke off the conversation. It was still raining, though no longer as hard. The thunderstorm moved away. When I stepped out for a moment, I saw that the sky was still navy blue, and the forest was sinking in the twilight of the approaching night. A cold wind was blowing, and time and again, new waves of rain came. It was quite warm under the lean-to, and we decided to wait until the storm quieted down completely.

"It might be worth asking Miss Petersen," William Tell said to me, "if she has tried to look for the Templar treasure in France!"

I repeated the boy's question to her.

"No," she said. "But I know about many such searches in France because they were made by my father's friends, members of the Society. Anyway, even Mr. Chabrol once looked for the Templar treasure. When my father and I stayed in Paris a few years ago as his guests, there was a lot of talk about this treasure in his house. I remember how impressed I was with his attempts to decipher the secret writing of the Templars. Because, you know, the Templars left a lot of bizarre signs on the walls of their castles. Mr. Chabrol collected them and, with the help of experts, tried to determine their meaning."

"Mr Wheels! Mr. Wheels! Ask her to draw them for us! They will be useful for scouting games," said Hawkeye. I turned on my electric flashlight and handed my notebook and pencil to Miss Petersen.

"Oh, I only remember a few. There were so many."

Karen began to draw, while explaining the meaning of the figures.

"This kind of cross points to a hidden object, perhaps a treasure. This sign—to a secret passage. This sign means *gold*. Here, you have *turn left*. And this means *nine yards*. Now, this sign comes from the walls of the Argina castle. These two overlapping circles say, *straight ahead*. This is a symbol for *danger*. This shield indicates *a well* and this sign—*a library*. Here is a sign symbolizing *ground level*. These last three signs come from the walls of the Templar castle in Charroux.

Medieval Mason's Marks

"You see, many of these signs weren't really secret signs indicating treasure. They were stone mason's marks. Back in the Middle Ages, builders drew no plans. The plan of the structure of a castle or a church or a tower was a secret carried in the master builder's head. This is how he protected his business but also the safety of his clients. A plan that was never drawn could never be copied, executed by another, or stolen and used to undermine a fortress.

"But the master builder had to communicate with his stone masons somehow—tell them how deep to dig a foundation or how far to take a trench and so on. So, he used these marks—we call them stone mason's marks—to give his men instructions: dig here; or dig nine yards from here; or drop a shaft behind this wall; or a well goes here. His men were capable stone masons, they knew how to cut, remove, carry, and place stone, sometimes huge blocks, sometimes seven floors up or down. They were not stupid men. But they could not read or write, so it was useless to scratch out in the stone "dig a well twenty feet from here." Instead, the master made a mark, which the stone masons understood. And these marks became secret knowledge. The stone masons took this knowledge from one construction site to the next.

And sometimes, to get a job somewhere, they had to show that they understand these secret marks."

I turned off the electric flashlight and put away the notebook with the drawings. It became dark under the lean-to again. But this darkness and the rain rustling outside fostered stories about old castles and treasure hunts. Miss Petersen told a story, and I translated it from English so that the scouts could hear it:

"Mr. Chabrol comes from a rather old French family, a very wealthy one. An old prayer book was once found in his grandfather's library, and it contained a note written in the margin by an unknown hand:

"'Look for the Templar treasure in the chapel,' the note said. 'The Saint and the Truth will show you the way.' This note so captivated young Chabrol's imagination that after graduation, having enough money to support himself, he took up collecting Templar memorabilia and searching for their legendary treasure. For a long time, Mr. Chabrol traveled around France, visiting former Templar castles. And in the village of Montcroix—that is, 'Mountain of the Cross'—he came upon a chapel that had once been part of a ruined castle. And in this chapel hung an old painting depicting some saint adored by an allegorical figure symbolizing Truth. Anyway, under the painting was an inscription: *Veritas*, which means *Truth*. Mr. Chabrol began to search the chapel and discovered that there were underground halls and corridors under the castle ruins. This was big news in France at the time and garnered him a lot of fame, but he never found any treasure.

"Well, OK. The Knights Templar were masters at building secret caches. They were bankers, after all, and they did handle very large amounts of cash. So, they made sure it was not so easy to break into their vaults. But the note found in the prayer book, as well as that painting in the castle chapel, date from a much later period, long after the destruction of the Templar order. Most likely, the note was made by someone who guessed where the treasure was located. But did he find it? So many madcaps in this story. I doubt he did."

"Now, in Southern France, on the banks of the River Rhône, there stands the castle of Agine," Miss Petersen continued. "In its name, etymologists have sought the sound of Argine, which is an anagram of the word Regina, meaning queen. And the Tarot symbol of hidden treasures used to be the "Queen of Clubs." In any case, the locals thought that the legendary Templar treasure was hidden there. So far, however, no search has yielded any results."

"Then, in the town of Die, in the Dróme department, one of my father's acquaintances owns a rather large piece of land, and on it are some remains of a former Templar castle demolished by Philip the Fair. My father's acquaintance even has a notion in which part of the wall to look for the treasure, since a mason's sign on the walls seems to indicate a treasury. But he never found the treasure despite a painstaking search. But a record from 1737 states that two urns weighing two quintals each, and a casket with three locks had been found when breaking a vault in the building abutting the wall. The urn contained gold and silver coins, while the casket contained gold and silver plate. But our friend believes that the main part of the treasure is yet to be discovered. He once managed to discover a statuette depicting a praying monk and a small jug containing coins. Both date to the 12th century. However, neither was a terribly valuable find. And so, our friend searches on."

A loud yet mournful roar suddenly resounded near us, and then a heavy thud. Terrified, we jumped out of the tent. The rain was almost over. The sky was clearing of clouds. And in the falling twilight, we saw a huge elk running through the clearing. The big, fawn-colored animal carried its horned head high. At the sight of us, it turned its muzzle toward us, its eyes shining menacingly. But it immediately crossed the clearing in a few huge jumps and, with a rustling of branches, disappeared into the thicket.

"Well, well, it was worth coming here just to see a sight like this," said Karen, delighted. I nodded my head.

"Oh, yes! Especially since our search for the school teacher has come to nothing. We're going back, aren't we?"

We helped Miss Petersen find her Lincoln. Inside, we found Mr. Kozlovski, as usual, dressed with studied elegance.

"Good God, how worried I was about you!" he exclaimed upon seeing Karen. "There was this terrible storm, and you were not back. I was just about to start searching for you!"

"Oh, yes? How nice of you, but how superfluous. Mr. Thomas

found me and protected me from the storm."

Kozlovski measured me with an offended glare. We all got into the Lincoln and drove out onto the road. Karen drove us to where my vehicle stood, hidden in the bush. We jumped in, and she and Kozlovski took off for Augustov. They led the way, and we followed.

I deliberately drove very slowly. Miss Karen at first tried to drive slowly also so that we may keep up, but soon she got bored with my speed. She accelerated, and the Lincoln pulled ahead.

"Mr. Thomas!" the boys were angry. "Why do you let yourself be left behind like that? You have the fastest car in the world. Show them what you can do."

I shook my head.

"No, my dear friends. I will not reveal my hand. I prefer that they think that my car is a worthless piece of junk. It may come in very handy someday."

CHAPTER SEVEN: THE BREAK-IN

Where is the Lady in Black? Fun and games at the club. I suggest drowning Kozlovski. A green flare. A race on the lake. Where is the mysterious document?

Night had fallen. In Milkokuk we found the teacher's cottage still locked up. But we saw no trace of the journalist, either. Her absence worried me a little.

"You will remain on guard here, as you did yesterday," I ordered my scouts. "You will pitch a tent in the orchard behind the hedge. Make dinner, and then take turns watching the lodge. In the meantime, I will go to the journalists' center on the other side of Lake Pomerania. It is about seven miles by road. It would be much quicker to just cross the lake, but..."

"You do not want to reveal your hand," said Tell.

"You got that right, smart cookie," I said, said goodbye, and jumped into the vehicle.

"Ah, Tell," I remembered something and called out to the boy. "Do you know how to handle a flare gun?"

"Of course! We all do!" Tell nearly took offense at my suspecting him of lacking skill in this area. "We learned that at the Boy Scout camp."

I took my flare gun out of its case and handed it to Tell.

"Just remember, don't shoot anyone with it. You could really hurt someone."

"Who do you think we are? Children?" Tell became indignant. "I'll only shoot if necessary, and I will do so over the water so as not to cause a fire."

"It is loaded with a green flare," I said. "If something important happens here, fire it, and I will see it and come immediately."

He saluted me in scouting fashion, and I took the circuitous route around Lake Pomerania.

The journalists' resort was located on a tall promontory jutting out into the lake. The shore was quite high and overgrown with pine forest. Colorful camping cabins stood among the trees, and there was a rather large brick building at the tip of the promontory. Downstairs, it housed a storage room for kayaks and motorboats. Upstairs, there was a canteen and a club room with large windows through which one could see a magnificent panorama of the lake and the opposite high shore.

I saw the Petersen's Lincoln at the edge of the resort and their trailer among the trees. The windows of the clubroom were glowing with lights because the resort had electricity. The sounds of live music flowed through the windows, and I could see people dancing. There was a party in the clubhouse.

I climbed the wooden steps to the terrace surrounding the club room. The music had just stopped for a moment, and through the wide-open door, several people slipped out onto the terrace to take fresh air.

"You've been watching the teacher's house nicely," I said with a wry smile. Dressed in a pretty dress and with a fancy hairdo, Anka came across the terrace towards me with Kozlovski in tow.

"Oh, is that you?" she was surprised. "It's been a very long time since you left for the Goat Market. I couldn't wait for you there—there was a party here."

"Well, sure," I nodded. "A party is always more important. What was this thing about 'reliable allies' and all?"

She became embarrassed.

Kozlovski said:

"I didn't know you were an ally of Mr. Wheels," he said with an exaggerated surprise. "Mr. Wheels seems quite quick in making friends and influencing people. That is, er, allies."

That said, he turned toward the door where Miss Petersen stood.

"Oh, my knight in shining armor!" exclaimed Karen. "Great to have you here. Let's dance, shall we?"

Anka pouted her lips.

"I was supposed to sit in Milkokuk and wait endlessly for the teacher to return while you were in charge of picking up beautiful girls.

Is that how the alliance works? Is that the division of tasks?"

Old Petersen came out of the club room. Kozlovski said to him in English:

"Of all of us, only Mr. Wheels is heading straight for his objectives. He knows where the greatest treasure lies, and he is going to get it, mark my words. And he's not after some Templar treasure at all."

"What?" Petersen asked.

"Oh?" laughed Karen. It turned out that Anka spoke English quite well and understood Kozlovski's words. She replied with studied venom:

"Because, you see, your treasure is where your heart is. Mr. Wheels has invested his heart in the right place."

I felt a strong urge to throw Mr. Kozlovski over the balustrade and into the lake. However, I was a well-mannered man, and there was nothing for me to do but respond in a polite tone:

"Mr. Kozlovski is right. Since I met Miss Karen, I have learned to value the treasure of the heart above the jewels of the Templars. Lucky thing, therefore, that someone had let the air out the air out of my tires the other day, or I would have never had a chance to get to know Miss Karen better."

"How cunning of you to have used that vehicle of yours to go after treasure," Anka commented icily. "No vehicle—no tires to deflate."

Captain Petersen turned to me with feigned seriousness:

"Let us in on your secret, as mysterious as the Knights Templar. Did you build your car yourself?"

"No," I replied with complete calm. "My uncle did."

I don't know what was comical about what I said, but everyone, Anka, Petersen, Karen, and a few journalists who came out to the terrace burst out laughing.

"And who was your uncle?" Petersen asked.

"An inventor."

"A famous inventor?"

"No, completely unknown."

"So this car is his only invention?"

And now the floodgates opened, and mean comments about

my unfortunate car came fast and furious—while the vehicle, clearly visible from the terrace, calmly glared at us with the bug eyes of its headlights. I had already become accustomed to such comments about its ugliness; they made no impression on me.

"In Denmark, you would be fined for disturbing public peace with an ugly car like that."

"There is no accounting for taste," I replied. But they continued to joke:

"You could show it at an amusement park for money," suggested one of the journalists.

"Oh, Mr. Wheels does that already, in the winter. In the summer, he drives it," said another.

The sounds of a sentimental slow dance sounded in the club room. My mockers broke off, and everyone went to dance. Karen had forgotten that she had offered to dance with me and took Kozlovski in her hand. Captain Petersen asked Anka to dance. I remained alone and studied my vehicle with a reluctant eye. So, what if it was fast and reliable and had a lot of other wonderful qualities if it brought ridicule to me? The truth was that I could not afford a beautiful car. I had received my monstrosity as a gift, but perhaps it would have been better not to have a car at all than to drive around in such a contraption?

Through the windows of the club room, I saw that Miss Petersen suddenly stopped dancing. And after a while, she came out to me on the terrace.

"Wait, weren't we supposed to have this dance?"

She smiled beautifully, and her big green eyes looked at me with undisguised friendship.

"Shall we dance?" she said, taking my hand. "I don't suppose you were offended by all those jokes?"

"We shall see who will laugh in the end," I muttered.

And I went in to dance with Karen. Captain Petersen danced with Anka next to us.

"Tomorrow, you will throw your car into the lake," Karen whispered in my ear. "And you will work with us. You will get an advance with which you will buy a nice new car. You saved me from the hands of those thugs. I will never forget it."

But I was profoundly shaken by the idea that I might throw my vehicle into the lake. No, it certainly did not deserve such a fate.

"It is a perfectly good car," I defended my wheels.

"There you are, starting that again! It's making people ridicule you!"

"I am not afraid of ridicule."

"But I am. And so is my father."

"I am sorry, but I do not see why I should care."

"So, Mr. Kozlovski was mistaken? Have I also misunderstood your words?" she asked flirtatiously. "I understood that you liked me."

"Oh, Miss Karen," I said and blushed terribly.

"Oh, I see. Well, I also like you. But I don't want you to be ridiculous. I would like to have at my side a man who is brave, like you, and, well, dashing. And don't ask me to propose to you... But I have heard from Mr. Chabrol that you are capable of great cunning when searching for lost collections. I suspect that you know in which Teutonic castle the Templar treasure is hidden. I am sure that thanks to you we will be able to find it. There will be a lot of good public relations in that. Later, you can assist my father in extracting gold from sunken galleons. You will be rich."

And these words suddenly sobered me up. I remembered the moment when, holding hands, Karen and I entered the forest while Kozlovski and Petersen let the air out of the wheels of my car and drove off to Milkokuk. These people were ruthless. I realized that I was, in this girl's eyes, just some young man with a funny car who might be useful in her treasure hunt.

"For you, Karen," I whispered, "I am ready to do anything. I will lay the treasure of the Templars at your feet. I will do anything you want. Except for one thing."

"Except what?"

"Except get rid of my vehicle. I love both you and my car."

"You're crazy," she hissed but turned red. Seeing my innocent expression, she tried to be sweet again. "Well, well. Keep your vehicle if you are so attached to it. It will be a sacrifice on my part. A sacrifice in the name of our affection."

I led us into an elaborate figure and saw Anka's eyes peering at me with an ironic smile. Karen and I probably looked comical. It might have seemed like Miss Petersen was whispering sweet nothings in my ear, and I had a look on my face as if I stood at the threshold of paradise.

"I will find the Templar treasures and lay them at your feet," I said in awe.

"We will find it together," she corrected me.

"Oh, no!" I said. "I will do it alone."

"Why? Don't you think it would be very beautiful to find the treasure together? You and I..." she said and smiled sweetly, although I could sense that she was getting irritated.

"I am ready for anything and everything," I whispered. "I'm even ready to drown my vehicle."

"Yes?" she whispered.

"But on one condition."

"And what is that?"

"I'll drown my car, and you drown Kozlovski. We will do it at daybreak. We'll tie a millstone around his neck and..."

She stopped dancing.

"Are you mocking me?"

"Aren't you mocking me?" I asked.

She gave no response. She took offense and walked out onto the terrace, leaving me in the middle of the dance floor, stranded among the dancing couples.

Ha, I thought vindictively. *I'm supposed to find the Templar treasure for you, and you're going to set me up like you did when I helped you pull your Lincoln out of the mud. Truly, there is no honor among thieves!*

Suddenly, through the huge windows of the club room, we saw a bright green light in the sky. It shot out from behind the forest-covered hills on the other side of the lake and floated high up, clearly visible against the black sky. It then burst into thousands of sparks that slowly fell downward into the murky surface of the lake.

"Oh, how lovely!" exclaimed Anka. "Fireworks? In Milkokuk?"

I jumped toward the door, where I nearly bumped into Miss Karen, returning from the terrace.

"This is a distress signal," she said to me. "A flare from

Milkokuk. Maybe the teacher has already returned?"

But I did not stop to talk to her. I ran downstairs and into the trees—to my vehicle. I got behind the wheel and started the engine. It took quite a long time before I found a convenient incline to the lake. And then, my vehicle rolled into the water with a huge splash. It seemed to me that someone was calling out to me from the terrace of the clubroom, but I didn't pay attention as a huge wave momentarily flooded my windshield. Only then did I see two speedboats detaching from the pier. In one sat Karen and Kozlovski, and in the other, Anka and Captain Petersen.

I revved up. The vehicle rocked on the waves, I shifted gears and pushed on. The powerboats, despite having shapes adapted to speed on water, fell behind. The twelve cylinders of the Ferrari 410 milled the turbine with such force that the car broke the resistance of the water, rose nose up above it, and glided across the lake like a hovercraft. What chance did one or even two-cylinder powerboats stand against it?

The other shore of the lake approached quickly. I reached the cove where I had spent the previous night. I went around the thicket of reeds, not wanting them to screw into the turbine, and emerged onto the meadow stretching along the shore. The motorboats were two hundred feet behind, but it didn't matter. Their passengers had to leave them at the shore anyway and do the remaining mile and a half separating the lake from the village on foot. But I was able to cover this distance with my car in three minutes. By the time they reached the shore, I was already disappearing into the forest. I felt anxious about the boys. But maybe the green rocket didn't mean danger at all, but only some other important event? *Probably the teacher has returned*, I thought to myself.

Soon, my headlights caught the outline of the first homesteads. Then, in a swift rush, I passed a few more huts on one side of the road and came to the hedge surrounding the teacher's house. At the wicket leading into the yard stood my three friends.

"What happened?" I asked, jumping out of the car. Only now did I notice that all three of them were very pale.

"Speak up at last!"

"We messed up," sighed Tell. "We were guarding the cottage

from the front, and meanwhile, someone broke in through the back kitchen window. Perhaps he stole the document. He robbed the place right under our noses."

"And you didn't notice a thing?"

"First came Hamster on his *Yunak*. He knocked on the door and, having convinced himself that the teacher was not there yet, drove away. After a while, that couple arrived in a blue Skoda. They knocked and also drove off to the lake. After that, no one came here. We did not hear any sounds. We decided to make the rounds every half hour and then we noticed that a shutter had been broken and the glass had been removed.

"Maybe it happened before we returned from Goat Market?"

"No," they all shook their heads. "We inspected the house when you left for the journalists' center. At that time, the shutter was certainly not broken."

We went to the back of the house to inspect the kitchen window. Someone had broken the hinges, then removed the glass and—presumably—climbed inside. What was he looking for in the cottage? It wasn't hard to guess. Someone had been too impatient to wait for the teacher's return and wanted to take possession of the mysterious document. Besides, he or she may have worried that after the teacher's return, the document would end up not in his hands, but in mine or the Petersen's? Because one thing seemed certain in all this: the burglary had not been carried out by the Petersens or Kozlovski. They were with me at the center at the time.

We discussed the burglary for some more time and then heard quick footsteps. It was Karen and Anka, and a moment after them— Kozlovski and Petersen. I showed them the broken shutter and explained the incident.

"Do you think the document was stolen?" Karen asked.

"Someone went in—probably to steal it. But did he succeed? I don't know what the interior of the apartment looks like and whether the document was easy to find. The mysterious burglar didn't have much time to search."

"Or is the thief still in there?" Anka said.

"I looked through the broken window and shone my flashlight

inside. I saw some kitchen appliances and a half-open door to the next room.”

“You have to get inside,” decided Kozlovski.

I protested:

“That would be breaking in! Besides, by going in ourselves, we might destroy some crucial evidence. We should notify the militia instead.”

I asked Tell to bring a toolbox from the vehicle, and I nailed the shutter back in place.

“This is the best,” I said, “This way, we secured both all evidence and the house. The rest is up to the militia in Ghiby. There is a telephone at the journalists’ center. After returning there, we will call the militia.”

Meanwhile, Captain Petersen, with Kozlovski as his interpreter, questioned the scouts:

“Dear boys, don’t you know a certain Malinovski?”

Tell rudely snorted:

“Everyone of us knows some Malinovski. There are hundreds of thousands of Malinovskis in Poland. Which Malinovski you are asking about?”

“O rascal! O crook! I will break every bone in his body!” shouted Captain Petersen. Hawkeye spoke up:

“Maybe the burglary was carried out by that Malinovski, for whom you are looking?”

“Malinovski?” Petersen marveled. “It’s probable. I would not put that past him. He extorted four hundred dollars and the secret of the Templar treasure from me. He could easily have come here looking for the treasure.”

Miss Karen squatted next to me.

“Are you still angry with me? It was not me. It was Kozlovski and the others who made fun of your vehicle.”

“We have an old Polish saying: he laughs best who laughs last,” I said.

Captain Petersen gave me a friendly pat on the back:

“I will buy this funny car from you. I will give you one thousand dollars.”

"What's that?" I was outraged.

"Not enough? Well, I'll give one and a half thousand."

"It's not for sale."

Kozlovski pulled me aside and whispered in my ear:

"Don't be stupid! Take the money and buy yourself a real car. What other lunatic will pay you fifteen hundred bucks for your wreck?"

"No!" I growled.

I had had enough of Kozlovski. He sensed this because he immediately gave up his persuasions and suggested that they return to the speedboats.

And they all left. I drove the car into the orchard and parked it near the boys' tent. We went to sleep right away, they in the tent, and I in the vehicle.

That night, there was nothing left to guard. I felt strangely confident that the mysterious document was in enemy hands.

CHAPTER EIGHT: THE MYSTERIOUS DOCUMENT

What did the burglar steal? The militia. Squirrel makes an interesting observation. Who's camping on the island? On the trail of the mysterious document.

In the morning of the following day, two militiamen on bicycles arrived in Milkokuk. The journalists' center had a telephone connection to the world through the post office in Ghiby, but that was always closed at night. Thus, the militia post had not been notified until early in the morning, and the officers arrived only now. We gave them a detailed account of what had happened in Milkokuk, but they were not great scholars of history, so they did not understand the business of the Templar treasure. I suppose that my person, as well as my bizarre vehicle, did not inspire much confidence in them, either. On the other hand, they took the break-in very seriously. Exciting stuff like break-ins happened rarely in their area. All the same, they ended up deciding to wait for the teacher to return to ascertain what damage the burglar had caused.

And, as luck would have it, the teacher showed up only an hour later. He learned only now about the newspaper article and the excitement caused by the news of a mysterious document in his possession.

"Dear God, and I didn't know anything! So many people here waiting for me!" the teacher was surprised. "We went hiking along the January Uprising Trail, and then the boys persuaded me to go further still, to the Vigry River. I had no idea that people were looking for me. And you think that this burglar wanted to steal an old document?"

"I'm sure of it," I said.

"I'm afraid he will be disappointed. I don't know Latin at all, I'm a mathematics teacher. But I like to collect various antiquities. This document is in Latin, and someone even translated it for me once. It seems that it concerns some economic affairs of the Templar order. It certainly has the seal of the Templars on it: two knights on a horse."

The Seal of the Templar Order

showing two knights (perhaps Hugues de Payens and Godfrey de Saint-Omer) on one horse.
Contemporary legend held that the symbol represented the initial poverty of the order; that
they could afford only a single horse for every two men.

The teacher became very upset and rushed into his house to ascertain what the burglar had taken. This short, thin old man was the epitome of modesty and kindness. One got the impression that what really bothered him about the whole story was not that he had been robbed but that the burglar may have suffered a disappointment, having gone to all this length to steal a worthless document. And he was embarrassed by the realization that while he was on a trip with his students, so many people—foreigners among them!—wasted their time waiting for his return.

His house was a veritable warehouse of the strangest of objects. On the shelves arranged along the walls lay stones collected during school geological excursions. In the corners stood clay pots of local craftsmanship and several wooden sculptures made by local artists. From under the bed peeked out the handle of an old raddle, which had probably not been used in a hundred years. On the walls, I saw two funerary portraits of noblemen and framed documents of all sorts: old land grant deeds from the period of the enfranchisement of peasants (1865), announcements from the new authorities from the time following the second partition of Poland (1792), some rather disconcerting old posters of amateur pop music and similar odds and ends.

"Oh, here! Here hung the Templar document," the teacher pointed to an empty spot on the wall. "It was framed behind glass like the rest. It is not there. It has disappeared."

The teacher circulated among his collection for another while to confirm what I had long guessed: that nothing else had been taken—only the Templar document.

"I found it right after the war," he said. "In the summer of 1945, shortly after the liberation of Pomerania, I went there with a school trip. We spent the night near a rectory ruined by an artillery shell. The pastor (it was a German evangelical church) had fled with the Nazis, but some books remained in his apartment. I took an old bible, oh, there, that one. It was printed in the 17th century in Königsberg. And inside it, I found this document with a Templar seal."

"Do you remember the name of the village?" I asked.

"Oh, no, no," he sighed. "After all, that was twenty years ago. Who would remember the name now?"

"And if you looked at the map and tried to retrace the route of the trip from memory?"

"That might be worth a try. And I will try it if it matters to you so much," he offered.

"Yes, it does," I said. We had to stop talking because the militiamen got down to the business of writing a protocol.

"Nothing left for us to do here. Let's go to Lake Pomerania. Lets camp there," I said to the boys.

And having said goodbye to the teacher, we left. After a while, we drove the vehicle into the cove, where I had spent the night before.

"Are you very upset by the theft of the document?" Hawkeye asked.

"To be honest, I don't really believe it's worth much. Only in penny thrillers mysterious documents surface up in treasure hunts. It is quite possible that it is a Templar document, but the Templars have left all sorts of documents, most of them pretty mundane. It seems naive to assume that this one concerns the treasure or will lead us to it."

"So why did we even come here?"

"Because even if the document is not helpful, I wanted to make sure that we have not overlooked any clues. And while I don't pin any hopes on it, I also don't have any other idea of how to look for the treasure, either. And when one searches for something and thinks about it constantly, sometimes, as if by accident, one comes across interesting clues that lead him to his goal. It may turn out, for example, that the document is not helpful, but, for example, the location where it was found is."

We pulled up at the lake. Tell and Hawkeye set about preparing a meal—it was past lunchtime. Squirrel borrowed my binoculars and climbed a tall tree to—as he said—"get an idea of the topography." After a while, he called out to us from the top of the tree:

"What a view! The lake is vast, and on the other side, I see a white birch grove... and, o-ho, there is Mr. Kozlovski kayaking across the lake, very bravely flailing his oar."

"Kozlovski? Where is he going?" I asked.

"To the journalists' camp. To those camping cabins on the other side of the lake."

"And where is he coming from?"

"It's hard to say because he's in the middle of the lake. Maybe he's just taking a pleasure trip."

"What else do you see?"

"To the right, some kind of a river flows into the lake..."

"That's the Maryha. But it does not flow in—it flows out. Or, more precisely, it flows into the lake at Ghiby at the opposite end of the lake, and at the end you are looking at, it flows out to join the Black Hancha."

"Ok. So this Maryha flows *out* through a field of tall reeds. And boy, is it beautiful there! The reeds sway in the wind and look like a field of grain. And from its center rises a plume of smoke... Wait, wait. There is a tiny island there. Probably someone is making a bonfire. These reeds are a real paradise for wild birds—there are so many of them! And there's Miss Anka kayaking towards us! She just passed Mr. Kozlovski, they waved to each other. And closer to us, some fishermen are pulling nets out of the lake."

"We can see them without binoculars, too," I said. "And we can also see our lunch. Come and eat."

Squirrel sat in the tree for a while longer, but since he didn't notice anything interesting, he eventually climbed down. We brewed coffee with condensed milk on the spirit stove. We cut fresh country bread bought in Milkokuk and spread it with delicious lard. Each of us took a huge slice in one hand and a mug of coffee in the other. We sat side by side and, eating, watched Anka approach over the water.

A recipe for lard *smalets* with onions and apple:
Dice pork belly. Set a large pot to medium heat and add pork fat. Render until all white is liquid and the bits start turning brown. This may take about 30-45 minutes. Add pork belly and continue rendering until meat bits start browning, another 30 minutes or so. Dice onions and grate apples. When the meat bits are starting to brown, add onions and apples. Sauté until onions are nicely golden brown. Then add minced garlic, pepper, salt, marjoram, and caraway seeds, stir well and cook for a couple of minutes. Set aside to congeal. Spread on thickly sliced bread.

"Enjoying your meal?" she greeted us, pulling up at the shore.

"Yes!" the boys replied.

I didn't say anything because I was still angry with her.

"What about the burglar, my fellow detectives?" she asked.

Her condescending tone upset me even more. I got up, walked to the car, and turned on the radio. A symphonic concert was on.

"Why do you say: 'the burglar'?" Asked Tell. "Maybe there were several of them?"

"And how do you know that there were several?" she wondered.

"We don't know. But it could just as easily have been one as several."

"Oh, you're all very unkind today. It is the bad influence of your chief, I bet. Hey, Mr. Chief!" she turned to me. "Why are you in such a bad mood?"

"I'm not in a bad mood. I'm just listening to a symphony concert."

She pulled the kayak up on the shore and sat on its bow.

"Don't you think that it's completely awful to come to a lake and then play the radio? Sound carries over water, and everyone around has their rest spoiled."

I turned off the radio. She was right. I also didn't like people playing their radios in nature.

I took a blanket out of the car and lay down on it. I wanted to show Anka that her presence was indifferent to me. I looked at the sky—clear and blue—and a hawk gliding high up in the air. It made wide circles, soaring high, then slowly gliding down, looking for prey. I thought of yesterday's break-in at the teacher's cottage. Maybe it was carried out by the three thugs who had tried to rob Miss Petersen? We didn't see them in Milkokuk after the incident in the woods, but that didn't mean anything. They could have driven back, hidden it somewhere along the forest road, and sneaked into the house under cover of darkness. Or how about that couple in the blue Skoda? I knew nothing about those two. Who knows if they were not a hundred times more dangerous than the Petersens? And finally, who was this Hamster fellow?

"Imagine the burglar's expression," I said to the boys, "when he finds out that the stolen document is written in Latin. Not so many people know enough Latin to read an old document. He will have to turn to someone to translate it for him."

"Do you think we could try to find out who in this area knows Latin to whom the burglars are most likely to turn?" suggested Hawkeye.

"Oh, there may be several such people. And besides, how do we know that the burglar isn't gone and somewhere very far away by now? And all because some stupid journalist wrote in a newspaper about the Templar treasure and about some document at the teacher's house in Milkokuk. And now all these suspicious types are here because of that article," I said, directing these words not toward the journalist but off into space.

"You are also a suspicious type," she said.

"Suspicious? Until now, I was just ridiculous."

"You can be sure," said Squirrel with indignation, "that if Mr. Wheels finds the Templar treasure, he will give it to a museum."

"Now you're not funny," Anka stated. "All the worse for you. As long as your opponent considered you a harmless freak, you were safe. Alas, your driving over the water has caused a great consternation last night. Perhaps your opponent suspects now that you are much more dangerous, too.”

“I am not afraid of him.”

“Do not be too confident. Your opponent has a wide range of available resources. He has money, which you do not have. He has a beautiful daughter who knows how to turn heads.”

“Who are you talking about?”

“Why, Mr. Petersen.”

“He’s not my opponent. Miss Karen has offered me cooperation. Perhaps I will accept her proposal.”

“What?” Anka became indignant. “No way. You will never do such a thing. I would never forgive you.”

“But I don’t need your permission,” I said. “You have betrayed us, and doubly so. You left the post you were supposed to guard. You laughed at my vehicle. That’s not what friends do.”

“Oh, you use big words to describe small things. I left the post because I am a human being. I need to eat and drink. And as you know, I have room and board at the journalists’ center. As for the other point, I acted that way on purpose. I didn’t want it to be known that I had entered into an alliance with you. Staying near the Petersens, I can keep an eye on them and hear a thing or two—provided they are not wary of me.”

“How very Machiavellian!” I exclaimed ironically. “But the Petersens are very careful and will not reveal their plans to a stranger. Or have you noticed anything interesting?”

“Not yet. But it could happen.”

We all laughed at the way she said it, and the scouts set about pitching their tent. The two fishermen dragged their nets on the shore. One of them approached us and offered to sell us fish.

“No way, too expensive,” I said when he mentioned the price.

“Too expensive? That’s what the gentleman on the island in the reeds paid us this morning. We were passing through Maryha by boat. He hailed us over and paid this price. I swear.”

“What gentleman was it?” I rose from my blanket, for I remembered the smoke rising from among the reeds that Squirrel had reported.

"Do I know what gentleman? A tourist."

"What did he look like? And is he still there? Because, you see, I am waiting here for my colleague. Maybe it's him?"

"Well, he looked like everyone else. He was in bathing briefs."

"Anything recognizable? Unusual? Scars? Strange hair color?"

"Nothing I cared to see," shrugged the fisherman, a little embarrassed. "The guy was in slippers," he added as if to explain why he hadn't looked too close.

He didn't like my insistent questions.

He asked me again whether I would pay his price, and since I refused, he took off and got into his boat. After a while, the two men rowed out to the middle of the lake again and started setting up nets.

"Can you lend me your kayak?" I asked the journalists. The scouts immediately understood what I meant and gathered around me.

"Mr. Thomas! Go with your vehicle. It will be fun!"

"No. The reeds are too dense, and my car could get trapped. A kayak will be more useful; plus, it will make no noise, so I may be able to sneak up on the man on the island."

Anka agreed to lend me her kayak, but on the condition that I take her along.

"I can sneak up on the enemy like an Iroquois!" she declared. "And I wouldn't forgive myself for the rest of my life if I didn't participate in this game."

Clearly, I had to agree to her terms because I could only get to the islet by her kayak. Besides, I did not expect to make any sensational discoveries. I simply wanted to find out who had spent the night among the reeds. In the current situation, given the general lack of clues, anything could turn out important. Squirrel climbed the tree again and reported that smoke was still rising from the sea of reeds.

"He is still roasting his fish," I concluded, jumping into the kayak. "We will find him still at the fire. He's not expecting a visit."

We paddled along the right bank of the lake toward the green sea of reeds into which the Maryha flowed. Anka had only one paddle, so out of necessity, I paddled while she sat in the front and tried to reason with me:

"Don't you realize that Karen is fooling you? She's making cute faces for the sole purpose of getting you to help her find the treasure. Of course, not to make money from the treasure—because as far as I've been able to figure it out, they are only allowed to take ten percent as the finder's fee, and they are too rich to care about a measly ten percent. But she has the ambition to be able to boast abroad: 'I discovered in Poland that Templar treasure which no one else could ever find.'"

"There is no point trying to fool me because I do not know where to look for the treasure," I said. "And, anyway, you seem to doubt that a pretty girl can like me?"

"Ah, no. You've taken offense again. But I warn you: Karen will do anything to achieve her goal."

"Do you care who finds the treasure?"

She became embarrassed.

"Well, no. But she irritates me. I would very much like someone to teach her a lesson. She imagines that everyone can be made to serve her. She is overconfident. She is conceited."

"First of all, she is a pretty girl, and maybe that's why, like any pretty girl, she has a lot of self-confidence. You're just being jealous."

She slammed her fist on the bow of the kayak, and it rattled like a drum.

"And you are naïve! I will not talk to you anymore about this!"

"Quiet!" I hissed. "You'll frighten our prey."

A wall of reeds rose in front of us. At first, they grew sparsely and paddling through was easy. The bow of the kayak separated the reeds, and we cut a path through them. But soon, the reeds thickened and entwined around the paddle, making it very difficult to push on. The forest of reeds surrounded us in front and to the sides and closed behind us. To avoid losing my sense of direction, I got up from my seat from time to time and looked over the swaying reeds to the wooded banks. Then, I began to paddle standing up and finally began to use the paddle like a punting pole to push off from the muddy bottom. Soon, however, the reeds became so tall that they obscured all view. I stopped, trying to figure out what direction to take.

And it was really, really hot in the reeds. It had been hot at the lake where we camped, too, but there, at least, we had a breeze from the water, which eased the midday heat a little. But now we were screened from the wind by the reeds, the sun was roasting us from above, and the water, full of rotting debris, was steaming like a Turkish bath, giving off, into the bargain, a faint but suffocating stink. Swarms of tiny but intrusive midges swirled above us, large dragonflies perched on the kayak shimmering in the sun. Shaken by the movements of the oars, huge spiders and disgusting beetles fell on us from the reeds. Somewhere in the thicket, wild ducks were quacking, frightened ducklings were squealing, and drakes were tooting in booming voices. High in the sky, a hawk circled overhead.

I was getting tired. I had lost all sense of direction. Perhaps, instead of approaching the islet, we were heading back the way we had come?

"We're lost," Anka declared almost gleefully as I crouched in the kayak and wiped my sweaty forehead with a handkerchief.

"You find satisfaction in this?"

"Definitely," she nodded. "At last, something interesting. After all, you don't think I've come with you because I like you?"

"I'm not so sure of it myself."

"I have been working in journalism for a very short time. I'm just out of college. So far, I haven't written anything special. And I would like to make a name for myself, attract the attention of readers. I would like to use my vacation to gather material for a series of sensational reports. Reports that will make readers hold their breath."

"And you came to Ghiby just for a holiday? You have not expected that all these suspicious types like me or the Petersens would descend on it in search of the Templar treasure?"

"Why, in fact, I expected it. After all, it was me... Well, I'm the person who wrote the article about the Templar document in Milkokuk."

"You!? You!?" I stammered.

"Go ahead and say it: 'You fool!' Yes?"

"Something like that," I said curtly.

"I know what you think. But it doesn't bother me at all. The main thing is that now I will be able to collect my material for the story. I will describe all these odd people looking for the Templar treasure. And among them, the pride of place will go to one Mr. Wheels. I will, of course, also describe how we got lost in the reeds. At this point, I will end one of my articles, leaving readers with a cliffhanger. And only in the next episode will I explain how we were saved."

"Then you already know that we will be saved? In that case, maybe you can tell me how because I want nothing more than to get out of here."

"Well, we either paddle forward or.... backward."

"Yes, but do you know which is which?"

She said nothing. It seems that it was only at that moment that she realized that we had indeed become lost and were surrounded on all sides by a green jungle.

Alright, that's not quite true. It was possible to go back, kind of, for we had left behind us a trail of broken reeds. But I still wanted to reach the islet.

I took the paddle in my hand again and tried to push on.

"You saw the mysterious document," I said. "So, I guess you can tell me whether it contains information about the Templar treasure."

"Of course, I saw it! I even had it in my hand! I saw it last year when I came here for a summer vacation. But I can't read Latin well[1] and didn't understand the contents of the document. I only know that the document was issued by the Knights Templar. And this is what I wrote about in my article."

"Pssst!" I hissed again, "I think we are near the islet."

The reeds thinned out. Four more yards, three more yards, I pushed a few more times with my paddle against the muddy bottom, and we emerged onto a patch of clear water surrounding a small island. Sharp, sable grass grew on it, a half-ruined shack made of branches stood in the middle under two dwarf trees.

One glance was enough to determine that the islet was deserted. The dilapidated shack was empty.

"So, there was no one here," Anka said. "And if there was, he's gone. And he didn't have to go through the reeds at all. He simply came on foot and left the same way."

She pointed with her hand.

---

[1] Until 1979, Latin was part of the Polish high school curriculum.

On the other side of the islet, huge pine trunks lay in a row like a causeway across the field of reed. Some were tied together, perhaps waiting to be floated downriver in the autumn. They formed a long footbridge between the islet and the mainland.

I jumped ashore and looked into the ruined shack.

"Someone was here, though. And not long ago," I said.

Next to the hut, I saw a recently put-out fire; the ashes were still warm. All around lay the remains of a meal of roast fish.

I whistled.

"And what's that?"

I picked up from the ground a few thin, broken slats covered with veneer. There were also pieces of broken glass in the grass.

"Do you know what this is? These are the remains of the frame in which the Templar document was mounted."

"So, this is where the burglar spent the night!" my companion exclaimed.

"Yes, he stole the document and hid here, on the islet. Here, he smashed the frame and took out the document. We have come too late. And we had a chance to meet him eye to eye."

CHAPTER NINE: LET US AMBUSH HIM

Malinovski again. The third way out. Petersen at home. To ambush or not to ambush. I put my cards on the table.

Returning to the camp where we had left the scouts, we spotted a motorboat bobbing by the shore. Kozlovski and the Petersens were talking to our friends.

"We've been waiting for you," Karen said as our kayak rode nose up onto the sand. Captain Petersen approached me, grunting angrily and waving a piece of paper.

"See this! I think I am going to blow a gasket!"

"We found this letter on the window of our car around noon," Karen explained. "Someone had put it behind the windshield wiper. We're here to ask your advice."

I picked up the note. It was written on a piece of paper torn from a math sketchbook. In a rather unstable hand—perhaps written with the left hand to disguise the handwriting—someone was informing the Petersens:

> If you want the templar document, put three thousand zloty behind the statue in the forest shrine on the road to ghilby. Do this at midnight, then return to your campsite, and in the morning you will find the document in the shrine.
> Malinovski

My reading the letter stirred up Petersen again, and he started thundering and cursing:

"There's that Malinovski again! He cheated me, ridiculed me, scammed me for four hundred dollars, and now he wants more: three thousand zloty! Thief, swindler, crook!"

"And what do you think?" Karen asked me. "Should we pay him that three thousand, or should we ignore the letter?"

"I won't pay it! I won't give him a penny!" roared Petersen. "He will take the money, and we will never see the document!"

"Calm down, Papa," Miss Petersen tried to calm Old Petersen down. "Let's first hear what Mr. Thomas thinks about it. Mr. Kozlovski advises us to pay him."

"And I advise against it. I strongly advise against it," I said.

Kozlovski spoke up:

"Oh, Mr. Thomas says this out of spite, to make me angry. Since I say 'pay,' he says: 'do not pay.' Because Mr. Thomas doesn't like me, he will always say the opposite of what I say. But in my opinion, the matter is simple: if you care about this document, then pay for it because I do not see any other way to get it."

"And why do you think we shouldn't pay?" Miss Petersen asked me.

"Ok. Fine. Mr Kozlovski is right. I don't like him."

Here, I made an exaggerated bow towards Mr. Kozlovski.

"But that aside, I suspect that the document is worthless. If it does point to the treasure, then why is Malinovski offering it to us for a mere three thousand zloty? He should be demanding much, much more. Or not sell it at all but take up the treasure hunt himself. Besides, we have no guarantee that this is not yet another scam. How do we know this person even owns the document? You put three thousand zloty at midnight at a roadside chapel and probably get nothing."

"Exactly!" boomed Captain Petersen. "Mr. Wheels is right. I won't pay a penny to that crook!"

Anka interjected:

"I agree with Mr. Thomas. It seems to me that one should not pay that thief. That is immoral."

"Oh, so you are an ally of Mr. Wheels now?" Karen mischievously squinted her eyes. "Mr. Thomas seems to be gaining followers by the hour! But I want to have the document!" she became angry. "If there is even a shred of hope that it will bring something new to the case, then I must have it, even if it means risking three thousand zloty."

"What?" Petersen was outraged. "You want to give Malinovski another chance to make a fool of me? I won't allow it."

But Miss Karen knew how to placate her father. Instead of arguing with him, she kissed him on the cheek and said:

"You promised me, Papa, that I would head this expedition. And for a stupid three thousand zloty, you want to break a promise you gave me?"

Petersen scratched his head.

"If I may suggest something," I said. "It seems to me that there is a third way. Instead of banknotes, you should put newspaper clippings in an envelope, put the envelope in the chapel, but not return to camp. Instead, lie in ambush somewhere near the chapel and capture Malinovski when he comes to collect the money."

"Well, I like this a lot better!" yelled Petersen and patted me firmly on the back. "This is what we will do. We will hide, wait in ambush, and capture Malinovski. Will you help me with this?"

"I will," I said. "I will lie in ambush with you tonight. But tomorrow morning, we will say goodbye. I'm leaving."

"Where to?" Karen asked.

I shrugged my shoulders.

"Will you let me read the contents of the document when you obtain it? No. Then I can't show you all my cards either. I am leaving to look for the Templar treasure. I consider staying here pointless."

"We will also leave. As soon as I get the document," Karen said.

"I'd like to point out one more thing," I said. "The document is the property of the teacher from Milkokuk. If you buy it back—or get it out of Malinovski's hands in any other way—you will have to return it to him."

"In order for you to get acquainted with it?" Miss Petersen asked ironically. "Yes, we will do that. But only when we have the treasure in our hands."

"Oh, sorry," Petersen interjected. "That's a no-no. If Mr.

Thomas takes part in the ambush and we succeed in capturing Malinovski, then Mr. Thomas will also learn the contents of the document."

Captain Petersen took a gentleman's approach to the matter. Neither his daughter nor Kozlovski liked it, which was not too hard to read in their faces. But Karen didn't want to argue with her father.

So, we discussed our plans for the night escapade, and then Kozlovski decided:

"Although I am against organizing an ambush, I will take part in it. Three of us have a better chance of capturing Malinovski than two."

"Well, at last!" Karen clapped her hands. "Because I already thought you were a coward."

Kozlovski smiled modestly.

"Some people," he said sententiously, "are inclined to view prudence as cowardice."

The Petersens got into their motorboat, and Kozlovski took me aside and began to reproach me:

"You are acting very inappropriately. We advertise Poland abroad, we encourage foreigners to visit our country, to come for holidays, to hunt, to fish. Many countries in the world live from tourism. We need them, these foreigners, and their hard currency. And therefore is in our national interest that the Petersens find the Templar treasure. And not only because ninety percent of the treasure will go to the state but also because when we advertise this fact abroad, many foreign tourists will be attracted to our country to look for treasures here like the Petersens. They will come to Poland and pay for their stay with dollars. This may turn out to be a far better business than hunting. And you are trying to compete with the Petersens! By doing so, you are, in fact, acting against our national interest!"

I was so amused that I snorted:

"You will forgive me," I said, "but I have a slightly different understanding of the interests of our country. Yes, foreigners should be encouraged to visit Poland. Let them hunt, fish, look for treasures. It is our duty to treat them with hospitality and make them feel welcome. Thus, I helped you when you found yourselves stuck in the mud, for which you paid me back by letting air out of my tires. However, I am of the opinion that foreigners should only pay for what they actually want and receive. Don't you understand that this story with Malinovski will make Petersens think we are a nation of crooks and thieves? And that will only deter others from coming to Poland. As for the treasure hunt, I will not give it up. I have the same right to it as the Petersens."

That said, I bowed to him politely and left, and the exasperated Kozlovski jumped into his motorboat. I breathed a sigh of relief when he disappeared from my sight.

The scouts immediately approached with a question:

"Will we take part in the ambush?"

I didn't think taking them with me on such a dangerous mission was a good idea. It was difficult to foresee what Malinovski might do when he realized that he had been tricked. I had no right to expose the scouts to any danger. The very idea made me feel uncomfortable. Besides, I realized, instead of thinking about capturing the criminal, I would constantly worry about keeping the boys out of danger.

They took my decision badly, but in the end understood that it was irrevocable, especially since I also advised Anka against participating in the escapade for the same reason.

"The fewer people hiding in the ambush," I said, "the better the chance that Malinovski will not guess anything. The three of us, Kozlovski, Petersen, and me, will be enough to capture one man."

Anka thought about it for a while and came to terms with my decision. She sat down next to me on the shore and said:

"And you won't tell me where you are going tomorrow either?"

"I don't know yet where I will go. Probably to Malbork."

"Will you take me with you?"

"You? What for?"

"I want to know how the search for the Templar treasure will end."

"But you consider this search the height of folly!"

"I do. Still, I am curious."

"About its outcome?"

"Not only that. Also about the adventures you will have along the way."

"Feel free to leave me your address. After the expedition is over, I will write you a letter telling you everything I have experienced."

"No. That's not fun."

"Your article caused enough trouble as it is."

"Oh! Are you still angry with me? I had no idea that it would cause such a ruckus. Anyway, I better warn you: I am coming along, one way or another."

"Where to?" I asked.

"To Malbork."

"But you don't know for sure that I will go to Malbork."

"Mr. Wheels," she said angrily. "Do not underestimate me. I can be useful. Please think about it."

She jumped into her kayak and paddled off to the resort for lunch. And I got in my vehicle and drove to Milkokuk to talk to the teacher one more time. On the way, I saw that the shores of the lake were empty; the blue Skoda was gone. I guessed that having learned that the mysterious document had been stolen, the couple decided to move on. Nor was there any trace of the three thugs; perhaps they, too, had given up the treasure hunt.

The teacher spread his hands helplessly:

"I can't. I tried and I really can't remember the name of the village where the ruined pastor's house was. I tried to trace my journey on the map. But my maps are not very detailed, and it was a small village."

So, again, I had nothing to go on. Disappointed, I returned to Lake Pomerania, where my three scouts had prepared lunch. I was very unhappy. It occurred to me that the militia should have been notified of Malinovski's letter. The militia, not us, was supposed to do things like ambush thieves. Still, Malinovski's letter was addressed not to me but to Petersen. It was Kozlovski's duty—since he was acting as their official guide—to inform the militia. I could, of course, get in the car and drive to the station in Ghiby. But what would the Petersens think of that? It would look like I was resorting to the worst possible tricks because of our competition. They trusted me with the information about the letter—and I should now head over to the militia without getting their permission to do so?

I eagerly awaited the coming of night. When it began to turn dark, I said goodbye to the boys and got into my vehicle. However, I did not motor across the lake. Having passed Ghiby, I found myself in the forest again, and here, about a mile from the journalists' center, I saw the forest shrine mentioned in Malinovski's letter. It looked quite original: in a deep tree hollow in an old, gnarly pine tree stood a statue of St. Anthony. We were supposed to place the money in this hollow, behind this statue. The location was well chosen, as a pine grove grew behind the chapel, and Malinovski—or whoever—would be able to sneak up from the back unnoticed. Then, all he had to do was take one step and reach in for the money.

Anthony of Padua (1195 – 1231) was a Portuguese Catholic priest and member of the Order of Friars Minor. He is one of the most popular saints in Eastern Europe today. The chapel most probably housed a statue like this one.

I stopped the car and thought for a long time about where we should hide. Should we hide in the grove behind the shrine? But then, our field of vision would be very limited. Or should we lie on the moss on the other side of the road, opposite the shrine? A sparse old-growth pine wood grew there, with clumps of juniper among the trees. We could hide behind one of the junipers. From there, we might be able to spot Malinovski as he crept toward the shrine.

After looking around some more, I drove to the journalists' holiday center. The Petersens were just finishing dinner and invited me to their caravan.

It was a beautiful caravan, comfortable and well-equipped. I watched it with real envy: I had always dreamed of having something like this. How useful such a caravan would be on my summer trips! Spacious, with two large windows, two folding couches, a table, a stove, why, even a miniature bathroom and shower!

Kozlovski watched my admiring gaze with satisfaction as if he were the owner of the caravan.

"Nice, huh?" he nodded. "The Petersens have a gas cylinder with them, too, a gas cooker, and even a gas heater in case of cold weather. And all those strange gizmos over there, in the corner, are their treasure-hunting equipment. They have all sorts of special detectors for detecting metals and open spaces underground. They even have a jackhammer for breaking stone walls. And you?" he asked me mockingly.

"I only have my wits," I replied.

"Well, you won't drill a hole in a brick wall with your wit. In contact with hard material, Mr. Thomas, your wit will blunt. You will see. It won't be long before you do."

"What are you talking about, Mr. Kozlovski?" Karen asked.

"I think this idea of setting up this ambush on Malinovski is very stupid," he said. "Either reject Malinovski's proposal altogether or accept it and pay for the document. But nono nono nono—on the advice of Mr. Wheels, you chose to set up an ambush. I don't think Malinovski will fall for it."

"Don't talk nonsense, Kozlovski," Captain Petersen got angry. "We will trap Malinovski! I get so angry when I think that this man is perhaps even now hanging around our camper, mocking me. He has been around here more than once, I am sure, since he put that letter under the windshield wiper."

Night was falling. I told Petersen about the place I chose for our ambush. The captain had also inspected the area around the shrine and agreed to my proposal to hide behind the juniper bushes across the road. We cut some newspaper and put a wad of clippings in an envelope. They were to mimic the bills that Malinovski demanded.

I reminded Petersen and Kozlovski of their duty to inform the militia of the burglar's letter.

"I think we can handle this ourselves," Captain Petersen slammed his fist on the table. "We are not committing any crime by trying to capture the thief. We will then hand him over to the authorities. And please don't argue about it. I have to capture this rascal with my own hands."

When I left the Petersens' caravan, it was ten o'clock in the evening, and in two hours, we were to leave our ransom for the stolen document at the shrine.

I visited Anka's cottage but did not find her there. I found her at the boat landing instead: she was sitting alone on the platform, with her legs hanging over the water.

I squatted down next to her. I wanted to say that if she really wanted it very much, I could take her to Malbork, but only on the condition that she gave up putting the person of Mr. Wheels in her article. But before I had a chance to open my mouth, Karen came in behind me.

"My goodness! What a romantic get-together! Am I not disturbing you?" she asked.

Without waiting for our answer, she also sat on the platform with her legs hanging over the water.

"Well, well, Mr. Wheels," she said. "You are leaving tomorrow. Where to?"

"'Your treasure is where your heart is.'"

"Exactly. How do you understand these words?"

"Well, to be honest, I don't know how to understand them," I said frankly.

"'Your treasure is where your heart is,'" said Karen again. "Now, remember. This was written by a monk to a monk. Where should a monk's heart, thoughts, and feelings be?"

"With God?" I replied.

"It is difficult to suspect Grand Master von Feuchtwangen of giving de Molay a lesson in religion. This is not a message for de Molay's immortal soul. So, where does God reside? In a church? I have a feeling that the Templar treasure was deposited in some church. This is what Feuchtwangen was trying to tell de Molay."

"I agree," I nodded. "The treasure was hidden in a church. But not any church. It must have been some church very well known to de Molay since Feuchtwangen gave no further clue as to its location."

"And we lack a clue as to the location of that church."

"There is no reason to believe that the treasure still remains in the same place. For instance, I do wonder whether some conspirators had not found the cache after the assassination of Grand Master von Orseln. Or even before it and then murdered him."

"Oh, no!" exclaimed Karen. "How would a word of that not get out? That would have been a colossal heist! It would surely have left some trace in the history of the Teutonic Order! I think the opposite happened. I think that the treasure was hidden in a way that made access to it difficult. Successive grand masters passed amongst themselves the secret of the treasure's location, but none, perhaps, ever saw it with his own eyes. And then, Von Orseln—took the secret to his grave."

"I will try to find some trace of it in Malbork," I said in all sincerity, "but I don't think that Malbork is the place we seek. The church at Malbork was destroyed during the war and has been partially cleaned up since—something would have come up."

"I heard that the underground sections of the church have not been destroyed," said Karen. "We have equipment which would allow us to scan for any underground structures. What shall we do, then, Mr. Wheels? Shall we go to Malbork as partners?"

"I do not think that the Templar treasure is there. The treasure was deposited in its hiding place even before Feuchtwangen arrived in Malbork. The castle was still under construction at the time, and that would have allowed for a vault or some other hiding place to be added to the design, but the castle was full of builders and masons and foreign knights, including those from France. And Malbork must have been teeming with spies of various powers. It would have been very difficult to hide the treasure there under those circumstances; and probably impossible to do it in such a way that the king of France would not get wind of it. If I were de Molay or Feuchtwangen, I would have deposited the treasure in some minor provincial castle, out of the way, out of sight.

The Castle Church of the Blessed Virgin in Malbork
was finally rebuilt in 2016

"I'll tell you what I will do, Miss Karen. I will lay my cards down for you to see. As I say, I will go to Malbork. But I am not going there for the treasure. Rather, Malbork Castle houses a museum. The people who work there are more familiar with the history of the order than I am. Maybe I can learn from them something that will direct me to the church or castle we seek."

"Well, then. I wish you the best of luck," Karen said.

She rose from the platform and, nodding to me, marched off to her cottage.

"Why did you reveal your intentions to her?" said Anka reproachfully. "She is a clever girl. She will use your clues against you!"

"There is no helping that. She has also told me a lot. Who knows? Maybe what I've just heard from her is my first real clue to the treasure."

"But she didn't say anything," Anka was amazed. "I heard her every word."

"Well, she did not come right out and say it. But it's obvious that she thinks the secret is contained in the phrase: 'Your treasure is where your heart is.' Until now, I've been inclined to regard it as morally uplifting words of encouragement. However, who knows if Karen is not right? Maybe this phrase does contain a clue. Maybe we have to concentrate on it instead of going from place to place and tapping on the walls of Teutonic churches? Perhaps it is better to lie down in the tall grass and ponder this sentence over and over again? Try to form an anagram from the first letters of each word? Or maybe just from the last letters? Perhaps the phrase should be read backward? People in the Middle Ages were fond of these kinds of ciphers, and Knights Templar excelled in them."

"Dear God!" Anka shook her head in disbelief. "And you will be constantly thinking about this sentence? Aren't you afraid that one day you will find yourself institutionalized, muttering to yourself, 'Your treasure is where your heart is'?"

"It's one possible outcome," I laughed. "In France, apparently, a number of people have ended up in institutions just in this way. Scores of maniacs are trying to find the Templar treasure. I hope that I manage to keep my wits."

"Common sense tells us to drop the case."

"Oh, don't worry about my head. There is a fundamental difference between me and those other treasure hunters. They are driven by a demented vision of immeasurable wealth that they want to possess in order to enrich themselves. And this can lead to a nervous breakdown. But I am not concerned with the wealth that I can possess. If I find the treasure, I will hand it over to the state. I treat the search as entertainment, a kind of calisthenics of the mind, a test of my intelligence and knowledge, an interesting puzzle. Crossword puzzle enthusiasts rarely end up in mental institutions."

I looked at my watch. I was eleven. It was time to set a trap for Malinovski.

CHAPTER TEN: THE CAP OF INVISIBILITY

Lying in ambush. What did we discover in the old chapel? Who wears a cap of invisibility? The man on the peninsula. Is Hamster Malinovski? Concerning the Yatvingians.

Midnight came. The journalist resort was plunged in sleep and darkness. No lights were on in any of the camping cabins, no murmur of conversation came from anywhere. We slipped out quietly of Captain Petersen's bungalow and, in a line, Petersen at the front, then me, then Kozlovski, set off along the forest road toward the shrine.

It was very dark: the moon hid behind the clouds. The road was barely visible before us as a lighter streak of darkness, and this made the trek easier. All around us, however, the darkness seemed impenetrable, and we could not see farther than twenty feet.

Captain Petersen put the envelope stuffed with newspaper clippings behind the figure in the shrine. Then, very carefully, so as not to make any noise, we hid behind a large juniper bush. Despite the dark, we could see the chapel and the saint's white figure shimmering in the gloom. We lay down on the moss next to one another so that—in case one of us noticed something suspicious—we could communicate without words, just by touching. We lay on our bellies, our chins on our hands, and stared at the shrine.

Time passed very slowly. I had my watch with its phosphorescent hands right in front of my nose. From time to time, I would glance at the watch and observe the bouncing seconds hand. The minutes dragged by slowly, and the hour hand stood motionless. We did not expect to wait for Malinovski too long. He had assured us that we could collect the document in the morning. Since the day would begin to break around three, we expected him to collect his money between one and two in the morning.

Around one o'clock, the sky cleared, and the night became quite bright. I could see the forest road, the shrine in the hollow of the tree, and the dark grove behind it. It was so bright that we even saw a fox silently slipping across the road. Malinovski would have to put on a cap of invisibility to approach the shrine unnoticed.

Then, a light breeze broke. The rustlings, whistlings, and cracklings it caused would obfuscate any sounds Malinovski might made sneaking up towards the shrine. On the other hand, they also proved beneficial to us, as they drowned out Kozlovski's yawns and Captain Petersen's loud breathing.

This waiting in ambush soon became very boring. Twigs and pinecones pinched me. I wriggled, trying to find a more convenient position, and was surprised at how loud the noise I made was. It was the same with Petersen and Kozlovski. Fortunately, the wind drowned out most of our noises. My eyelids were heavy and closed every now and then, and I had to pinch myself to stay awake. Kozlovski fell asleep several times and began to snore, only to be awakened by Petersen's rough poking.

It was one in the morning. Then two. And finally, three. The forest turned gray, dew began to fall, and the air became very cold. We were cold, and our legs and backs were numb from lying still in the same position.

And still, Malinovski had not come.

I would have given a lot to be lying in my car or on a mattress in a tent instead of in the woods on the cold moss. I missed my cigarettes, and I was sure Petersen missed his pipe. He wriggled incessantly.

At four in the morning, Kozlovski rose from the grass and said:

"I'm sick of it. It was a crazy idea. Someone fooled us. No one came to collect the money."

He walked over to the shrine. He looked behind the statue, where the envelope lay.

"Dear God!" he exclaimed. "There is another envelope here!"

"What?" The captain jumped up from the moss. We both ran up to the shrine.

Kozlovski was holding... two envelopes! The first was the one we had put there, the one with the newspaper cuttings. On the second, someone had written in Polish in the same hand as in the original letter from Malinovski:

For Mr. Petersen

"It's for you," Kozlovski said and handed the letter to Petersen.

The captain opened the envelope and took out a small sheet of paper and a scrap of parchment snipped off from some larger whole, bearing a few characters in beautifully calligraphed Latin script and... the seal of the Templar Order.

"Read it. It's in Polish," Petersen said and handed me the note. I read it aloud, translating it into English:

Dear sir,

You have tried to deceive me by leaving scraps of newspaper for me instead of money. I should take offense and cut off all contact with you, but i came to the conclusion that you simply do not trust me and underestimate my wit. As proof that you can trust me, i am giving you a piece of the document you seek. You can have the rest tomorrow if tonight at midnight you put real money behind the statue in the shrine.

However, as penalty for the fact that you have tried to trap me, i raise my price from three thousand to five thousand zloty. And i assure you that if you try to deceive me again or lurk at the shrine, i will know about it and i will break off all further contact with you, and you will never obtain the document you seek.

Malinovski

When I finished translating, there was a long moment of silence. We felt foolish. We had let ourselves be tricked. We had lain in ambush for almost four hours with our eyes fixed on the shrine, and meanwhile, Malinovski approached it and discovered that the envelope contained not money but scraps of newspaper. Not only that—he then walked away from the shrine, wrote a new note somewhere in hiding, and brought it back! Again, all while we were watching!

"He must have the cap of invisibility," I said.

"Oh, Malinovski, Malinovski," groaned Captain Petersen and clenched his fists in helpless anger. Kozlovski triumphed:

"And did I not say not to play games with Malinovski? But no, you listened to Mr. Wheels instead, and now Malinovski raised the stake to five thousand zloty! We lost two thousand zloty because of, excuse me, stupid advice. Now what?"

Petersen shrugged his shoulders:

"I don't know what. I best confer with Karen. She is the leader of the expedition."

We went to the journalists' center. I felt terrible and went last because I was ashamed to think how Karen might react when she read Malinovski's letter. The mysterious Mr. Malinovski turned out to be a hundred times smarter than all of us combined. And not only that! He also had some mysterious powers at his disposal—powers that allowed him to become invisible.

I spat at the thought.

"A devil, not a man."

"What? Do you believe in the devil? In witchcraft and ghosts?" Petersen asked.

"I have not until this morning. But only magic can explain the fact that Malinovski planted the new letter right in front of our noses," I said.

"We must have fallen asleep. All three of us," Kozlovski said. "And none of us noticed it. And just at that time, Malinovski approached the shrine."

Karen was of the same opinion. She looked at the snippet of parchment while Kozlovski translated the letter for her. Finally, she said with derision:

"I will give five thousand to this fellow Malinovski and invite him to partner with us in our treasure hunt. He seems to be a man worth much more than all three of you combined. You fell asleep! Was the moss so soft?"

"I did not fall asleep! Not for a moment, I swear," Petersen raised his hand in an oath.

It was obvious that she did not believe him. I did not try to convince her that I had not slept either and yet somehow could not explain how Malinovski had approached the shrine undetected.

We studied the scrap of the document planted by Malinovski. It had been cut in a very clever way: it proved that it was most likely an original, but it was difficult to see whether the whole document represented any value to us.

"Let me decide our next step," Karen stated. "No more ambushes, please. I will put that five thousand zloty in the shrine myself, and later, I will go to collect the document—again by myself. I am sure that if we act loyally, Malinovski will not deceive us. And we will get the mysterious document. And you, gentlemen, will be kind enough to stay away from the shrine tonight."

"Oh, I will be very far away," I said. "I'm leaving for Malbork."

"Very well, we will see which one of us makes more progress," Karen said. "You made fun of Malinovski, and see where that got you."

"I never made fun of him," I said. "I never joke about thieves. They do not arouse hilarity in me but anger. If you care for my advice, you should report him to the militia."

"No!" Karen stomped her foot. "I've had enough of your advice. I think you better leave for Malbork now."

I shrugged my shoulders and said:

"In such case, a very good morning to you all."

And I went to my vehicle. Petersen caught up with me and put his hand on my shoulder.

"Do not be angry with Karen, Mr. Wheels. I share your opinion, but this time, I must yield to my daughter. I have promised her that she will lead this expedition. Nevertheless, I hope that you and I can join forces to capture Malinovski in the future. I think I can count on you in this matter, right?"

"Yes, you can," I nodded.

We shook hands. Petersen went back to his daughter, and I got into my vehicle, drove into the lake, and motored across the bay to the Boy Scouts' camp. I confess that Karen's words had stung me. Malinovski—a burglar and a brazen crook—had triumphed over me, and I couldn't help thinking about it with irritation.

My arrival at the camp woke up the scouts. They crawled out of their tent and barraged me with questions, but my unhappy face immediately told them of my defeat. I told them what had happened at the shrine.

"I swear I didn't sleep. I didn't sleep a wink," I said.

Hawkeye raised his big nose skyward and snorted like an ogre.

"This is a very mysterious story. Did you find any tracks at the shrine?"

"I didn't even look for them. It was fairly dark when we left."

"Ha! You should have raked the area around the shrine! Then every trace would have been visible on the ground," said Hawkeye. "Indians do this as a matter of course!"

Squirrel was of a different opinion:

"It's all because you didn't take us with you. I would have hidden in the branches of the tree. From there, I would have certainly seen this fellow Malinovski."

The most serious response, as usual, came from Wilhelm. He asked simply:

"Now what?"

I shrugged my shoulders.

"In the afternoon, we leave for Malbork. There's nothing here for us to do, my friends."

They made big eyes.

"Mr. Wheels!" cried out Hawkeye. "You can't let that crook Malinovski take Miss Petersen's money, can you?"

"You want to let this thief triumph over honest people?" seconded him outraged Squirrel.

I opened my hands helplessly.

"Miss Karen forbade me from setting another trap. I vowed to comply. She wants the document and agrees to pay for it. I can't prevent her from doing so because she's ready to think I'm not so interested in capturing the thief as in preventing her from obtaining the document.

I see no other way out of the situation but to roll up camp and leave for Malbork. I am sure that sooner or later, Malinovski will fall into our hands. He certainly won't leave the Petersens alone, he will be hoping to extract more money from them. The villain has become totally brazen. And this will eventually doom him. I am sure of it."

They realized that I was right. There really was nothing left to do but give up trying to catch the thief. I had set my departure for Malbork for twelve sharp, and it was barely six in the morning. I climbed into my car, changed into my pajamas, and covered myself with a blanket. Since I was to drive all the way to Malbork, I needed some rest after a sleepless night.

The boys did not go back to sleep. At the lakeshore, they started a general washing, then dressed in their scout uniforms and prepared breakfast.

Despite my fatigue, I could not fall asleep. I was disturbed by the bright sunlight coming through the windows. I watched the boys busying themselves by the lake, and through the opened windows, I could hear their every word. They thought I was asleep, so they behaved freely, and at such times that one learns best of other people's character.

Here was Hawkeye, known to his parents as Little Peter. Long nose and sharp, curious eyes. He walked into the lake with soap in hand and a towel over his shoulder. On the sandy bottom, he espied some kind of a creature.

So, instead of bathing, he brought his face closer to the water's surface and followed the creature out into the lake until the water reached his nose. Then, having given up watching, he returned closer to the shore and set about washing up.

"Who will Hawkeye be when he grows up?" I wondered. "Will he be a scientist? No, he doesn't have enough patience for that. His mind is very inquisitive and logical; he has both the ability to think clearly and the necessary curiosity, but he lacks patience. That's the greatest difference between him and William Tell. Tell is serious and calm, rather mature for his age. He wants to be a doctor like his father. And if he becomes a doctor, his patients will be able to have confidence in his diagnoses. And Squirrel... Squirrel is the baby of the group. Active, cheerful, constantly whistling something under his breath, constantly looking around the treetops as if his only real dream was to climb trees and observe the world from above. Maybe in the future, he will want to climb the highest mountain peaks? Or will want to see what no one before him has ever seen? Will he become an explorer of the white spots on the map of science?"

"I'd like to be grown up already," said Hawkeye, coming out of the water. "I will join a militia officer school and work in the criminal police. I will deal with crooks like Malinovski. I will become their terror. They will tremble at the sound of my name."

"Oh, yeah?" said William Tell. "For now, Malinovski is laughing at us all. Mr. Wheels is a hundred times smarter than you, and yet Malinovski has tricked him. As for me, I wouldn't want to grow up any time soon."

"No?" asked astonished Squirrel. "And why not? It's nice to be an adult. I think I'd like to work at a newspaper like Miss Anka, travel to remote parts of the world, and write reports about how people live there."

"You'd better learn to write school essays first. You make spelling mistakes all the time. Any editor-in-chief will throw out a journalist who submits such trash," laughed Hawkeye. "And I think Tell is right. It's probably not a good idea to become an adult too quickly. When we grow up, we'll have serious jobs, and we won't be able to travel with Mr. Wheels."

"Why! When I grow up, I will build a vehicle like Mr. Wheels has. And I will also drive around looking for adventures."

"Oh, come on," William Tell waved his hand dismissively. "You would like to be everything at once: an anthropologist, a journalist, Mr. One-man-band. If you want to be everything at once, you will become nothing, do you understand that?"

"Adults very rarely have adventures like Mr. Wheels," said Hawkeye. "They don't have time for it. My father works as a foreman in a cotton factory. He is only interested in machines. At home, he talks about nothing else."

And listening to him, I thought that Hawkeye would become neither a scientist nor an investigator, as he imagined, but just what his father was: a foreman at a weaving mill. Or maybe he would go one step higher and become an engineer at that factory.

But now, Squirrel interrupted the serious conversation and called out in broken English, with a tone of voice mimicking Captain Petersen:

"Are you perhaps Mister Malinovski?"

The boys burst out laughing. And when their laughter died down, Tell said:

"It seems to me that we are laughing at ourselves. Because so far, it is Malinovski who is on top. Under our noses, he broke into the teacher's cottage and stole the Templar document. Then he managed to slip the ambush, too."

"Oh, don't believe that!" Hawkeye came to my defense. "Mr. Wheels can't be tricked, period. If he didn't notice Malinovski sneaking into the shrine, it's only because he was busy pondering the meaning of the word: 'Your treasure is where your heart is.' This is, after all, the key to the entire riddle, not Malinovski."

"...where your heart is. I don't understand any of this," sighed Squirrel.

I didn't understand anything, either. Falling asleep, I repeated in my mind: '...where your heart is'.... 'your heart'.... 'your heart'... As if from behind a thick wall of fog, I still heard Tell's voice:

"We should help Mr. Wheels. Malinovski is probably hiding somewhere in the area. It is unlikely that the boys from Milkokuk would not have noticed a stranger hanging around the lake. Let's go to the village and talk to them."

I wanted to jump up from my bed and forbid the boys to stray from the camp—after all, we were to leave for Malbork at twelve. But then I thought to myself, *Alright, let's see what they can learn*, and I fell into the embrace of sweet and heavy sleep.

When I woke up, it was already past twelve. On the grass next to the car lay a pile of stuff packed for the journey: rolled blankets and mattresses, a tent in a bag. On the handle of the vehicle hung a note:

Didn't want to wake you but we discovered something interesting. Follow the signs. The Three Yotvingians

"Well, yeah," I muttered to myself. "Here we go again."

Willy-nilly, I got dressed and started to look for the first sign.

And there it was: an arrow laid out with sticks pointing along the shore:

A little farther on, I discovered an arrow with a double head scrawled on the sand:

This meant: "Go fast."

So I went faster until I found myself on a narrow path climbing a steeply elevated shore of the lake. A pine forest grew here, and a piece of paper hung on a tree trunk, and on it was drawn a long line cut in two places by two perpendicular short lines:

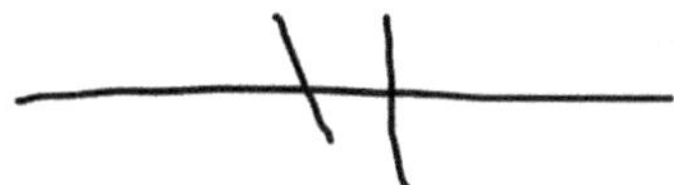

This sign meant: "Advance carefully."

I obediently slowed my pace. The path continued along the shore of the lake. Suddenly, it ended. Here, the elevated shore was cut right across by a rather shallow ravine through which a silted stream flowed into the lake. It was the same stream in which the Petersens' car got stuck the other day. On the trunk of an alder tree, I spotted a piece of paper again, this one with a zigzag line drawn on it, cut perpendicularly by two dashes:

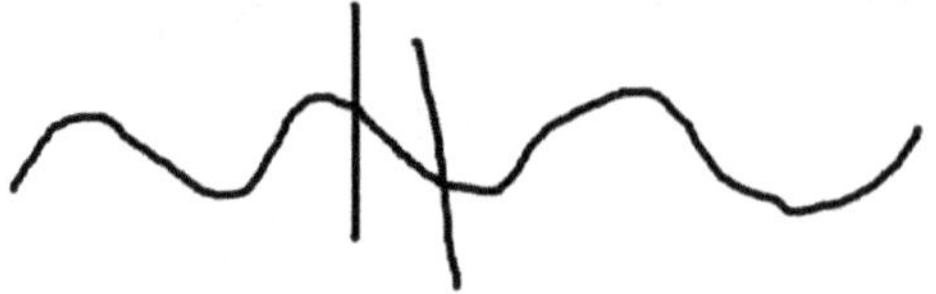

I remembered that this symbol meant: "Ford the water."

Something's telling me my Yotvingians are fooling me, I thought.

I took off my shoes, rolled up my pants, and, wading in the water up to my ankles, crossed to the other side. Here, I climbed up the steep bank again and found another piece of paper. On it was a large rectangle, and inside it, a smaller one:

This meant: "Wait here."

I waited. Five minutes. Ten. Fifteen. I was about to move on when, as if from under the ground, William Tell sprang up in front of me.

"Quiet!" he whispered, putting his finger to his lips. He sat down on the grass next to me and whispered in my ear:

"Two hundred feet ahead begins a low peninsula jutting out into the lake. Our leather-clad motorcyclist with a *Yunak,* a.k.a. Mr. Hamster, camped there in a tent. The boys from Milkokuk told us about him. Maybe this is Malinovski? Just moments ago, he packed up his camp, put his tent in a bag, and strapped it to his motorcycle. But he hasn't left yet. He's just sitting on a fallen tree trunk, occasionally glancing at his watch as if he expecting someone."

I nodded as a sign that I considered the explanation sufficient. Now, Tell led me in the direction of the peninsula. We left the path and trudged through the bushes to the shore of the lake. The terrain was still high, then it just broke off perpendicularly, as it had next to the stream. From there, looking down, we saw the alder-covered peninsula. In the bushes on the shore lay Hawkeye and Squirrel.

Tell and I snuck up and lay down next to them. The spot was perfect for watching the entire peninsula. I immediately spotted a black *Yunak* leaning against the trunk of an alder tree. A little farther away, on a fallen tree trunk, right by the water, sat a young man in a leather biker suit. He was looking toward the other shore of the lake, where the colorful cottages of the journalists' resort were clearly visible.

He seemed impatient. He looked at his watch, then lit a cigarette, then looked at his watch again. Suddenly, he pulled himself up from the tree trunk and, standing up, looked eagerly toward the other shore. And then we saw it, too: a blue kayak, with two people, coming towards us. At the sight of the kayak, the motorcyclist extinguished his cigarette and retreated into the bush, hiding so that the newcomers would not see him.

I saw that only one person in the kayak was rowing: a man sitting in the back. At the front sat a woman with a backpack in her lap. I recognized her. It was Anka. The rowing fellow was that young smart-aleck journalist who had made such a cruel mockery of my vehicle.

In a few moments, the kayak rode nose up on the sand of the beach. Anka jumped ashore.

"Thanks for the ride! See you next week!" she said, bidding farewell to the fellow who had brought her. The journalist turned the kayak around and paddled back to the resort. For a while, Anka stood uncertain at the tip of the peninsula, looking around in all directions. Finally, she sat down on a fallen tree trunk and lit a cigarette. Only now did Hamster emerge from the bushes and approach her. They shook hands, pecked cheeks, and spoke with each other so quietly that we could only hear the murmur of their voices. Then Anka got up, and they walked over to the *Yunak* hidden in the bushes. Hamster grabbed the handlebars of the motorcycle and pushed it out onto the path. Hamster kick-started the bike and Anka took her place on the back seat.

And then they sped away, bouncing on the alder roots protruding from the ground. They disappeared from sight around a bend in the path, though we could still hear the rumble of the engine for a little while, growing ever more distant.

"They had a date, Miss Anka and Hamster," said Hawkeye. "He was waiting for her."

"She never told us that she knew Hamster," said Squirrel bitterly. "I bet that's Malinovski. And she is in cahoots with him."

"She's been lying all along. From the very beginning," Tell was indignant.

"No, no, boys," I shook my head. "We must not be so suspicious. First of all, we do not have any reason to think that that was Malinovski. There are a lot of tourists in this area. Maybe it's just Anka's boyfriend? Or friend? Or even a journalist colleague?"

"A boyfriend?" ironized Hawkeye. "So why didn't he go to the resort to collect her but waited for her here, on the other side of the lake? Why did he hide in the bushes so that he would not be noticed by the fellow in the kayak?"

I shrugged my shoulders.

"Ok, to be honest, I don't fancy that guy in the kayak either. Anyway, I really don't understand any of this. I confess that these mysteries are a little too much for me. It seems everyone has a secret. I would like to get out of here and into the open and deal with just one mystery: the Templar treasure. Back to camp, boys," I ordered.

I decided to delay our departure. We bathed in the lake, because it was hot, then we sunbathed on the shore. While cooking lunch on the spirit machine, I asked the boys:

"Why did you call yourselves 'Yotvingians'"?

"Because you said it was a mysterious tribe," explained Tell.

"And we want to be mysterious," added Squirrel.

I laughed:

"The Yotvingians were not mysterious to the people of their time. They are mysterious to us because they were exterminated by the Teutonic Knights and left behind no written record. We know very little about them, and this is why they seem mysterious to us."

"Did they live here? By this lake? In these woods?" asked Squirrel, looking around.

"Yes. Perhaps also on this lake. Certainly in these forests. All this part of the country was once inhabited by the Yotvingian tribe and the

Teutonic Knights came here to exterminate them."

"Did the Yotvingians resist the Teutonic Knights?"

"Their misfortune was that they had not managed to form a unitary state, like, for example, Poles or Lithuanians. You know, a state with its own king, its own army, its own administration, its courts, a tax system. Yotvingia was just a stretch of small statelets, each of which functioned like an independent nation, sometimes ruled by the local strongman, or the landlord, or a head of the village elected at a village rally from among the wealthier villagers. This lack of a unified central authority doomed them. They were tough warriors, brave, bold to the point of madness, but they had almost the entire Europe against them. Pope after Pope declared a crusade against them. The Teutonic order came here all the way from Palestine to attack them, only two knights at first, but soon hundreds; then they were joined by crusading knights from all over Europe on short crusading trips.[2] I guess it was a kind of medieval form of football hooligan tourism. The Ukrainian Princes of Vladimir and Halich attacked them from the south, too, as well as the Polish dukes of Mazovia. You see, according to the notions of the time, fighting pagans was a 'sacred duty.'

"And yet, the Yotvingians defended themselves against the invasion for half a century. Their battle tactics were those of guerrilla warfare: they avoided battle in the open field but harassed the enemy by suddenly falling out of the forest while they rested or while they were on the march. But the long term outcome was never in doubt: the Prussians had to succumb to the more powerful enemy. In bloody battle after battle, they surrendered settlement after settlement, tribe after tribe, to the Teutonic Knights. By 1283, the Order took control of all of the Prussian and Yotvingian lands.

"Then, the Teutonic Knights systematically exterminated the indigenous population, burning their settlements and killing the people or chasing them off into the wilderness. They only spared those who accepted baptism and agreed to serve in their army. And soon, where the Yotvingians had once lived—a tribe of fifty thousand people—all that was left was uninhabited wilderness, which the Order decided to

---

[2] Like Bolingbroke, the future King Henry IV of Shakespearean fame.

keep that way. For several centuries, no one settled here. Only the forest, ever denser and wilder, grew on the burnt-out places of the former settlements. From time to time, groups of hunters from Polish Mazovia cautiously ventured into these lands, peasants began to look in—in search of forage, and from time to time, a military detachment crossed the barren wilderness: Teutonic, Polish or Lithuanian."

A Map of the Baltic Tribes just as the Teutonic Knights were preparing to attack them..

"Are all the Yotvingians dead? Every single one of them?" Squirrel asked.

"Some Yotvingians escaped to Lithuania and Ukraine, where they gave rise to several noble families.[3] Some were resettled by the Teutonic Knights in the vicinity of Jeshgon, Pashleka, and Ilavka or to the Sambian Peninsula. Those Yotvingians retained their language, customs, and distinct dress until the 16th century. And some think it

____

[3] Your translator's great-grandmother maintained with all seriousness that she came of Yatvingian stock.

possible that some Yotvingian villages survived here and there in the deepest forest. In recent years, scientists have been looking for their traces in the ground and in the speech of the people living here today, for traces of old cemeteries and former fortified settlements destroyed by the Teutonic Knights."

"And then? What happened then?" the boys asked.

"Well, then the Polish settlement happened. At first timidly, and then in an ever-increasing wave, peasants from the area around Warsaw began to settle here. And after the fall of the Teutonic state, when it submitted to Polish kings in the second half of the 15th century, Polish kings granted these unoccupied lands to Polish magnates, churches, and monasteries, who then, in order to exploit them, settled peasants and craftsmen here. Settlements such as Augustov, Seyna, Suvalki, and Krasnopol were established then—Polish towns on what had once been Yatvingian land and later became a wilderness. People cleared the wilderness, and grain began to sway on the land reclaimed from the forests."

"So this forest is what remains of this old Wilderness, right?"

I nodded.

"There are still stretches of total virgin forest in the Suvalki region—forest that has been forest for as long as history remembers, since before the Teutonic Knights and even before the Yotvingians. And Yotvingians continue to fascinate scholars and amateurs alike. You see, foreign chroniclers, even the unfriendly ones, such as the Teutonic chronicler Peter of Duisburg, wrote about them that they were a people who valued freedom more than their lives, hated any kind of coercion, and therefore did not want to accept the Christian religion because it was imposed on them by force."

And as we sat there contemplating the strange and cruel twits of history, a wind suddenly arose. The water of the lake frowned with a million wrinkles, and a quiet wave began to splash against the sandy shore. The forest swayed and rustled in the wind, and in its hum, we seemed to hear the clash of weapons and sharp battle cries in a language nobody remembered. And the waves of the lake whispered mysteriously as if to add their own testimony.

CHAPTER ELEVEN: MALBORK CASTLE

Herman von Salza. How the monastic state was born. Malbork. Why was the custodian murdered? A skirmish in the castle corridors. The story of an altarpiece. A letter from Baphomet. The basilisk. Trapped.

An hour later, we set off for Malbork. We drove along the highway that runs through Augustov, Elk, Mrongovo, and Olshtin. Just as in the Suvalki region, we passed through beautiful countryside rich in dense forests and gorgeous lakes. Behind every bend of the road vistas of endless woods or vast stretches of lakes full of wild birds opened up before us.

Here, too, the Teutonic Knights had made a bloody mark on the land. They exterminated its original inhabitants and brought in foreign colonists in their place. They built powerful castles of red brick, where steel-clad monks with swords in their hands and crosses on their coats kept a watchful eye for any sign of rebellion or heretical worship.

"And it all started pretty innocently," I told the boys as we drove. "The Teutonic Order—the Order of the Knights of the Blessed Virgin Mary was founded in 1189 in Palestine during the siege of Acre as a military order of German knights. It had few members and rather poor prospects because German knights were not very interested in the wars in Palestine. How little anyone cared for the order is perhaps best illustrated by the fact that we do not even know the names of its first three grand masters.

"But the fourth grand master, Herman von Salza, was something else," I continued. "Elected in 1210, he was a man of humble origins but of great intelligence and diplomatic skill. Having soon realized that the Teutonic Order had no prospects in Palestine, he turned his attention to Eastern Europe. He was a trusted advisor of German Emperor Frederick II, who was constantly in conflict with the Pope, and the Pope kept excommunicating him."

"Ex-what?" asked Squirrel.

"*Ex-com-mu-ni-ca-ting.* It meant that the Pope excluded the emperor from the Church. As long as the emperor remained excommunicated, he could not attend mass or take communion."

Hermann von Salza (1165 –1239)
was the fourth Grand Master of the Teutonic Knights,
serving from 1210 to 1239

"Big whoop," said Squirrel. "What did he care? He was the emperor, wasn't he? He didn't have to go to mass. He could order it brought to him."

"Well, yes. But the fact that he was excommunicated meant that oaths sworn to him on the Holy Bible were no longer valid. And this meant that his knights, lords, and even peasants were now free not to serve him or not to pay him taxes if they didn't feel like it."

"Ouch."

"Ouch it is! Of course, few of the emperor's subjects would rebel—Frederick was not a bad emperor—still, it is pretty inconvenient if *the Pope* goes around telling all your men that they don't have to serve you. Luckily for the emperor, Herman von Salza was a good diplomat and more than once acted as a mediator in these disputes between the Emperor and the Pope and was usually able to bring the two men to an agreement again. This gave Herman great influence with both the emperor and the Pope.

"Now, just at that time, Andrew II, King of Hungary and a cousin of the emperor, was having trouble with his pagan neighbors, the Cumans, and needed soldiers. And he liked the idea of using monks. Monks, you see, take no pay, so as soldiers, they are pretty cheap. They also vow to be obedient, which Andrew's subjects often were not. So, as far as Andrew could see, there was a lot to like about the Teutonic Order. He proposed to Hermann von Salza to bring the Teutonic Order to the eastern ends of his kingdom to help him fight against the Cumans.

"And Herman knew a good thing when he saw it. He quickly accepted the proposal and established a colony of the Order in Transylvania. Unfortunately, that did not last. Fourteen years later, King Andrew expelled the Teutonic Knights from his kingdom."

"Why?" asked Tell.

"Because the Teutonic Knights began their stay in Transylvania not by fighting the pagans but by playing political tricks. When he brought the Teutonic Knights to Hungary, King Andrew assumed that all these new shiny German knights would come under his authority. But the Teutonic Knights had a different idea: they put themselves under the protection of the Pope in order to become independent of the king. And soon they began to violate Hungarian laws and ignore the orders of the king. Now, King Andrew had a short fuse, and the Teutonic knights in Transylvania were still weak. He drove them out."

"Good for him," said Squirrel.

"Good for him and potentially a publicity disaster for Herman and his Order, were it not for the fact that almost immediately he received a similar invitation from a Polish prince, Conrad of Mazovia. Now, Conrad was a minor princeling ruling a small town near today's Warsaw, and he was having the same sort of pagan problem with the local Prussians that King Andrew had with the Cumans.

"And so, he invited the Teutonic Knights over here. The rest is history. You learned in school how close to destroying Poland the

Teutonic Order came in later centuries. And when you learned about it, you probably asked yourself, why did Conrad do this? Could he not see what was coming? Was the danger from the Prussian tribes really so great that Conrad had to bring in the power of the Teutonic Order into the country? And I guess the answer is that, no, Conrad did not see what was coming."

"But he had a problem with the Prussians, yes?" asked Hawkeye.

"Yes, he did. And the Teutonic Knights and their propagandists later exaggerated the Prussian problem in order to present themselves in the eyes of Europe as saviors and defenders of Christian Poland. And in so doing, they justified Conrad. But the truth is that while the Prussians were a pain, Conrad picked on his Polish neighbors because he dreamed of conquering the capital of Poland, Cracow, and of crowning himself king. So, he did not want to divert his forces to defend himself from Prussian raids. Bringing in a handful of monastic knights and settling them on the Prussian border seemed to him a cheap way to buy himself security on that side. So he granted the Teutonic Knights a few villages for income but without conceding suzerainty."

"Su-what?" asked Squirrel.

"*Su-ze-rain-ty*. Political power. This is an important word. For example, I own this car. It is my car. I can drive it, or use it to secure a loan, or sell it, or give it away. But because I am a citizen of Poland, the Polish state has *suzerainty* over my car. In extraordinary conditions, for example, in times of war, it can say: 'Mr. Wheels, the nation needs your car for self-defense; we take your car, thank you very much.' And all I can do is take them to court to claim that they should pay me something for it. This is the difference between ownership and suzerainty. You see?"

"Ok. So, Conrad gave these villages to the Order but reserved 'suzenty' for himself?"

"*Su-ze-rein-ty*. Yes. Basically, he said: I give you these villages so that you can use them as a source of income, but they remain part of my principality."

"And?"

Emblazonment (Flag) of the Grand Master of the Teutonic Order

"Ha! So, what do you think the Teutonic Knights did? They crafted the endowment document in such a way that it implied that Conrad of Mazovia had relinquished all his rights, suzerainty included. Like these five villages now became an independent state. You see? Thus, treachery and deceit lay at the root of the future power of the Teutonic state."

"And he signed it? What a dimwit!"

"Well, let's not condemn Conrad too harshly. Today, from the perspective of history, we judge these matters differently. Today, we know that these two knights who came to Poland in 1230 eventually grew into a huge military power, which did not just wipe out the Prussians but very nearly wiped out our country, too. But things were different back then, at the beginning. The first stronghold these two knights built was just a single tower, and they called it *Vogelsang*, or Bird's Song. Do you know why? Because it was in total sticks. All you heard was foxes and birds."

"Wait, wait," said Tell. "Did you say *two* knights? Like—two guys?"

"Well, yes. Two knights. Though you must remember, in those days, 'a knight' meant a guy clad in iron on a powerful warhorse. He went into battle, and by sheer weight of his animal and his horse, he carried everything before him. He was, basically, the medieval equivalent of a modern tank. And like a modern tank, he needed support: men who looked after his armor and his horse, men who helped him get on the horse and handed him his lance, and then all those people who took care of tents and provisions and so forth. And when it came to battle, they all fought. So 'one knight' meant maybe seven or ten men. So, these first two knights who came to Poland led a force of maybe fifteen or twenty.

"But there really were only two knights—Konrad von Landsberg and another knight, unknown by name. It was only as a result of Conrad's complaint to Herman von Salza that the Order sent in a new commander, Herman Balk, who arrived in Poland along with more knights of the Order."

"In fact, it was such a small group that the first Teutonic expedition against Prussia had to be supported by Conrad's troops. And later? At the beginning, Polish troops assisted the Teutonic Knights in their conquests on Prussian soil. Conrad of Mazovia, with his son Casimir, brought his men. From Silesia came Henry the Bearded. From Greater Poland came Ladislaus Odonits, and from Pomerania came Duke Sviatopelk with his brother Sambor.

"This was the first Northern Crusade, and it inflicted the first great defeat on the Prussians. More than five thousand of them fell on the battlefield on the Jeshgon River, and part of their lands, Pomezania, fell into the hands of the Teutonic Knights. Without in any way diminishing the strategic abilities of the Teutonic leader, Herman Balk, who was a brave knight and an excellent commander, we must say that without the help of Polish knights, the Order would never have succeeded in capturing Pomezania. But with their help, they did, and Pomezania became the nucleus of the future Teutonic state."

We passed Olshtin, then Elblong—both of them old cities originally founded by the Teutonic Order—and camped in a wood by the road. The following day, we arrived in Malbork, and we headed straight to a campground near the Nogat River—a branch of the Vistula. The Teutonic Castle, which we had seen from very far away, did not seem as impressive from this perspective. Only later, as we approached it from the riverside, did we see how magnificent it was.

There were a dozen different-colored tents at the campsite by the river and their owners' cars stood next to them. We directed our vehicle to the far-left corner of the field, a relatively secluded place. We parked the car, and on both sides of the vehicle, we pitched our two tents, one for the boys and one for me. It wasn't until two o'clock that we went to dinner at the campsite restaurant, creatively called 'By the Nogat.' Over dessert I explained to the scouts my plans for our stay in Malbork.

"I have been here twice," I said. "The Malbork complex is actually two huge castles connected to each other: the Middle Castle and High Castle. You will see for yourself that they have many halls and rooms, dozens of corridors, labyrinthine undergrounds, and hundreds of nooks and crannies. The castle has been destroyed, rebuilt, and remodeled many times, but even so, it will be a long time before all of its secrets are properly investigated and revealed because, in addition to the mysteries from Teutonic times, new ones have come from the period of the last war. Nazis used Malbork Castle as a fortress against the combined Soviet and Polish armies, and immediately after liberation, very strange things happened here, the discovery of the folding altarpiece of Ulrich von Jungingen among them."

"Whoa!" cried Squirrel. "Ulrich! Ulrich the Bad! He had a *folding* altarpiece? Lets' hear it!"

"Oh, surely you know this story," I tried to wriggle out.

"No, we haven't heard it. We want to know. It may come in handy for us when we visit the castle," said Tell.
I ordered another coffee so that my mouth wouldn't get dry and proceeded to tell the story.

"At the battle of Grunwald in 1410," I began, "the victorious Polish army took Teutonic prisoners, battle flags, arms, horses, the contents of their camp, as well a beautiful, intricately carved field altarpiece of the Grand Master Ulrich von Jungingen. The Grand Master had prayed before it before the battle. King Yogaila offered the captured altarpiece to the Gnezno cathedral and it lay in the church treasury until the partition of Poland in 1795. In 1795, the Germans looted it from the treasury and transported it back to Malbork, where it remained until World War II. In 1944, Germans defended themselves long and hard in Malbork Castle against the Russian and Polish armies. When Malbork fell, Polish soldiers found many valuable items in the castle. However, it was difficult for ordinary soldiers to figure out the value of these items, and the German custodian of the castle hid many precious objects and then went into hiding himself. The Polish commander of the city of Malbork posted military guards against looters prowling the area but many art objects of the castle were missing.

Ulrich von Jungingen (1360 – 15 July 1410)
was the 26th Grand Master of the Teutonic Knights between 1407 and 1410. His policy sparked the Polish–Lithuanian–Teutonic War and led to disaster for his Order and his own death at the Battle of Grunwald. Like every Polish schoolboy, Squirrel is familiar with the name.

"One day," I continued my account, "someone revealed the custodian's hiding place. It seemed that now it would be possible to recover all the art objects of the Malbork Castle. But to the astonishment of the soldiers, when they arrived at the indicated address, they found the custodian dead. He had been shot that night, probably so that he could not reveal the secrets of the castle.

"His death and the reports that some unknown individuals were prowling about the castle aroused the vigilance of the town's commandant. At that time, there were still quite a few Germans living in the city of Malbork, and many survivors of the German army were hiding among them. Late in the evening, in mid-May, a soldier rushed into the commandant's headquarters with a report that a group of people had made their way into the castle through a breach in the shell-shattered walls. An alarm went up, and a group of soldiers set out for the castle. It turned out that the visitors were in the High Castle, in some rooms near the former castle treasury. The Polish soldiers ambushed them in an alcove of the corridor. The thieves began firing automatic weapons and managed to escape through the breach in the wall. The Poles gave chase and found a German soldier's coat and, in it, documents with the address of one of Malbork's German residents.

"And in the treasure room, they found a freshly made hole in the wall. Presumably, something had been buried in the wall, and this "something" was then stolen by the thieves. The soldiers immediately attempted to search the house of the German resident, but as they approached the house, a man jumped out of the window and fled. The chase yielded no result, but the search of the house yielded great results. In the basement, under the kitchen, they found wrapped in the coat of a German soldier—the field altarpiece of Ulrich von Jungingen. It had most likely been walled up in the Malbork treasury and was the target of the night theft. You can see it at the National Museum in Warsaw. And in the Malbork treasury, guides still show the place in the wall where it was once buried," I concluded the story.

By the time we left the restaurant, it was already four in the afternoon. I realized that it was high time to go to the castle because a tour, even a cursory one, would take at least two hours.

We marched quickly along the castle moat and up to the main entrance of the Middle Castle. In place of the old drawbridge, there was now a long, permanent bridge of wooden logs. Two museum guards stood at the gate to check tickets. Visitors could only enter with a guide, so we had to wait, but not very long because a group of perhaps thirty tourists was already waiting at the gate. We decided to take the tour with them with them.

The folding "field" altarpiece of Ulrich von Jungingen
Made in Elblong (Elbląg) in 1388.
It was a medieval fashion to have such portable, folding altarpieces, some painted, others carved, which one would unfold and pray before while on a journey. They were usually very small, this one is the size of a large coffee-table book.

Up close, the castle looked imposing. It was a huge, austere, reddish-brown mass. Its high defensive walls dropped off vertically into a deep moat, now dry and overgrown with grass but once filled with water from the river. Behind the defensive walls, various castle buildings piled close together, rising ever higher all the way to the towers of the High Castle, which, seen from below, seemed to reach the sky. How small and weak a medieval knight, armed with a sword or a crossbow, must have felt before these walls mighty and hard, which seemingly nothing could crush!

In former times, the castle had looked even more magnificent. It was surrounded by the civilian settlement with its own walls and towers, and these were further defended by another moat and the Nogat River. An attacker who broke through those defenses now faced the even higher defensive walls of the Middle Castle. Then, between the High and Middle Castles ran another precipitous moat and another steep wall several stories high. And behind this defensive wall stood the towers of the High Castle, each designed as a fortification in its own right.

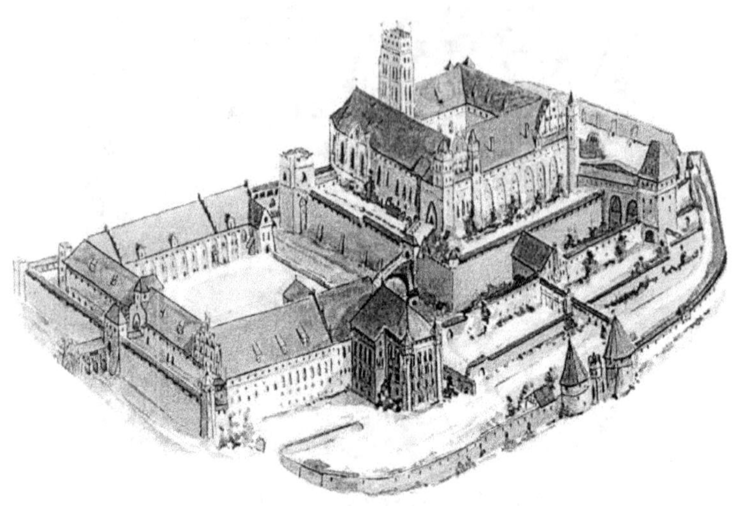

Aerial view of Malbork Castle today.
Middle castle on the left, High Castle on the right.

"*Ex luto Marienburg*," I said quietly.

"What does that mean?" asked Tell immediately.

"The Teutonic Knights were very proud of their fortress—one of the largest medieval castles in Europe. They compared it with the world's most beautiful cities and said, rather poetically, that while Milan was made of marble, and Buda[4] was made of sandstone, Marienburg—in other words, Malbork—was made of mud.

"Of mud?" asked puzzled Tell.

"Yes, of mud, that is, of clay. Of brick. It is said that to reinforce the mortar, it was mixed with chicken and cattle blood."

Meanwhile, an elderly lady approached us. On her sleeve, she had an armband with the sign: *Guide*.

"Ah, God," she said at the gate to one of the guards, "one more tour! And I have guided four tours today! Would you count the

---

[4] Part of today's Budapest in Hungary

participants, because I think my brain is just not working anymore. This morning, I led a tour of twenty people into the castle and led twenty-two people out. A while ago, a tour of twenty-eight people left the castle, and I would have bet my head that thirty had entered."

"It's all from fatigue, ma'am," said the janitor. "We always have too many visitors at the beginning of summer."

We lined up in front of the gate. The guide waved her hand and, giving up on counting us, began her lecture:

"The Teutonic Knights began to build the Malbork keep in 1272, and the castle around it in 1279-1280. They named it Marienburg, or the City of Mary. Today's appearance of the castle does not give a full idea of what it looked like in the 13th century because it has been remodeled several times since then."

Slowly, trundling loudly over the wooden logs of the bridge, we entered the castle gate. Suddenly, someone touched my shoulder. It was an usher guarding the gate.

"Are you with these three scouts?" he asked.

"Yes, I am. Why?"

"Some gentleman left a letter for you. He told me that a gentleman with three scouts would come. He asked me to give you this letter."

And he handed me an envelope.

"This is some kind of misunderstanding. I don't know anyone here," I said, taking the envelope.

I opened it and read it:

Mr Wheels. I advise you to leave Malbork and stay
away, or it will be the worse for you. Baphomet

"Is this indeed for you?" asked the guard curiously.

I nodded:

"Yes, thank you, sir. This is a letter for me. And where is the gentleman who handed it to you?"

"I don't know. He toured the castle this morning and, I imagine, has left by now. Perhaps he was with the tour that left for

Cracow half an hour ago."

I thanked him and caught up with my group, which had just entered the grounds of the Middle Castle. The guide narrated:

"First the High Castle was built, which you will see further on. But once Malbork became the capital of the monastic state and the Grand Master moved here from Venice, the High Castle proved too small, and the Teutonic Knights proceeded to enlarge the fortress."

I caught up with the boys and discreetly showed them the letter and explained how it came into my hands.

"I don't understand any of this," whispered Tell. "Who is *Baphomet*?"

I leaned toward them and whispered:

"The devil."

"What?"

"This was the name of a mysterious and enigmatic idol that, according to their accusers, the Knights Templar allegedly worshipped in the secrecy of their chapels. Philip the Fair, the King of France, appointed a Micky-mouse court to investigate this accusation; the court did as it was told—found the Templars guilty of devil worship—and burnt them at the stake."

"And this Baphomet... is here?" the boys said in surprise. The guide stomped angrily on the stone floor of the courtyard and called out:

"Hello, young people, please keep quiet and come closer. Here I am, wearing out my throat out, trying to tell you about the history of Malbork, and you're whispering to each other and learning nothing. Please come closer. Oh, yes, here. And you too," she pointed an accusatory finger at me and pierced me with a stern gaze.

I blushed as the entire tour gave me the evil eye. I obediently stood next to the guide. For the next few minutes, I was her most eager listener.

Stopping here and there for an explanation, we walked through the huge courtyard of the Middle Castle. Here was the monumental building of the grand master's palace, decorated with columns and pointed arches in the Venetian style. Here was the grand refectory, where foreign knights—"guests" as they were called—took their meals.

In the grand master's palace, the guide showed us secret openings in the walls through which the grand master's men could surreptitiously observe the behavior of the knights and eavesdrop on their conversations in the refectory. There was a hunting scene painted on one of the walls of the refectory, and the secret spy holes were located in the eyes of the animals depicted in the scene. The grand master was afraid of conspiracies and intrigues, and the "eavesdropping apparatus" was supposed to help him figure out which knights were possibly ill-disposed towards him.

"How was such a man dealt with?" the guide explained. "Well, he would be egged on to get drunk during a feast, and then when he went to the lavatory located in the High Castle, in a tower called Gdanisko, a trapdoor would suddenly open under him, and he would fall thirty feet down. He smashed his head against a special ledge designed for that purpose, and his body would be carried away by the swift current of the river flowing under the tower."

And a drawbridge, a gate, and a courtyard surrounded by buildings: the courtyard of the High Castle, the oldest part of the fortress. In one corner stood the church of the Virgin Mary, demolished during the last war and still only partly restored,[5] and beneath it, in its crypt, the chapel of St. Anne, the resting place of the grand masters of the order. One entered the church from the courtyard through the so-called Golden Gate, with a beautifully carved portal.

Our footsteps rang out in the stone courtyard surrounded on all sides by stone cloisters.
"Knightly tournaments were once held here," said our guide, "and the audience gathered in the two levels of the cloisters watched the bouts. How loudly the steel-shod horses of the Teutonic Knights must have rumbled here! How loudly did the clash of swords ring out!"

Her words were quite poetic, but she did not allow us a moment for daydreaming.

"Here you see the great kitchen of the Order. It is authentic, never destroyed or rebuilt. It is preserved just as it looked years ago. Whole animals were spit-roasted inside this gigantic fireplace and then

---

[5] At the time of writing. It is restored now.

delivered to the dining hall using a special chute. Next to us was the bakery, located below the monastic treasury. In 1364, when the Order was at the height of its power, the treasury contained, in addition to the usual coin, four hundred silver drinking cups used by the Teutonic knights and their guests during special feasts.

The cloisters of the High Castle in Malbork

"Now, old chronicles preserve an interesting story that, at one time, the bakers punched a hole in the ceiling and got at the coin that way. However, they immediately began to spend the money, the matter came to light, and they were caught."

We climbed the stairs to the second floor and, through a narrow door, entered the realm of the Order's treasurer.

The sight of the treasury clearly disappointed the scouts. They had associated the word "treasury" with the image of a chamber full of chests filled with gold, precious stones, and golden vessels. And here? A tiny, empty chamber, some stains on the walls, a faded wall painting in which one could barely make out the outline of a terrible dragon, a basilisk. According to the general belief of the time, basilisks were real creatures and the best guardians of gold.

The boys were the first to leave the treasury, followed by the rest of the tour. I tarried behind.

Your treasure is where your heart is, I said to myself. *Where is the Templar treasure? Where are their jewels, their gold?*

I meditated in the deep silence that fell in the tiny chamber of the Teutonic treasury. I heard the distant footsteps of the tour from the courtyard, and as I strained my ears, it seemed to me that I could hear the clinking of the coins that had once been counted here.

"Why have you stayed behind?" I heard the sharp voice of the guide. "I noticed that you are not listening to me at all but thinking about something completely different. And here I am, wearing out my throat to explain things to you."

Having properly upbraided me, the guide turned around and stomped out into the cloister.

"Now I will show you the famous cell in which Kaystut, prince of Lithuania, was imprisoned by the Teutonic Knights," she said in a somber voice meant to awaken a feeling of dread in us.

She led us into a narrow, short corridor with double iron doors and a portcullis. A slit window in the thick walls let in a little light. The stone floor rang out underfoot; the sheet metal-clad walls breathed cold.

"It seems that there is no way to escape from here," said the guide. "Yet Prince Kaystut escaped from Teutonic captivity. According to legend, he did so with the help of Alfa, a servant of the Teutonic order, a Lithuanian by birth, who was kidnapped as a child and baptized by the Teutonic Knights. The noble appearance of Prince Kaystut awoke patriotic feelings in the boy."

As the tour left Kaystut's gloomy cell, I approached the slit-window and tried to look at the sky. Prince Kaystut, captured treacherously, probably looked out through it in the same way.

Who is this mysterious Baphomet? I wondered. *And why does he mind my presence in Malbork?*
I twitched. Behind my back, the iron hinges creaked. I looked over and saw the cell door closing. An iron bolt rattled, and then a latch slammed shut.

Someone had played a silly trick on me.

I was locked up in Prince Kaystut's cell.

I ran to the iron door and tried to jerk it open. It did not budge. I pounded it with my fists, but the thick iron only clanked with a faint, hollow sound. No one could hear me, even if they passed near the cell.

Kaystut (Polish: Kejstut, Lithuanian: Kęstusis)
(died 1382) was an important prince of the Lithuanian Gedymin Dynasty.

CHAPTER TWELVE: MALBORK CASTLE AT NIGHT

A god with a human face. Why was von Orseln killed? Ghosts in the castle. An eavesdropping apparatus. What does the triangle on the wall mean? Go, go, go, get him!

A deafening silence fell all around me, so profound that my ears began to ring. Thick walls clad in sheet metal did not allow any sound to pass through. Besides, by now, the Castle was empty, all visitors had left. I sat on the stone floor in the dim light coming through the slit window and tried to think about my situation.

I assumed that the guide would notice my absence at the exit (after all, she probably remembered me, having called me to attention so many times?). She would probably raise the alarm; the museum ushers would set out to look for me and find me locked in this prison cell. Of course, I knew that my three young friends would notice my absence immediately, but they would think that I remained on the castle grounds on purpose, and not only would not raise the alarm, but they would try to trick the guide into thinking that I had left before the others. I would, of course, be released from my confinement the following morning when the first tour came to visit the cell. I tried to imagine the tour guide's expression when she saw an imprisoned man!

Of course, she would tell all the museum staff about this, and from then on, they would all keep a beady eye on me. Their distrust would prevent me from coming into closer contact with the museum staff and would make it difficult to get the kind of historical information I was hoping for when I arrived in Malbork. Was this what the mysterious Baphomet wanted to accomplish when he locked me in Kaystut's cell?

It seemed clear to me that behind this name hid some competitor of mine in the search of the Templar treasure. The proof of this was the name he had taken for himself. It showed that he (or she) was well-versed in the history of the Templar order. I decided that this was no one from the Petersen group, as they had stayed at the lake to buy back the stolen document from Malinovski. Nor could it have been

Malinovski himself, for he, too, had had to stay at the lake to collect his money.

So, who was this Baphomet? I was stumped. I sat on the stone floor and, pulling my knees up to my chin, rested my head on them. Next to my cheek was the watch on my wrist, but even though the passing of time ticked incessantly in the seconds hand, no one came to release me from my prison cell.

The narrow trickle of light streaming through the window grew dimmer and dimmer, like a lamp that ran out of fuel. The night was coming, and with it disappeared my hope that I would be released that day.

I thought about the Lithuanian prince who had sat imprisoned here. Six hundred years have passed since then. The same thick walls, the same stone floor, the same iron double doors blocking one's escape. How many moments of dark doubt did the Lithuanian prince experience here?

At the time, the Teutonic Knights were at the zenith of their power. Having united with the Order of the Knights of the Sword in Livonia, they acquired territory so large that they rivaled the largest kingdoms in Europe. To them belonged today's Pomerania, all of what was later called East Prussia, a part of Lithuania, today's Latvia and Estonia. Only a small patch of Samogitia separated the Teutonic possessions in Prussia and Livonia and in its territory raged constant battles: the Teutonic knights wanted to connect their two possessions by conquering Samogitia. And Samogitia was part of Kaystut's patrimony.

Teutonic Order reached the peak of its power by then. And all that remained of the Templars were demolished castles and infamy, slanderous court documents, trumped-up accusations, coerced false confessions that no one could retract because those who had made them under torture were now long dead, burned at the stake. The French authorities, possessed by their frantic search for the Templars' treasure, accused the monks of having denied Christ, spitting on the cross, and worshipping an idol made of wood and leather with a human face and a huge beard. The name of this idol was—Baphomet.

In fact, no image or statue of this deity was ever produced by either Philip the Fair or anyone else. Philip had simply invented this Baphomet for the sake of his case. No Baphomet had ever existed. Most rulers of the time gave no credence to the nonsense accusations against the Templars about the worship of this invented deity.

And now this bearded Baphomet wrote a letter to me? I pondered.

Meanwhile, my prison cell plunged into a profound darkness, which only seemed to deepen the silence in which I was lost. I had lost hope that I would be released that night. Curled up in a corner of the cell, I tried to fall asleep.

I don't know how long I slept. Maybe a few minutes, or maybe an hour? I was awakened by some rustling and then a quiet screech.

Rats? I thought with revulsion.

The rustling sound repeated. And then the quiet screech. Both of these sounds came... from the direction of the door. Suddenly, the bolt slammed open, and the heavy door of the prison cell groaned.

A stream of electric light burst into the depths of the cell and began to glide across the stone floor. Finally, it hit me in the eyes, blinding me.

"Who is this?" I called out.

"Mr. Wheels! Mr. Wheels!" I heard the happy voices of my scouts.

The light dimmed and changed direction. I picked myself off the floor and jumped over to the boys.

They were not alone. They had with them—a girl of about twelve. She had red hair pinned up in a ponytail. She was the person holding an electric flashlight in her hand.

"This is Mr. Wheels," the boys introduced me. "And this is Eve. Eve lives in the Middle Castle. Her mother works in the museum archives."

"Who locked you in here?" she asked.

"I don't know. Probably this fellow," I said and showed her the note from Baphomet.

It turned out that the boys had noticed my absence on the way out of the castle. But, just as I had assumed, they thought that I had stayed behind of my own free will. Accordingly, they told the guide that

I had left a little earlier than the others because I had been in a hurry to catch a bus.

But then, an hour passed, and I still did not return. The boys waited for me near the gate but now did not know what to do. Finally, after much discussion, they came to the conclusion that if I had intended to stay behind of my own accord, I would have warned them about it. Then, they remembered the threatening letter from Baphomet and became concerned.

And while they were discussing this at the castle gate, they noticed a girl who passed freely several times in and out of the gate, not minded by the guards. They guessed that she lived on the castle grounds. And when she came out of the gate once again and went to the store to get some groceries, the boys got into a conversation with her. They told her about us and me and initiated her into the purpose of our journey.

The girl—her name was Eve—had once read in a youth newspaper about my discovery of the Dunin Collection. And this broke the ice.

She took her shopping to the castle apartment. Then, she came out again to see the boys and led them all the way to the bank of the Nogat. They walked for quite a long time along the high castle walls, then waded through some bushes until they finally came to the dry bottom of a deep moat. The girl led them to a small wooden gate, which she opened with a heavy key. They entered the area of the garden where monks had once grown their vegetables. Then, they climbed up some wooden steps. And, through a dark corridor, holding hands, they entered the castle.

Finding me was an easy matter. After all, they remembered that I had disappeared while visiting Prince Kaystut's cell. So, they decided to start their search there. They opened the cell door and found me.

"I wonder if Baphomet left with the tour or stayed in the castle," Eve said.

"He has left," Tell stated firmly. "The guide counted the people taking part in the tour. Only one was missing—Mr. Thomas."

"But we don't know him," I said. "We don't know what he looks like. Maybe he entered the castle with the tour, locked me in a cell, and stayed behind somehow?"

"It's a good idea to look around in any case," Eve advised. "We have a flashlight, and I know all the crannies here."

"Sounds like a plan," I nodded. "Baphomet, it seems, is a dangerous opponent."

"We have to take off our shoes and hold them in our hands. Every step sounds like a gunshot within these walls," Eve said. "During the night, the museum's janitors patrol the entire castle several times. Someone once started a fire in the Middle Castle, and since then, they have been very careful that no stranger strays here at night. During the day, too, visitors are not allowed to separate from the tour group."

We obediently removed our shoes.

"We'll start from the second floor," decided Eve. "There is no need to push into the attics because they are locked. I doubt Baphomet went there."

We climbed the stairs to the second floor and walked quietly as ghosts along the cloister that circled the courtyard. We passed the doors to the granaries, the knights' chambers, the convent refectory. Eve carefully checked that all the doors were locked. Guides had keys to some rooms and opened them during the tour, showing the interior architecture and old paintings on the walls.

Then, Eve led us to a cramped secret chamber. It had two windows, or rather, openings looking out into the interior of the castle church. This was where monastic knights were locked up for penance. Such men were not allowed to participate in the rite of mass, but in this chamber, in seclusion, they could still watch the ceremony. The church was now destroyed, and through the windows, we could see its ruins and the starry sky.

Then, on the second floor, we stood in front of the Golden Gate—the former entrance to the church—which was closed to the public because, on the other side, there was nothing but ruins.

Eve shone a shaft of light on the beautifully carved portal.

"Look," she said, "here are the imaginary figures of the "wise virgins," and on the other side of the "foolish virgins.""

"And you are a *smug* virgin. And there isn't one of those on the portal," Hawkeye said teasingly.

"I am a Wise Virgin," Eve cut him off and grabbed Hawkeye's long nose with two fingers. He squealed like a mouse and, from then on, stayed away from the girl, no longer trying to tease her.

Eve lowered her voice:

"At this gate, the Grand Master Werner von Orseln, was murdered in 1330... He was killed as he left the church after hearing mass."

I shuddered. I looked at the low, dark opening of the Gothic door. Right here, at this gate, not only the thread of Orseln's life had been cut, but also the trail that led to the Templar treasure.

"And why was he murdered?" asked Squirrel, who had probably forgotten what I had recounted during the first day of our trip.

"Nobody knows," replied Eve. "He was killed by a monk named Neudorf. The Teutonic Knights said that Brother Neudorf was insane. Others claimed that it was a personal revenge: that the Grand Master excluded Neudorf from some expedition to Lithuania.

"Yes," I nodded. "This last version does seem likely. You see the life of a monastic knight was by no means sweet or comfortable, especially in the 14th century, when the Order maintained strict discipline. The monastic rule provided for severe punishments, even for the slightest transgressions. For transgressions in eating, drinking, or speech, the monk was beaten. For brawling, disobedience, or spending the night outside the convent or camp—the culprit's cloak was taken away, and he was sent to do manual labor along with the slaves. For spending two nights outside the convent or camp or plotting against his superiors, he suffered a year of such demotion. For fleeing from the battlefield, deviating from the faith, and corruption in office, the penalty was expulsion from the Order without exemption from the vows, which threw such a person completely outside the bounds of society. So, life in this castle, under the eye of the Grand Master, was not easy, especially for young, energetic men who joined the order because they wanted to see action. They reared to go to war. It seems possible that a knight who was excluded from an expedition because of some minor infraction might get mad and attack somebody."

"My mother said," said Eve, "that some old documents contain another version of von Orseln's murder. That the Teutonic Knights invited some Lithuanians to a feast in Skirstimon in 1328, got their guest drunk, and then murdered them and burnt the castle. This cruel and perverse murder was supposedly the cause of Neudorf's insanity. Unable to endure the cruelty of his brothers, he killed the Grand Master."

"And he did this two years after the events in Skirstimon?" I said doubtfully. "I don't think so. The grand masters dealt with the general affairs of the Order—international affairs and so on. The practical business in Prussia—such discipline of the local brothers—fell in the purview of the National Master. When the Teutonic Knights treacherously attacked Pomerania,[6] a Christian province, they did it on the orders of the National Master. European opinion was so outraged that the Grand Master, Siegfried von Feuchtwangen, had to flee from Venice to Malbork because he suddenly faced a court case before the Papal Curia. Old records say he was furious that his subordinates in Eastern Europe had attacked and seized a Christian country.

"The national master at the time was a fellow named Henrik von Plotzke. He was responsible for that attack. He was a hard and cruel man, and he led a party of hawks. He had a simple notion of business: attack, attack, attack. Take what you can and keep it. The hell with the international reputation—"How do you eat international reputation?" he used to say. He did not hesitate to commit the most despicable crimes in order to gain new territory for the Order, whether Christian or otherwise. Feuchtwangen's successor as Grand Master, Charles of Trier, came into conflict with this hawkish Henrik, and this conflict became so heated that the Grand Master left Malbork in 1318, went to Germany and—renounced his office. Although the general chapter never accepted his renunciation and Charles of Trier remained in office until 1324, he never returned here. And the very next Grand Master was— guess who—Werner von Orseln. We know that he was a dove and favored a peace settlement with Poland in 1330. But he was assassinated."

"So, you think that von Orseln was killed on the orders of

---

[6] Pomerania was an old province of Poland with Gdansk as its capital.

Henrik von Plotzke?" Tell picked up.

"Well, no, not on the orders of hawkish Henrik because he was already dead by then. He died in 1320 during another expedition against Samogitia. But, of course, his ideas and its supporters—hardline men convinced that force was the only way—remained very powerful. By that time, the Teutonic Order had already become very secularized. It forgot that it had been established to propagate the Christian faith. I mean, seriously, what was the point of a Christian military order fighting the Christian king of Poland? By attacking Poland, the Order showed that it became an ordinary state, ruled by people who had little to do with religion and thought only of ever-new conquests and consolidating their power. But since they could not speak openly about their intentions, they decided to drive the policy of the Order by secret terror. They instituted a "Secret Tribunal" inside the Order."

"What?"asked Hawkeye.

"Well, they decided that they alone knew what was best for the Teutonic Order and that their enemies were brain-washed doves and had to be dragged, by hook or crook, to do the right thing. And the crook they invented was this "Secret Tribunal.""

"And what was that?" asked Squirrel.

"Well, well. In one of these castle towers, knights in black face masks assembled at night so that no one, not even the other members at the meeting, would know who they were. These masked monk-knights then tried in their absence those whom they accused of betraying the Order's most vital interests—basically, the weak-kneed doves. To them, any leniency shown to any of the opponents of the Order was equivalent to "treason." My guess is that just such a secret tribunal sentenced Werner von Orseln to death for trying to make peace with Poland.

"In fact, now that I think of it, I wonder if it may have reached their ears that Werner von Orseln intended to return to the survivors of the Templars residing in Scotland the Templar treasure. Von Orseln's intentions would have been known to his confessor, also a brother of the order. Was the confessor part of the "Secret Tribunal"? The Teutonic Knights were by now accustomed to breaking all oaths and pledges and were outraged at the idea that Von Orseln might keep a promise and return their deposit to the Templars. Of course, the "Secret Tribunal" had no idea where the treasure was located. But it seemed to them that finding it would be an easy matter. Therefore, they passed a death sentence on von Orseln."

"How did they do it?" asked Tell.

"First, there was a secret ballot. And when it became clear that a death sentence had been passed, the future executor of the sentence was chosen by lot. Balls were cast into a special urn, as many as the tribunal members. All except one were white. Whoever pulled out the black ball had to become the executor of the sentence. And since the members of the court wore masks, no one knew either who issued the death sentence or the name of the murderer until he carried out the assassination. After that, all members of the court had the duty to protect the murderer from punishment.

"In my opinion, Knight Neudorf was a member of the tribunal and drew the black ball. He murdered the grand master, thus carrying out the sentence of the "Secret Tribunal." It seems that in order to save him, the members of the "Secret Tribunal"—men usually recruited from the highest authorities of the Order—came up with the story of Neudorf's insanity in order to save his life. One way or another, negotiations with Poland were broken off, and a year later, in 1331, the Teutonic Order attacked Poland. What followed was a three-corner war between Poland, the Teutonic Order, and their allies, the Czechs. And it ended with us, thank God, beating the bejeezus out of both of them. But it was a close-run thing."

"And the Templar treasure?" Eve asked.

"Von Orseln probably took its secret to the grave. But maybe not the whole secret. You see, it seems to me that the Grand Masters never possessed the full secret of its location. I doubt de Molay naively assumed that the Teutonic Knights would never try to defraud him. The world is full of thieves, some of them come in priestly robes. These "priestly" guys knew each other and were perfectly aware of how they operated. So, I suspect that the deal was this: Siegfried von Feuchtwangen allowed for the Templar treasure to be buried in one of his castles, but the hiding was done by the Templars themselves to make sure that they were the only ones to recover it."

Suddenly, I stopped because Eve grabbed my hand and squeezed it tightly, ordering me to be silent. By now, we were in the upper gallery of the courtyard. We heard footsteps in the courtyard and looking down, saw—gasp!—two shadows run across it in the dark. They disappeared into the cloister at the opposite end. Everything was silent again. We waited for the two shadows to reappear, but they did not. Only after a while we heard the sound of someone else: slow footsteps approaching from the side of the Middle Castle.

"Who was that?" Tell asked.

"I have no idea," said Eve.

"Was that the night watchman?"

"No. *This* is the night watchman."

The watchman's footsteps came closer: he was walking slowly with a lantern in his hand, looking around in all directions. Eve pulled us back into the penitential chamber. We crowded together, holding our breaths, and waited for the watchman to pass by. After a while, the echo of his footsteps moved away and eventually disappeared.

As silently as we could, we ran out to the gallery and looked down. We hoped the two mysterious shadows would reappear in the courtyard. We waited with bated breath for quite a long time. We were already starting to think that they would never appear again when somewhere down below, under the cloister, we heard a whisper of conversation. Then, we saw two people slowly move in the direction of the Middle Castle.

Still barefoot, we dashed down the stairs. We entered the courtyard just in time to see the two shadows pass the castle gate and enter drawbridge leading to the Middle Castle. A moment later, they were lost in the dark.

"Do you think they've gone down to the basements? I don't think so. I think maybe they went up to the palace of the grand master?" Eve whispered in my ear.

She led us upstairs. Through an unlocked door, we entered a dark corridor. We passed the entrance to the underground and climbed the stairs. We walked holding hands, without a light, because didn't want to warn the mysterious visitors of our presence.

Suddenly, we heard a sound as if of a stream or of a water tap turned on right next to us. We stopped and pricked our ears.

No, it was not a running tap. It was the murmur of a conversation. But it was a strange murmur, coming, as it were, from the floor. We slipped into a niche where there was a stone bench. We sat down. And then the murmur of the conversation became even clearer, although it still came from the ground.

After a while, we realized that there was a small opening in the walls of the niche. Perhaps it was a duct from the central heating system? Or was it part of the "surveillance apparatus" installed in the grand master's palace? Whatever the reason, sitting on the stone bench in our niche, we could clearly hear the conversation taking place somewhere else—we did not know where—but somewhere in the castle. Could it be that the two people were talking to each other right next to us—in an adjacent room?

A woman's voice said:

"I'm starting to get sick of it. This is not how I imagined our vacation. It's the second night we're staying in the castle and roaming the underground in the dark. Eventually, they'll catch us, and we'll spend the rest of our vacation in jail."

A man's voice answered her:

"Don't worry! We're not doing anything wrong. Even if we do get caught, we will explain that we wanted to spend a romantic night in the old castle. At most, they will fine us for trespassing. Besides, it was you who suggested that we spend our vacation searching for the Templar treasure."

Woman:

"Because I thought it would be fun. But this is grim business. Did you have to lock up that guy in there?"

Man:

"I didn't want him getting in our way. Do you think I don't know who he is? He is following us. I'm sure that's the guy who robbed the teacher in Milkokuk and then pretended that he knew nothing. He's a clever fellow, and I felt that I had to neutralize him."

I whispered to Eve and the boys:

"Behold your mysterious Baphomet! Or rather, two Baphomets."

"This is the couple in a blue Skoda," I heard Tell whisper.

"I don't understand what you are looking for in the castle," the woman's voice said. "Do you think the treasure is somewhere here, and over so many hundreds of years, no one has found it?"

"I've told you a hundred times: I am looking for a mason's mark in the shape of a triangle. The Templar mason, Peter of Avignon, always used it to mark his buildings."

"And what if you find the sign?"

"That will mean that we have found the treasure!"

"I don't understand this bit," the woman replied.

"Well, you do remember the letter from my friend in France? As the issue of moving the capital of the Teutonic order from Venice to Prussia became urgent for Feuchtwangen, the Teutonic Knights had to choose a site for the new capital. Feuchtwangen then asked de Molay, with whom he was on friendly terms, to lend him a good architect. The Teutonic Knights were good at building defensive towers and other fortifications, but this time, they needed something else: they needed a castle that could serve as a capital. And in 1306, Peter of Avignon came to Prussia to begin working on a palace that might serve the needs of the grand master."

"Great. Now what?"

"Well, just think for a moment. What did this mean? It meant that such a palace would be built on Templar lines. It would have plenty of secret passages, dungeons, trapdoors, and hiding places. It had to have devices for secretly spying on diplomatic missions, eavesdropping on conversations, and so on, without which one could not imagine conducting great politics. And I think that when later, the scheme cooked up by Philip the Fair hung over the Templars, they buried the treasure here, in that building built by Peter of Avignon, whichever one it is. With Feuchtwangen's permission, of course. Then, the Templar affair started in France, Peter of Avignon was recalled and was put on trial along with all the others. He was sentenced to death and burned at the stake like the rest. And someone else completed the building started by him."

"And you think that there is a building here, in Malbork, built by Peter of Avignon? And that the treasure is hidden in it"?

"Exactly! Now, we don't know if he built a whole building or only started one. But if he only started one, it would still have his mark on the walls—perhaps on its foundations. But it will have this triangle mark. And that's where we should look for the treasure."

"Isn't it well known—isn't there some kind of a record when the various buildings of Malbork Castle were erected?"

"Yes, some, but we do not know which part was erected by Peter of Avignon. I have my friend's letter with me. Shine your flashlight for me, and I'll read it to you."

We heard the rustling of paper, and the man began to read:

"He writes something we had not known. Not just that the Teutonic Knights were moving their seat here and building a capital but that the Templars sent their builders here. He says that some correspondence has been preserved in France between Feuchtwangen and de Molay on the subject of building *a capital in Prussia*. And here, listen, he quotes verbatim what Feuchtwangen wrote about that future capital: 'I would like this capital to become the heart of our Order, to be great and magnificent, to inspire awe and admiration. We should also give it a beautiful, spiritual name. Why shouldn't we call it something uplifting, like *Your Heart*? For then, each of our knights, whenever he thinks of it or speaks of it, will remember that it is not only the heart of the order but also his own."

"Dear God!" I whispered. "That I have not thought of this!" And I gave myself a solid slap on the forehead.

Next to me, I heard the boys gasp, too. They, too, understood that we had just found the solution to the riddle: 'Your treasure is where your heart is.'

The woman's voice said:

"*Your Heart* is Malbork, then. The capital of the Order. So this is where you should look for the treasure if you take the slogan literally. Yes?"

"Exactly!" agreed the man. "All we need to do is figure out which building here was erected by Peter of Avignon! Because that's where we should look for the cache. Then, my friend writes, give me more light here!..."

And just at that moment, we heard a muffled cry as if the

woman was frightened by something. And then a muffled but menacing male voice resounded through the "eavesdropping apparatus":

"Freeze! Hands up, or I shoot! Put your hands where I can see them! Right there! Stop right where you are! Now, you! Put the letter on the floor and step back under the wall! Fine. Good. Now turn around to face the wall!"

"Please, sir, don't hurt us!" the woman pleaded.

"Oh, be quiet! I won't hurt you as long as you don't raise a racket," the new voice said. "There, I'm taking the letter. And you stand there quietly and count to a thousand before you move."

And then there was silence. A menacing, depressing silence.

"Eve! Where are they? Where is it happening?" I grabbed the girl's arm.

"I have no idea. They're probably underground somewhere."

I experienced a terrible feeling of helplessness. Somewhere next to us, or below us, a mysterious thief had just taken a letter that contained information regarding the location of the Templar treasure. I heard every word the bandit said, and yet, I was unable to do anything. I had no idea where he was.

"Into the courtyard! Let's go to the courtyard!" I said in an urgent whisper. "The robber will have to come out from the underground that way."

Barefoot, on our tippy-toes, we ran down the stairs to the darkness-filled courtyard of the Middle Castle. But we arrived too late. All we heard were the running footsteps on the drawbridge leading to the High Castle.

We threw ourselves into a mad dash after the receding footsteps. Behind us, somewhere far behind, someone called out something in a threatening voice—probably the castle watchman, who also heard the steps of the fleeing man.

In a few giant leaps, the thief ran up to the second floor of the High Castle and disappeared into the corridor leading to the tower called Gdanisko. Then, as he reached the stairs, we saw for a moment his slim figure outlined against the starry sky.

The Gdanisko tower of the castle of Malbork
Gdanisko (in German: "Dansker") were fortified towers in Teutonic castles built on the water
where ships from Gdansk could arrive to deliver supplies.

We ran after him along a narrow corridor. But he suddenly veered off onto a wooden gallery. It led downstairs, all the way to the foot of the castle, where there used to be a place for the knights to exercise their horses. Barrelling down the wooden steps two at a time, we briefly saw the villain reach the wall and grab hold of a thick rope hanging from the blanks. He must have been a very athletic man because he climbed up the rope as deftly as a circus gymnast. He perched himself on the wall, pulled the rope up behind him, and dropped it down on the other side. He grabbed it again and—disappeared from sight.

We stopped helplessly at the foot of the high wall over which the robber had just passed with such ease. High up on the wooden gallery, a light shone, and we heard the stomping of the running watchman.

"We should get out of here," said Eve. "Instead of catching this villain, the caretaker will catch us. I don't know how we can explain our visit here.

"Good idea," I said. "Let's get out of here, and let's let the caretaker catch Baphomet and his wife. They could use some rest in detention."

Eve led us to the same gate in the wall through which she and the boys had entered the castle. Again, she led us among bushes and thickets along paths known only to herself, and finally, we found ourselves on the bank of the Nogat. Exhausted by the chase and the fast march through the bushes, we sat down to rest and talk.

"I would give a lot to know what other information that letter contained," sighed William Tell. "Perhaps we should have pursued that villain further?"

Eve shrugged:

"Who stopped you, Mr Eager? Honestly, by the time we ran all around the castle to the place where the villain jumped off the wall, he would have been a mile away. But go right ahead."

"Eve is right," I said. "It really made no sense to continue the chase. Besides, Baphomet probably knows by heart all the information in that letter. Tomorrow, I will find Baphomet and talk to him. Nevertheless, tonight brought us great success: we now know how to understand the words: 'Your treasure is where your heart is.' The treasure is hidden in the capital of the Teutonic Knights, Malbork. We also know about the architect of the Templars, Peter of Avignon. And what are you thinking about so intently?" I turned to Hawkeye, who sat rubbing his long, inquisitive nose.

"I wonder why the bandit took the letter?" Hawkeye said.

"Oh, elementary, Hawkeye," cried Squirrel. "He wanted to get the information contained in the letter."

"Well, sure. What is there to wonder about?" nodded William Tell.

But Hawkeye kept rubbing his nose.

"I'll tell you what there is to wonder about. It's really not that simple at all. Like us, hidden in some nook or cranny, he overheard Baphomet's conversation with his wife. So, instead of going in with guns blazing and taking the letter, he could have quietly waited for Baphomet to reveal all the information to his wife. After all, it is not the letter itself that is important, but what it says. And this he could have learned by just waiting. So why did he take the letter?"

"Maybe he was afraid that he would not remember the information and preferred to have it in writing?" Eve said.

"Wow, I didn't think about that! Have it in writing!" said

Hawkeye sarcastically. "No, Eve, I don't think so. I think that tomorrow, or the day after tomorrow at the latest, the Petersens will receive an offer to buy this letter."

"What?" shouted the boys in astonishment. "You think this was Malinovski? Didn't Malinovski have to stay at Lake Pomerania to collect the ransom?"

I said:

"If he has a fast car, he could have been able to collect the previous night's ransom and been here by late afternoon. But to do that, he'd have to have been a man of iron constitution: he didn't sleep last night, then drove all the way here, and then spent tonight on a dangerous escapade, running around the castle and jumping over walls. I think that Malinovski is not acting alone. He has an assistant who stayed at Lake Pomerania while Malinovski himself set off for Malbork."

"He followed us, in other words," said William Tell.

"Not necessarily. Maybe he followed Baphomet's blue Skoda? It seems to me that this is how this business stands: this bandit is either Malinovski or his sidekick. He came here on the trail of Baphomet, who has overnighted in Malbork Castle twice, looking for the sign of the triangle. The bandit also spent the night in the castle, following Baphomet in order to see if he found anything. Then we arrived.

"At this point, Baphomet noticed us and decided to neutralize me by closing the door of Kaystuts's cell. This was also to the advantage of this Malinovski. But neither he nor Baphomet anticipated that you people would free me from my cell. Trailing Baphomet, Malinovski, like us, probably overheard his conversation with his wife and interfered, entering with a gun in his hand and snatching the letter because he came to the conclusion that looking for the sign of the triangle would be a waste of time. Better a sparrow in the hand than a pigeon on the roof. Better to get a few thousand zlotys from the Petersens than to waste his time trailing Baphomet further. There you have it, the whole mystery of tonight's events."

"Do you also think that the Petersens will now receive an offer to buy Baphomet's letter?" asked Hawkeye.

"I am sure of it," I said. "As soon as they arrive in Malbork, they will find a letter offering them valuable information."

"Captain Petersen is going to be mad again," said Squirrel and began to imitate the Captain by puffing out his chest and shaking his fists.

The boys burst out laughing. I rose from the grass.

"Let's go to sleep. Eve is probably sleepy, too."

"Me?" Eve was offended. "I can chase thieves all night. I like such occupations very much. I will join you. I have learned that treasure hunting is my specialty."

"And how will you explain to your mother coming home so late?" I asked.

"I'll tell her everything," she said.

"What? Do you want to tell her about our business?" the boys were outraged.

"Oh, sure. I'll let her in the secret. I am sure she can help us. She knows the history of the Teutonic Knights very well, and there is much to learn from her."

We said goodbye to Eve and, circling the castle, headed to our campsite. Despite the rather late hour, many windows in the modern apartment blocks built next to the medieval castle were still lit up. These blocks had been built after the war on the ruins of the old town. Only one beautiful historic building had been restored to its former glory: the old town hall, located on the road from the castle to the town.

Near the city hall, we crossed paths with a lone woman coming towards us from the direction of the town. We were still busy talking about the events in the castle and did not pay attention to her. Besides, it was dark, the streetlights were far apart, and the face of the walking woman remained in the shadows. But nothing could escape the sharp eye of Hawkeye. He stopped abruptly and said:

"Good evening, Miss Anka! What a nice meeting!"

CHAPTER THIRTEEN: GOOD MORNING, MR. BAPHOMET

Blabbermouth. Face to face with Baphomet. Baphomet trembles. Mr. Motorcycle. Night on the Nogat. Another letter.

"My goodness! What a surprise! Is this you? Here? At midnight?" I called out in astonishment. Anka was taken aback but soon regained her confidence.

"Any time is a good time for a joyful reunion with friends," she said. "And what night expedition are you returning from, good knights?"[7]

"And you?"

"I'm coming from the post office. I had to call my editorial office in Warsaw, and it took forever to get a connection. And you, fine knights? Returning from the castle?"

"The castle is closed at night," said Hawkeye. "We only wanted to see its silhouette in the moonlight. We're going to sleep now."

"Oh, how sad that your romantic expedition was spoiled by Mother Nature. There is no moon tonight," she said.

"And have you been in Malbork for long?" Squirrel asked as if to change the subject.

"Since this morning. You, on the other hand, probably arrived in the afternoon. I was walking by the campground about two in the afternoon and saw you guys puttering around."

"What?" asked Tell.

"I am referring to your vehicle. You gentlemen left Milkokuk late. I wonder if anything interesting happened at the lake. What news of our friend, Mr. Malinovski?"

"You should know best what is up with Mr. Malinovski," Tell said indignantly.

"Me?" she made a puzzled expression.

---

[7] All school kids in Poland have to memorize a fragment of a poem about the war between the Teutonic Knights and the Lithuanians which starts with the words:
From where were the Lithuanians returning?
They were returning from a night expedition.

"Yes, you! We think that you are a very suspicious person," burst out Squirrel. "We trusted you! But now we no longer trust you. You think we didn't see you leaving with that motorcyclist?"

"Oh, detectives, detectives!" she gasped. "But I have told you that I was coming to Malbork! Mr. Wheels did not want to take me with him, so I had to find some other means of transportation. A certain young, friendly man offered to take me by motorcycle. Was I not to take the opportunity? Now, I confess it was a hard trip. I nearly gave up the ghost. He was speeding that *Yunak* like the devil, my head nearly fell off for all that rush of air, and my insides turned over in terror. But, as you see, I am alive and well in Malbork. I'm staying for a few days in this big block of flats over there. I rented a room in a private apartment. Block number 4, apartment 10. You are very welcome to pay me a visit during the day."

I asked politely:

"And could you tell us why you came to Malbork?"

She shrugged her shoulders.

"Dear God! This is the tenth time I'm explaining this. I want to write an article on the nutjobs looking for the Templar treasure. And since the treasure hunters have all moved to Malbork, I have had to come here, too."

"You said: 'all,'" I picked up. "Anyone else besides us?"

"Well, I have seen that couple in a blue Skoda. And just a moment ago, I saw Petersen's Lincoln. And now I found Mr. Wheels and his jolly band."

"Please do not call me Mr. Wheels," I said sternly.

"And we're not a jolly band," said the boys.

"My, my. You really don't like me," said Anka regretfully. "And I will never hear about your adventure tonight?"

"Never," said Tell.

Squirrel proudly puffed out his chest:

"You won't hear anything from us. Too bad, for we would have a story to tell..."

He did not finish. Hawkeye and Tell clapped their hands to his mouth. All we heard was a stifled mumble.

"For God's sake, let go of him, or he'll suffocate!" I shouted.

"Chatterbox! Blabbermouth!" shouted both boys. "From today on, you're no longer 'Squirrel.' Now you're 'Blabbermouth.'"

They let go of the boy, who, panting heavily, began to explain himself:

"Well, I didn't say anything..."

"Blabbermouth! Blabbermouth!"

Anka pretended to be angry:

"Enough of this! You little kids march off to sleep! It's already past midnight!"

Then she turned to me:

"How are you not ashamed, Mr. Wheels, dragging these boys about town this late at night? It seems that I will have to write to their parents and complain about you."

"Why the concern for the boys all of a sudden?" I asked acidly. "Yes, they have been going to bed a little late, true. But they are learning all sorts of interesting things."

"I can just imagine what horrible things they are learning from you," she sighed.

"I teach them to be upright and honest. Your example, on the other hand, is demoralizing. At first glance, you appear a very nice person while in fact..."

"While, in fact, what?" she became indignant. "You know nothing about me. You're jumping to conclusions based on appearances. You are as naive as a child. Why, without me, you will only put yourself in danger. Out of the goodness of my heart, I have decided to look after you. And you—!" she stopped to catch her breath. "You are the most naive of your entire treasure-seeking bunch. Well, goodbye to you, Mr. Wheels—er—Mr Thomas—and to you, young gentlemen, and sleep well, and see you some better day," she waved her hand and marched off in the direction of the apartment blocks.

"God forbid such a caretaker," I muttered under my breath.

"Maybe she is not all that suspicious after all?" said Squirrel tentatively.

His conciliatory do-goodness irritated me.

"You are welcome to submit to the tender mercies of this lady, if that's what you want. As for me, I prefer to stay without a babysitter."

"She is actually very charming," noted William Tell.

"*Actually, actually*," I mocked him. "What do we *actually* know about who she *actually* is? And maybe she is charming, but I prefer to stay away from her. You just wait. She will write about us in her newspaper, and the whole country will laugh at us."

We entered our campground. Only now did we notice the blue Skoda at the far end of the camp.

"Good grief! Are we blind or something?" I slapped my forehead. "We had Baphomet right under our noses all afternoon!"

A little further on, we saw the Lincoln with its camper. Kozlovski was pitching his tent near the mobile home.

"And a good evening to you, sir," we greeted him in a chorus.

"Well, hello, gentlemen," replied Kozlovski. "And where might you be returning from?"

"We are *returning from a night expedition*," we all answered in a chorus. Our salvo summoned Miss Petersen from the cabin.

"Have you found the treasure yet?" she asked mischievously.

Squirrel burst out:

"We are one step away from finding it! Mr. Wheels already knows what that line 'Your treasure is...'"

He did not finish. The hands of Tell and Hawkeye slammed his mouth shut lightning fast.

"Blabbermouth! Blabbermouth!" they shouted at him. Miss Petersen folded her hands imploringly:

"Let go of the poor boy! He will suffocate!"

But the mischievous smile disappeared from her face. The boys let Squirrel go, and he lamented in a weepy voice:

"Why get all uptight like this? I didn't reveal anything, did I? Am I not allowed to open my mouth anymore?"

Alas, Kozlovski had heard Squirrel's words. He interrupted the apparently daunting task of erecting his tent, approached Karen, and told her in a whisper that we had obtained some new information about the Templar treasure.

I tried to hurry the boys back to our camp, but Karen did not let us leave. She closed in and began to grill me:

"You were right, Mr. Wheels. The document turned out to be

worthless. I spent a lot of money on it. Do you know what it contained? It concerned not the treasure, but the purchase of seven oxen for a monastery farm. From dawn till dusk, my father rages against Malinovski. My only hope is that now you will be willing to cooperate with me. We returned the document to the teacher in Milkokuk, as you told us to, and I lost my only clue to the treasure. Will you help me now?"

"Why me? Malinovski will help you," I said. "Tomorrow at the latest, you will get an offer to buy valuable information form him."

"What are you saying? Did you see him?" She asked with astonishment and—I thought—perhaps a trace of fear.

"No. Well, I mean, in a way, yes, we did see him. We caught him in the act of stealing a letter with what seems like useful information. We chased him, but he got away. Stealing and robbing seem to be his way—he is rather good at it. And I am sure he stole that letter hoping to sell it to you. And since he has already managed to extract a sizable sum of money from you, I am sure he will try to do it again."

"How do you know that the information is valuable?"

"Because I know the contents of the letter."

She sprang to her feet.

"Oh yeah?" she said. "You know it? So, the boy was right! You are one step closer to finding the treasure, and I'm—I'm nowhere. In that case," she stomped her foot, "let Malinovski bring his proposal as soon as possible. I will pay any price."

And she strode away to her camper.

I wanted to say something else, but she didn't seem to want to hear anything. She was annoyed that I knew more than she did. How very much she wanted to find the Templar treasure!

"No, I am not one step away from anywhere," I muttered and slipped into my tent. My three friends were already snoring in theirs.

I woke up quite late. I looked outside. The sky was covered with dark rain clouds, and it was drizzling. This weather put me in a very sleepy mood, so I was about to dive back into my sleeping bag when I noticed Mr. Kozlovski returning from town. That got me out of bed— I was curious to see where he had been. But as I emerged from my tent, I saw another group: they were folding their tent, getting ready for departure. The woman was wiping the window of the blue Skoda and her husband was taking down their tent. I got dressed and walked up to them.

"Good morning, Mr. Baphomet!" I called out to the squat, pudgy gentleman struggling with his tent. "How did you manage to get out of the castle? Did the night watchman give you any trouble?"

The pudgy gentleman looked at me with shock, and his wife, still busy with the car window, turned pale. She, too, was pudgy—she looked like the female edition of her spouse. They both resembled each other like a brother and a sister.

"And are you leaving us?" I asked politely, as my previous words had not been answered.

"Yes," Baphomet said curtly.

"In that case, it's a good thing I caught up with you now so that we may have a chance to chat before you leave."

Baphomet became even more frightened, and his spouse turned even paler.

"I won't say that I'm very happy about yesterday's adventure. You cannot even imagine how unpleasant it is to be locked up in a prison cell. I've never been to prison before. How about you?" I asked Baphomet.

"I've never been to jail either," he groaned.

"But you could," I said, making a stern face. "I don't know if you know this, but locking up someone against his will is actually a felony in this country. You locked me up in Kaystut's cell, and now I can lock you in a jail cell."

"But I... I did nothing of the sort!" Baphomet wriggled awkwardly. His wife folded her hands in prayer and said pleadingly:

"Oh, good sir! Take pity on him! He did it out of stupidity. I swear to you that we will not search for the Templar treasure anymore. We will never get in your way again. We're giving up the search. We're leaving".

"Why? It was so pleasant to compete with you," I said.

"Ah, please," groaned Baphomet's wife. "This is not something for us. We are quiet people. My husband works as a chemical engineer. It's all my fault. I'm to blame for everything. I read about the history of the Templar treasure, we wrote a letter to my husband's friend in France—he is a historian—and that's how our misfortune began. I persuaded my husband to look for this treasure during our summer holiday. But as of today, we won't bother you anymore. We are leaving."

"You are not bothering me," I said. "Rather, I must have been bothering you since you felt you had to lock me up in Kaystut's cell. However, I have no hard feelings about this little practical joke. My friends soon freed me from the cell, so this unpleasant adventure did not last long. Later, I even tried to come to your rescue when you were attacked by the masked thief, but I couldn't find you. To make matters worse, the castle caretaker got involved in all this, and I had to flee."

The couple was clearly terrified. I guessed that they did not believe me and took me for the masked bandit who had taken their letter.

"Good Madam, Sir," I said solemnly, putting my hand to my chest as a sign of great sincerity. "The basic mistake you have made is this: you assumed I was your enemy. But I am not your enemy. I am only your competitor. I did not break into the teacher's house. And I did not attack you last night to take your letter away."

I told them about the story with Malinovski's letters and the ransom the Petersens deposited in the forest shrine. I also explained to them how it happened that I heard but did not see the attack of the masked bandit.

"I think Malinovski will now try to sell your letter to the Petersens," I said. "I am outraged by this bandit's insolence. Therefore, I turn to you with a request: help me in my fight against him."

"Never! No!" shouted Baphomet's wife in horror. "We are peaceful people. We give up the treasure hunt. We are leaving. Ah, if you could only imagine how I felt when the bandit aimed his gun at us!"

"Well, I wonder if it really was a gun," Mr. Baphomet shook his head. "I am starting to suspect that he threatened us with a flashlight, and we, terrified like sheep, did not look carefully at what he had in his hand."

"Flashlight, gun, who cares! It doesn't matter!" cried Baphomet's wife. "We fell up to our necks with the wrong sort. We are leaving. We need time to recover after all these adventures.”

“Well, you see? My wife won’t let me help you,” Baphomet opened his pudgy hands in a gesture of helplessness.

I nodded my comprehension.

“And maybe she is right! Fighting bandits is an occupation for the state, not for us. But you probably don’t want the bandit to benefit from attacking you?”

“It’s all the same to me,” said Mrs. Baphomet cautiously. “I just want to leave here as soon as possible.”

“And you?”

“It depends on what you want.”

“Very well. I want to know what information about the Templar treasure was contained in the letter from your friend. In this way, I will know just as much as the bandit does. Perhaps I will then be able to guess his next move and catch him.”

“Fine! I will tell you. Naturally, I will!” Baphomet seemed relieved to learn that this was all I demanded of him. He had expected, the poor man, that I would ask him to chase dangerous criminals at night, perhaps even—gun in hand. “I will tell you everything I know. Very well. Here it goes.

“My friend wrote to me that Siegfried von Feuchtwangen, speaking of the future capital of the Teutonic Order, may not have had Malbork in mind. You see, Malbork Castle already had a name. It was called *Marienburg*, not ‘Your Heart.’ My friend thinks it is possible that Feuchtwangen intended to build a new capital somewhere else and that that somewhere else is where Peter of Avignon went to work. But then, before that work could be completed, Feuchtwangen’s move to Prussia became urgent. And since the construction of the new capital had only just begun, Feuchtwangen settled in Malbork, where there was already a castle of a relatively large size. Besides, just at that time Peter of Avignon returned to France and was burnt at the stake, which probably put an end to whatever construction project he was carrying out here. And, anyway, after the Grand Master’s move to Malbork, the plans to build a new capital were abandoned altogether, and the efforts of Feuchtwangen’s successors went into expanding Malbork Castle instead.”

"So perhaps *Your Heart* is not Malbork at all," I muttered to myself.

Mrs. Baphomet, hitherto pale with fear, now swelled with satisfaction. She said proudly:

"You see? You see? My husband knows history really well! He is a chemist, but history is his hobby. And you know? He once took first place in a television tournament! He won twenty thousand zloty for his answers on medieval history. So, I urged him to get involved in the search for the treasure of the Knights Templar. I thought that we might get lucky again. But it turns out that in this business, you need not just brains but also fists. Who knows, maybe a gun, too. And for this, my husband is not suitable. And that's why we're leaving."

Mrs. Baphomet was relentless. She was fed up with the nightly visits to the castle, and above all, she was terrified of the mysterious bandit.

"We spent the whole night hiding in the castle cellar," she said. "The caretaker chased after you and the bandit. He never realized that someone else had remained on the castle grounds. In the morning, when the first tour showed up, we simply joined it and left the castle with it. It had been so cold in the basement that our teeth were chattering."

The couple set about rolling up the tent. They were in a great hurry; they wanted to leave Malbork as soon as possible.

They drove away in their blue Skoda, and I gave them a friendly wave goodbye. I became fond of them during that one conversation. They were not bad people. And they gave me precious information that just might lead me to the treasure. And that was probably the most important thing.

Upon returning to our encampment, I found the boys busy preparing breakfast. It was raining, so the boys hung a tarp on four pegs and under this improvised roof, they were making coffee on a spirit machine.

At our neighbors'—that is, Petersen's—home, life was also beginning to stir. The captain brought a bucket of water from the well, and through the open door of the camper, I saw Miss Karen frying scrambled eggs on the gas stove. Kozlovski was helping her and they were talking about something, gesticulating vigorously; she was probably narrating to him her conversation with me.

Petersen was apparently not thrilled with the content of this conversation because, having brought the bucket, he set it so violently on the floor of the camper that the water sloshed out in all directions. Then he turned around and marched out, and came to visit us. We made him room under the tarp and treated him to a mug of coffee.

"Yes, yes, Mr. Wheels," sighed Petersen. "My trip to your country has been a disaster."

"Well, it is beautiful here," I said. "Forests and lakes…"

"Yeah, well, but no treasure and no Malinovski," he growled. "My daughter told you how the ransom story ended? The document was worthless. Malinovski had extorted five thousand zloty for it."

"Oh, don't get worked up. We have a proverb in Poland that goes like this: *a wolf that makes a few catches will soon be taken itself.* It means that every criminal get caught in the end. Malinovski fooled us twice, but he may not succeed a third time. As they say in Latin: *Omne trinum perfectum.* Which means: three times lucky."

"You linguist, heh!" Petersen chuckled. "My daughter told me that Malinovski would soon approach us again with an offer to buy information."

"I hope that this time you will show a little more sense. You really should turn this business over to the militia."

"I was of that opinion, too," he nodded. "But you have had enough time to get to know my daughter. She is as stubborn as a mule. She insists that she must find this treasure. I don't know what to do with her. She is ready for anything, it seems. I quarreled with her this morning because of this damned Malinovski. But arguing won't accomplish anything. I feel helpless and bound by my promise because—indeed—before we left for Poland, I had promised her the leadership of our expedition. But allow me to say this: no matter how my daughter behaves, I want you to consider me your friend. I care nothing about the Templar treasure. I won't even blink an eye if you, not Karen, find it. My goal is to capture Malinovski and put him in jail."

"In this regard, you can count on my help," I said solemnly. "Malinovski must be punished. I will not rest unless he is."

We shook hands firmly. Just at that solemn moment, Miss

Karen came out of the camper. She was dressed in a waterproof jacket—probably going for an extended walk.

"My, my, Mr. Wheels wins ever more admirers," she said tartly. "Even my father has moved to your camp. But come hell or high water, I will not give up my treasure hunt. I'm going with Mr. Kozlovski to visit Malbork Castle."

And she and Mr. Kozlovski marched off.

"Follow them," I whispered to the scouts. "Pay attention to what they look at in the castle grounds. Maybe Karen knows more than we do, after all?"

The boys followed Kozlovski and Karen, and Petersen returned to his camper to eat his scrambled eggs. I got busy washing dishes after breakfast. And as I was washing them, Anka turned up.

"Here is the most appropriate occupation for you," she greeted me with irony. "You wash dishes beautifully. I could safely say: you're the right man in the right place. You sent the boys on a mission, and you're taking care of the kitchen."

"Why do you say that I sent the boys on a mission?"

"I met them on the way. First came Miss Petersen and Kozlovski, and behind them came your scouts. And their faces looked as if they had been entrusted with a task of utmost importance. They didn't even want to talk to me."

"Because they don't trust you."

"And all because I dared to come to Malbork on a motorcycle. Well, clearly, Mr. Wheels does not like motorcycles. Otherwise, he would ride a motorcycle, and his name would be Mr. Motorcycle. And do you know what? That would be a nicer nickname!"

"Thank you kindly. I think I will stay with mine."

"Whatever you think is right," she shrugged her shoulders. "But you can not resent me for choosing a motorcycle. You refused to take me."

"So, who is this Hamster fellow?" I asked.

"Hamster?"

"Yes, this Mr. Motorcycle."

She shrugged her shoulders:

"I know him as much as you. He showed up at the journalists' center to rent a motorboat. I asked him to drive me to Malbork. He agreed. He said he was on vacation and had nothing better to do than to give rides to pretty girls on his motorcycle."

"Ugh," I muttered.

"Am I not pretty?"

"Pardon me if I do not comment."

"Well, he found me pretty. I told him to wait on the other side of the lake. And do you know why? I didn't want anyone to see me riding away. I thought I would give you a huge surprise in Malbork."

"Oh, the surprise was huge," I said.

"What I didn't take into account was that Mr. Wheels' favorite occupation is spying on his neighbors."

"I do have other hobbies. For example, washing dishes," I said.

I arranged the clean dishes in a drying box and wiped my hands with a cloth. And as I did that, a man dressed in a striped sailor's T-shirt approached us. He was small, wearing very short shorts and that striped blue and white shirt.

"Well, hello, distinguished lady and gentleman," he greeted us. "I am here to rent kayaks to tourists. If you would like to kayak with your beautiful lady on the Nogat, come to me. I have a marina down there," and he pointed in the requisite direction.

"Can't you see it is pouring?" I said.

"Does the rain bother you?" the man was amazed to hear that and came a little closer. "To a true athlete, the rain makes no difference. It is not like you are made of sugar."

"I'm not made of sugar. That's true," I nodded. "But don't like getting wet."

"Then you do not want to go kayaking? You can rent for one hour, or two, or even the whole day. My rental company is widely known. A good company, I tell you. You can arrange a beautiful ride with this lady who is clearly in love with you."

"No. Thank you," I said.

Anka blushed.

"Ah, that's not gonna work, is it?" sighed the gentleman in a sailor T-shirt. "And who might live in this house on wheels? Maybe he could use a kayak?"

"He is a foreigner," I explained. "Danish. But you can speak to him in English. If you want, I will serve as a translator."

"Ah, well, English. I think I can handle that. As they say, an honest man will always get along with an honest man. A lot of foreigners come here to see the castle and rent kayaks from me, so I learned to say this and that in many different languages."

He went to the Petersen camp and knocked on the door of their cabin. Captain Petersen came out to see him—he had just showered and was stripped to the waist. I saw a blue anchor tattooed on his hairy chest.

"Mr. Sailor," said the man in a sailor shirt. "I rent kayaks."

"What's that?" asked the captain in English.

"I rent kayaks. Ka-yaks," explained the man in a sailor shirt, gesticulating.

"Kayaks?" repeated bewildered Petersen. "What is this *kayaks*?".

"Yes, kayaks," said the man in a sailor shirt. "You, sir, are a sailor, I can see, so we'll get along. I charge very little. I rent for an hour or two, even for the whole day."

Petersen scratched his head because he understood nothing of what the man was saying to him. Just in case, he asked him:

"Don't you happen to know Malinovski?"

"Malinovski?" the eyes of the little man filled with astonishment.

"Malinovski, yes, Malinovski," Petersen repeated. The man in a sailor shirt tapped his finger on his chest:

"I am Malinovski. Have you heard of me? I didn't know that my company was so widely known in the world. *I am Malinovski*," he repeated in English.

At this, Petersen roared like a wounded buffalo:

"Malinovski, you are Malinovski! You are Malinovski!"

"Yes, sir, I am Malinovski, exactly," nodded the man in a sailor T-shirt cheerfully. Petersen threw the towel he had slung over his bare shoulders onto the grass. And then—as huge as a gorilla—he grabbed the neck of the tiny man and began to shake him like an old rag.

"Are you Malinovski?" he yelled. "And you come to scam money again? You are a swindler! You are a thief! I have you, at last! I will skin you alive!"

Petersen's shouting lured people out of their tents. A ruckus ensued. People assumed that the foreigner had caught a thief who wanted to rob his cabin. So this one and that one poked angrily at the guy in a sailor T-shirt. And the captain still held him in his big paws and shouted:

"Thief! Burglar! Fraudster! He scammed me for four hundred dollars! He scammed me for five hundred zloty for a worthless document! Oh, Malinovski, you will atone for all your evil deeds!"

I struggled to squeeze through the crowd surrounding Petersen and Malinovski.

"Call the militia!" cried the people. "He must be handed over to justice! To jail with the thief!"

And everyone considered it his duty to poke the poor man in his lower back while he babbled unintelligibly, trying in vain to explain something that could not be explained.

"Mr. Petersen," I said. "This is not Malinovski."

"What do you mean: not Malinovski?" roared the outraged captain. "He says he is Malinovski!"

The small man moaned:

"Yes, yes, I am Malinovski. Let me go, people. I confess, I am Malinovski. Everyone knows me here! I rent kayaks!"

"Do you hear? He's Malinovski!" thundered Petersen. "Do not defend him!"

A young lady with huge glasses pointed at me:

"And this fellow is probably Malinovski's accomplice. They probably rob tourists together."

I felt someone poke me in the back. Someone else grabbed my arm.

"Catch thief!" yelled some bulky lady in voluminous pants. "Even on holiday, there is no peace from them!"

I jerked once and again to pull my arm out of someone's grasp, but several hands gripped me tightly.

"Look how he wriggles!" someone cried out. "Hold him, or he will run away!"

"Mr. Petersen!" I called out to the captain. "Mr. Petersen! This is not *that* Malinovski! It's *another* Malinovski!"

But Petersen did not hear my voice, lost in the general uproar.

I spotted Kozlovski in the crowd. But he, instead of saving me, egged everyone on.

"That's right! Hold him! Take him to the militia!"

I was poked, pushed, and pinched.

"Oh, you scoundrel! You just wait! I will deal with you!" I shouted to Kozlovski.

"Look, people, he is threatening us!" squealed the lady in glasses and pinched me so hard that I wailed like a wounded wolf.

Finally, Anka came to my rescue. She explained to each and every one that there was a mistake—as a result of the fact that Mr. Petersen does not know Polish and Mr. Malinovski does not understand English.

"Hot damn!" spat Petersen. "A stupid story. And you, Mr. Kozlovski, still added fuel to the fire instead of resolving everything!"

"And what was I supposed to do?" asked Kozlovski, surprised. "I simply assumed that you had finally caught Malinovski and that this Malinovski turned out to be Mr. Wheels!"

"Thank you," I said. "Keep this up, Mr. Kozlovski. There will be a reckoning."

Suddenly, Petersen dashed like a prancing deer to his Lincoln. From behind the windshield wiper, he took out a piece of paper folded in four. He unfolded it, glanced at it, and, in two bounds, found himself next to me.

"You read this! It is in Polish. The signature is sure familiar!" and he gnashed his teeth in helpless anger.

I read the note and translated it into English:

Dear Ms. Petersen,
I have acquired new and valuable
information that will lead you to the
treasure. I want twelve thousand zloty
for it. Please come today at eleven P.M.
to the fifty-kilometer mark at Hoynitse.

I will be waiting for you. Only please
come alone, otherwise I will not appear.
And please, no more tricks.
Malinovski

CHAPTER FOURTEEN: KAREN IN DISTRESS

Should I stay or should I go? Where is your heart? Plans for a new expedition. Karen in distress. The chase. In Hajikove.

It was raining. We were sitting in the cozy interior of the Petersen's camper—Anka, Karen, the captain, Kozlovski, myself, and the boys. Through the low window of the trailer, we could see the brown silhouette of Malbork Castle, misty in the rain, and through the other window—the black depths of the Nogat River, streaked with rain.

Captain Petersen opened a bottle of French cognac for the adults, and opened a bottle of orange juice for the boys. Karen held the letter from Malinovski in her hands and seemed to be reading it for the tenth time, although we knew that she was only running her eyes over the letters, as she did not know Polish. We waited anxiously to see what she would decide. She was very beautiful in her reverie, with her straw hair falling over her shoulders. When she squinted her eyes, urgently thinking about something, her long eyelashes cast shadows on her cheeks and made her look even more beautiful.

Suddenly, she jerked her head, throwing back her hair, and said:

"I will accept this proposal. I'll take the car and drive to the fifty-kilometer mark."

"I knew this would happen," Petersen sighed. "My daughter is crazy."

"Miss Petersen, Mr. Petersen, I strongly advise against it. I advise against it this time," Kozlovski said. "This is dangerous. To go alone to a night encounter with a bandit, someplace in the woods or in the field? No, I advise against it. Strongly."

"Especially since this is probably a new scam," added Anka.

"No," I shook my head. "Malinovski is a crook, and I would like to see him behind bars. But this time, he actually has valuable information."

And I recounted our night adventure in the castle but avoided any details of the contents of the letter.

"Nevertheless, I share Mr. Kozlovski's view," I said in

conclusion. "I also advise against anyone going alone to meet Malinovski. And, by the way, why did he deviate from his old system of you putting the money somewhere and him putting the document there later? Why does he want to meet you in person? And why does he set the meeting so far away?"

"Maybe he wants to communicate something important to me," Karen wondered.

I shook my head.

"I know what's in the letter. And I know that this time, too, Malinovski could have demanded that the ransom be placed in some nook in town. But instead, he asked you to meet him at the fifty-kilometer mark. I'm afraid for you, Karen."

The girl looked at me angrily:

"Your concerns can neither help nor harm me. You're not worried about my safety. You just do not want me to obtain the information you already have. But I will get that information, and I will find the Templar treasure. I will do so even if I have to risk all our money."

I turned red at this accusation. I hesitated for a moment, but the thought that Karen suspected me of selfish calculation weighed on my decision.

"Miss Petersen," I said very quietly but with such emphasis that the whole room became completely silent. "I'll tell you what's in the letter. I will lay all my cards on the table if you agree not to go to this meeting. In fact, once you find out what the letter contains, you will no longer need it. No," I said, "I am not doing this driven by concern for your safety or your money. But I don't want this thug to benefit from his nefarious activities. Let him wait in vain at the fifty-kilometer mark. No one will bother to drive fifty kilometers to see his sorry person."

Anka grabbed my hand and squeezed it tightly.

"Don't give away your secret. If you do, you will lose your chance of finding the treasure first! You have gained this information through wit and gumption. And you have no obligation to Miss Karen. There is no need to tell her your secret. This magnanimity goes too far."

"A point well taken," I said stubbornly. "Nevertheless, I will do as I said. I'm looking for this treasure because it is fun. And I am afraid that Malinovski will spoil it. If something bad happens to Miss Karen, I will feel responsible."

The conversation was conducted in English, but now Anka turned to the boys in Polish.

"Do you know what Mr. Wheels is going to do? He intends to reveal the contents of the letter to Miss Karen so that she does not go to meet Malinovski."

Tell shrugged his shoulders:

"Don't you know Mr. Wheels? It was clear from the beginning that he would do something like that."

I smiled at Tell. I was pleased that the boys considered me a man of honor.

"Mr. Thomas," Anka turned to me angrily. "I am sorry to say this, but I think that you are being stupid. Maybe you are in love with Miss Karen, I don't know, but if you are, you are going to be disappointed."

"Tough luck," I said. "I can't do otherwise. And not because, as you say, I'm in love, but because I don't want anything bad to happen to anyone. If something bad happens, I will never forgive myself that my ambition prevailed over my honesty."

Karen, Petersen, and Kozlovski looked at me intently. Karen had a mocking smile on her lips: she was convinced that when it came down to it, I would hold back and not reveal the letter's secrets.

But then I started talking. I told them first about Siegfried Feuchtwangen, who asked James de Molay to send him an architect to build the new Teutonic capital, which was to be called *Your Heart*. I told them about Peter of Avignon, who came to Prussia to build that capital. And I told them that I guessed that the treasure was buried in whatever building Peter of Avignon built or started building in Prussia. And then—I told them—he was summoned to France and died at the stake. He never completed the construction he had begun.

And then I told them that because Feuchtwangen had to move from Venice to Prussia in a hurry, he chose Malbork as his capital. He chose Malbork because it was already built. But was Malbork the place where Peter of Avignon had begun the construction of the new Teutonic capital? That question remained unanswered. A triangle sign left on a wall somewhere may perhaps indicate where Peter of Avignon had worked.

"And that's all that the letter contains. And this is what Malinovski wants to offer to you for twelve thousand zloty," I said in conclusion. "Now, you no longer have to go to meet the thief."

"Thank you sincerely," Petersen rose and gave me a bear hug. "You are a true gentleman. I am glad that my daughter will not go to the fiftieth kilometer. Malinovski can wait there all night. For the first time, we will leave him out to dry."

Only Karen did not express her gratitude. A mocking smile appeared on her lips again.

"How can I be sure," she said, "that you told the whole truth? That you did not conceal any detail? Where is this mysterious Baphomet, who could testify that the letter did not contain other, more important information?"

"Baphomet gave up his search this morning," I said. "Malinovski's attack scared him to death. He wanted nothing to do with the treasure anymore."

"Did he leave?" asked Karen. "It is very convenient for you that he left, for he cannot confirm or deny the veracity of your words. And am I supposed to trust you—you, my competitor for the treasure? After all, it is enough for you to conceal one small detail, one piece of information, perhaps concerning the place where Peter of Avignon began to erect the Teutonic capital. And you will swipe the treasure from under my nose."

"The letter did not say where this place was," I said. "Baphomet didn't know it, either. Baphomet spent several nights in the basement of Malbork Castle searching for the sign of the triangle and did not find it."

"I don't believe you," hissed Karen. "I do not know what it is, but I sense that there is a trap hidden in this sincerity of yours. You are very clever. You have fooled everyone with your sincerity. But not me. That's why I will go to the meeting with Malinovski. And I am not afraid. I am not afraid of anyone. I have to find this treasure, and I will find it."

"And good luck to you, Ma'am!" exclaimed indignant Anka. "I

expected you to behave just like this!"

She turned to me and continued in Polish:

"She not only did not thank you, but she called you a liar."

Anka was right. I felt I had been slapped in the face. I got up from my seat and bowed politely to everyone.

"A very good night to you all. Miss Karen will do as she wishes. But please remember that I have done everything in my power to ensure that you avoid danger."

I left the Petersen house, and the boys and Anka followed me out. The boys, whom she told about Karen's reaction to my story, were outraged.

"This Miss Karen is a viper!" cried Squirrel. "I am telling you, this bandit will attack her and kill her."

"Don't talk nonsense, Squirrel," I said. "Let's go to dinner at our favorite Malbork establishment. *By the Nogat*, the best restaurant this side of the Castle. We'll eat something good, and our mood will improve immediately. Will you come with us?" I turned to Anka.

"Fine," she said in a rather unfriendly tone. As angry as she was with Miss Karen, she was still angry at us, too.

"And then we will pay a visit to Eve," said Hawkeye.

And before he could put in another word, Squirrel shot his mouth off:

"We met her at the castle, and she invited us to visit tonight. You will be able to talk to her mother about the Teutonic capital."

"Do not worry," William Tell consoled Anka. "You'll find that even though Miss Karen has learned all of Mr. Wheels's secrets, she still won't be able to find the Templar treasure. She is too greedy."

"Oh, kiddos," laughed Anka. "Do you know why Malinovski is able to trick you all? Because he does not believe in the Templar treasure! For him, the real treasure are the Petersens, whom he will continue to fleece."

"You speak as if you knew Malinovski," said Hawkeye, suddenly suspicious.

But Anka shook her head.

"I don't know him," she added. And then she added:

"Yet. But I promise you that I will be the first to unmask him.

And soon!"

I pricked my ears. It suddenly occurred to me that Anka had also picked up some scent. But she would never be as magnanimous as I was, and she would never reveal her hand.

We had dinner and then went to the castle, where Eve was already waiting in front of the drawbridge. She led us to a tiny apartment within the old walls, where we met her mother, a gray-haired lady with large, horn-rimmed glasses. I thought I saw amusement in her eyes.

"That's right," she admitted, treating us to tea and cookies. "I find it very amusing to think that there are people who are seriously looking for treasures. Do you really believe that this treasure exist?"

I confess that I was a little embarrassed.

"You think that treasure hunting is a meaningless activity? Only children believe in legends of buried treasure, right?"

"Ah, no," she said. "And, in any case, meaningless or not, everyone has the right to dispose of their free time as they see fit. Some fish, others hunt, others travel or play bridge. I don't see why treasure hunting should be inferior to those. If there's anything that amuses me here, it's that you make a rather amusing bunch. You and the three boys and the young miss."

"I'm very sorry, but I'm a serious person," objected Anka. "I am not looking for treasure. But I am interested in *treasure hunters.*"

Teasing and joking, we drank tea and then started talking about the Teutonic Knights, the Templars, and their treasures. I had no reason not to trust Eve's mother, and Anka had heard what I told Miss Karen, so I presented my clues to the Templar treasure with all sincerity.

"It seems that the challenge facing us now," I concluded, "is to find out whether there was, or could have been, some place other than Malbork where Feuchtwangen had planned to erect his capital, a castle to be called *Your Heart.* For if there was, then that is where the Templar treasure is."

Eve's mother thought about my words for a while.

"I would very much like to help you, but unfortunately, it seems that I cannot. We know from history that Feuchtwangen moved from Venice to Malbork in September 1309, and Malbork became the capital of the Teutonic state by virtue of his arrival. His move was linked to the Teutonic seizure of Pomerania—Feuchtwangen was in fact fleeing from Western public opinion. It seems clear that the fate that befell the Templars must also have worried Feuchtwangen, too, and probably hastened his departure from Venice.

"There has long been a debate among historians why Malbork was chosen as the capital—many think that Elblong would have been the better choice. The situation within the Order at the time was probably of some importance in this regard: in Elblong, the partisans of the national master, Henry von Plotzke, were very strong and he was Feuchtwangen's main opponent. The grand master perhaps preferred to settle in the relatively small city of Malbork. It only grew later, once it became the capital.

"Of course, it is possible that Feuchtwangen had been considering the possibility of moving the capital of the Order from Venice to some other castle still to be built or under construction. But we, Polish historians, are not aware of any such information. You say this Baphomet's friend in France had seen a document suggesting as much?"

"From what I remember of the letter, the wording wasn't clear, but it suggested that it may have been a place called *Your Heart*."

"*Your heart*?" Eve's mother wondered aloud. "In German, that would be *Dein Herze*. Or in Latin: *Cor tuum*. I have a dictionary of Polish place names. Let's see if we can find a locality with a similar name."

We got busy browsing the dictionary but with no results.

"But, Ma'am," I said. "Over the years, this name may have changed. And perhaps it only appears in the dictionary under the new name? We've been looking in the dictionary under the letters C and D. Maybe we should to look under the letter K?"
We turned to place names beginning with K. I ran my finger over the names and suddenly my finger stopped.

"Kortumovo," read the boys.

"Kortumovo?" Eve's mother repeated.

"*Cor Tuum*. Kortum. Kortumovo," I said. And I read a brief description of the village:

Elblong (Polish: Elbląg, German: Elbing)

Founded in 1230, Elblong was not only larger than Malbork but also safer, both because it was further away from the Polish border and also because it had its own access to the sea.

"Kortumowo, a village in Helmno County, on the lake of the same name. In the village, there is a church dating back to the beginning of the 14th century dedicated to the Blessed Virgin."

"Teutonic Knights seized Helmno early on," Eve's mother said. "And if the church was built at the beginning of the 14th century, it would have been at the time when Feuchtwangen was perhaps thinking of building a new capital. Perhaps, Mr. Thomas? Perhaps you should go there? You will get a much better idea once you see the Teutonic remains on the spot."

"Yes," I nodded. "We will leave for Kortumovo tomorrow. Only I have a very special request," I turned to the boys. "Keep your mouths shut about this."

"We may have to cut Squirrel's tongue out," Hawkeye said grimly.

"Dear God, what do you want from me?" said Squirrel defensively.

But Eve clapped her hand in joy:

"Alright! Well, I am going with you! You will see that I will be very useful!"

Eve's mom protested, as moms usually do when their children

come up with crazy ideas. Eve argued that the idea was not so crazy: the three boys had been traveling with me for a long time, and nothing bad had happened to any of them. Then, Anka assured Eve's mother that she would take the girl into her tent and take care of her. The mother slowly softened and stopped protesting.

"Are you also going to Kortumovo?" I asked Anka. "May I ask what means of transportation you plan to use?"

"Certainly not a motorcycle," she replied. "I think it will be more convenient to go in your car."

"What? My car can't accommodate such a big bunch."

"In that case, I'll ask the Petersens to drive me there in their Lincoln."

I gave her a long, hard stare.

"This is the most ordinary piece of blackmail I have ever come across," I said.

"You expressed it very aptly," she nodded. "Until now, I have tried to convince you using persuasion and smiles. And since that didn't work, I decided to resort to other means. So, Mr Wheels, what is it going to be? Shall we go together, or should I ask Miss Karen for a ride?"

"You may come with us," I groaned.

And I glanced at my watch and found that it was past ten in the evening. I rose from the table.

"Now, please excuse me, but I have to leave. I have a very important matter to attend to in the city. You boys can still play with Eve for a while. But I ask you to be in the tent in half an hour."

"I am also leaving," said Anka and began to say goodbye to Eve's mother, the girl, and the boys. We left the castle.

"Good night, young miss," I held out my hand to Anka. She pushed it away and said abruptly:

"I know where you are going. You are going to the fiftieth kilometer. You are worried about Karen. You are in love with her. This girl hates you, she thinks you are a liar and a cheat, but you are blind and do not see it. Do you not understand that she does not care about you at all? She only thinks about finding the treasure. And you only enter into her calculation insofar as you can help her find it. You tell her your secrets, and even that only creates resentment in her. Why do you want to go there? I understand your intentions are kind, but you will find that Miss Karen will reject your help. She will suspect that you only want to snatch that letter from before her nose."

I pushed her away gently but firmly.

"What if something bad happens there?" I said.

"What does it matter to you? She is of age. We have all warned her about that meeting."

"I cannot think like that. Besides, why do you not want me to go?"

"I am afraid. Malinovski is a crook; he could even be a killer for all we know, and you are as naive as a child. When it comes to Karen, well, I think you should let events take their natural course. I hate that conceited girl. But I like you. And I don't want you to expose yourself."

"No, no," I shook my head. "I understand and appreciate your concern for me, but I have to go."

And leaving Anka in front of the castle, I ran toward the campground where my vehicle was waiting. The Petersen's Lincoln was no longer in the parking lot: Karen had gone off to meet Malinovski. I looked at my watch: twenty minutes to eleven. Would I manage to cover fifty kilometers—thirty miles—in twenty minutes?

I started the engine, and—like a ghost emerging from the night—Kozlovski sprang up next to the car.

"Where are you going?" he said snarkily. "Miss Karen forbade anyone to follow her. Malinovski might panic and not sell the letter."

I shrugged.

"Give me a break with Miss Karen, will you? I've had enough of her. She called me a cheat and a liar. I don't want to have anything to do with her. I'm going to dinner. Will you come with me?"

"No," replied Kozlovski haughtily.

Relieved, I took off and after coming out onto the main road, took a turn out of the city. I found myself on the highway, stepped on it, and flew over the bridge over the Nogat in a mad rush. The road to Starogard was narrow, full of blind turns, and because I really stepped on the pedal, I had to brake time and again, as I made sharp turns with a shrill shriek of the tires.

I made the decision to go to the fiftieth kilometer very late, too late, and now I had to make up for lost time. No, it was not at all about capturing Malinovski. I was going to the fiftieth kilometer to make sure that nothing bad happened to Karen. She offended me with her suspicion, but it didn't matter when I realized that this stubborn girl might find herself at the fiftieth kilometer at the mercy of a bandit. No, I was not in love with Karen. I simply considered it my duty to protect her from danger. I trembled at the thought that the thief might murder Karen for her gold watch, her diamond ring, or the diamond brooch she always wore pinned to her blouse. It seemed to me that, unless I went, I would be complicit in whatever evil happened to her.

So I rushed to make up for the delay. Trees, fences, and telegraph poles flew past me on both sides of the road. In my high beams, time and again arose ghostly, glaring signs like "Caution, dangerous turn," "Caution, four dangerous turns," "Caution, unguarded railroad crossing," "Caution strong winds." Time and again, I overtook horse-drawn carts with barely visible reflector lights. I kept at the pedal, spinning faster and faster.

The ghostly bluish displays of my dashboard glowed menacingly. Seventy miles.... seventy-five miles... eighty miles, showed the speedometer dial.

Now, the highway exited the woods and turned into a wide and comfortable highway. I increased my speed to ninety. I flew over a viaduct above the intersection of two roads: from Gdansk to Grujondz and from Malbork to Starogard. Ten more miles and I saw the lights of Starogard.

The highway bypassed the town. I reduced my speed a little since more vehicles appeared on the road, mainly a lot of motorcycles.

Eleven o'clock was still five minutes away, I thought, but when I looked at the dashboard, I realized with trepidation that it was already eleven. And there were still ten kilometers to go.

I pressed harder on the accelerator. The speedometer hand jumped sharply, the rush of wind hit the windshield with a rumbling sound. The howling of the wind distempered me. It sounded ominous.

Again, a sharp turn. I braked but was thrown almost to the very edge of the road. I nearly rubbed my fender on the concrete posts at the side of the road. Like a row of one-eyed cyclops-dwarfs, they shone red furious with their reflective glass.

Around the bend, the road straightened again and ran through a dense forest. I was closing in on Zblevo. Way ahead of me on the road, I saw the taillights of a car standing on the side of the road. I recognized the lights of the Lincoln.

I took my foot off the accelerator and put it on the brake pedal, slowly reducing my speed. I didn't want to stop because if Malinovski was late for the meeting, Karen might resent me for arriving early and scaring him off. I intended to pass Karen's car, drive on, and then turn around.

My high beams touched the Lincoln. I saw that the car was empty. Another moment and I saw Karen. She was standing next to the car, and a man's shadow loomed beside her. No, she wasn't standing. She was tugging at the man. She was pushing him away, shouting something, but the noise of my engine drowned out her words.

I slammed the brake. The tires squealed, the vehicle stopped dead in its tracks and almost keeled—I felt its backside lift for an instant. I came to a full stop sideways on the road, about three feet from a tree.

I jumped out of the car. At most, fifty feet separated me from Petersen's car, but the lights of the vehicle and the squeal of the brakes had warned Malinovski of danger. Karen had not turned off her car's engine, and she left the key in the ignition. Malinovski now pushed the girl away from him—he pushed her so hard that she staggered and fell. He then jumped into the Lincoln. The engine whined. Another moment and the Lincoln tore away from us in the fumes of spinning tires and fell into the night. Its taillights dissolved in the dark.

I ran up to Karen and helped her up from the ground.

"He ripped the gold watch from my hand and took the diamond brooch," she said, panting heavily. "He wanted to pull the ring off my finger, too, but I defended myself, and then you came. But I have the letter," she triumphantly showed me the paper, which she held tightly in her hand.

"Congratulations! By the way, I don't know if you noticed this, but he stole your car, too," I said. Only at that moment did she realize that Malinovski had fled in her Lincoln.

"Dear God! What to do? We should probably notify the

militia? And I thought he was a gentleman thief! And he turned out to be a common thug."

She didn't even ask why I had come.

"We'll try to catch up with him," I said, jumping into my vehicle.

"My Lincoln? In your jalopy?" she said with astonishment, in which I clearly heard contempt for my vehicle.

"Come on! Hurry up!" I ordered. "You don't know cars any better than you know people. You trusted a carjacker and came off badly. A Lincoln seems to you the eighth wonder of the world."

I turned on my second set of high-beam headlights, which I normally only used when riding on the water when the waves covered my highway lights. At this hour, the highway to Zblevo would be empty, so no one would be dazzled by the glare of my lamps. Soon, my speedometer indicated ninety miles per hour.

"Do not delude yourself into thinking that you can catch up with a Lincoln," said Karen. "It has eight cylinders. It can do one hundred twenty miles per hour."

I said nothing. I just stepped on the gas. After a while, the speedometer hand touched one hundred and ten. For a brief moment, I dipped my headlights because a car came from the opposite direction. We passed each other with a wham, then the highway lit up in front of me again and I looked for the taillights of the Lincoln.

I was sure that Malinovski was not driving at his top speed. He probably felt uncomfortable in his vehicle—he may never have driven a Lincoln. Besides, he was probably not of the best opinion of my vehicle and didn't think he needed to make a special effort to elude me. I expected to catch up with him soon.

I stepped on the accelerator some more. When the speedometer hand touched hundred and twenty, Karen gave a muffled sigh. I didn't want to go any faster, even though my car was capable of higher speeds. But I had old tires; I was afraid that they would not hold up at such speeds. If one of them blew at this speed—we would crash.

"Your Lincoln has eight cylinders?" I asked Karen.

She nodded uncertainly.

"This hearse...this hearse has twelve."

"What?" gasped Karen.

"Twelve," I repeated. "How much power does your Lincoln have?"

"Two hundred and eighty horsepower."

"This engine has three hundred and fifty horsepower. And its top speed is one hundred and seventy miles. And if I changed the gear ratios, it could reach two hundred. It could go faster, still, but ordinary tires burn at such speeds."

"Dear God! It's like a Ferrari 410!"

"Well, it *is* a Ferrari 410. Only—it had a... *body job*, you might say."

She said nothing more. She just looked at me, at my dashboard, and at the road ahead.

Finally, we saw the taillights of the Lincoln. I reduced my speed a bit. We were way past Zblevo now, on the highway to Chersk.

"Well, now he will not escape us," I stated with triumph.

"And, wouldn't you know it," Karen suddenly giggled. "There is enough gasoline in my car for seventy miles at most. Do you know the mileage of a Lincoln? We get 14 miles to the gallon. On a good day."

"That's a nice number," I laughed. "But even there, I am not impressed. My hearse gets 9 miles to the gallon. Ten downhill and with a strong wind in the back. You can go bankrupt driving this thing. But unlike the fellow in front of us, we have a full tank."

We caught up with the Lincoln. The bandit—as I predicted—had not expected a chase. He was driving a mere ninety. But when I tried to overtake him he looked behind and recognized my vehicle. He immediately swerved to the left side of the road to prevent me from forging ahead. And he added gas.

And now, a proper chase began. I tried to overtake him again, now from the left, now from the right, but each time, he blocked my way with the Lincoln's wide bum. At times, he pretended to give up, and when I started to overtake him, he pushed against my car with the side of his and tried to push me into the ditch or against the tree trunks flashing past us on both sides of the road,

In a mad rush, we blew past Chersk. I no longer tried to overtake him but just drove about fifty feet behind him and waited patiently for the Lincoln to run out of gas.

"I arrived at the fiftieth kilometer punctually at eleven o'clock," Karen recounted. "I stopped the car but did not turn off the engine. You must have noticed—there was a dense forest growing on one side of the road? After a few minutes, a man came out of the forest. He had a bandana on his face with holes for his nose, eyes, and mouth. The get-up made me laugh. I opened the window and, without getting out of the car, I said: 'I brought the money. Give me the letter.'

"Without a word he took the letter out of his pocket, but did not hand it to me, but waited for me to slip him the money. Finally, we made the exchange but the moment I extended my hand with the money toward him, he probably saw the gold watch on my wrist. He grabbed my hand, twisted it tightly, and jerked the door open. He pulled me out of the car, ripped the watch from my hand, grabbed the brooch on my blouse, and yanked it out along with some fabric. There, you see, there is a hole in my blouse. He wanted to pull the diamond ring off my hand, too, but luckily, you arrived just in time. But I have the letter. I held it tight in my hand the whole time."

"You will find that the letter contains nothing more than what I have told you. This idiotic adventure was completely unnecessary. With the loss of your watch, brooch, and car, you are paying very dearly for your distrust of me."

"Oh, I think we'll get the car back," Karen said, "Twenty more miles and he'll run out of gas."

We now saw streetlights in front of us. This was Hoynitse. We drove through the city center and suddenly, I saw that Malinovski turned. He went not for Chlukhov, as I had expected, where there was a good road, but to the right, onto the road to Bittov. This alarmed me. I guessed that the bandit had realized that he was low on gas and would now try to either lose us or dump the car and disappear into the roadside woods.

The highway climbed upwards, and a mile and a half outside the city, it forked.

"He is going to Hajikoveh!" I yelled out, braking sharply and turning the steering wheel.

I knew this area well. I had been to Lake Hajikovski several times—it was renowned for its beauty. Dozens of beautiful villas and luxurious camping cottages stood on the high shore here, and there was also a Tourism Office and a youth hostel. Long wooden piers ran out into the lake, with dozens of private boats and motorboats rocking on the waves. Was the bandit going to try to lose us in Hajikoveh?

Another sharp turn. We drove down the only street of the settlement, and suddenly, the taillights of the Lincoln lit up. The bandit braked abruptly just before a cafe located on the left, in a small garden on the high shore of the lake. I also stopped. We heard a door slam and saw a black shadow disappear into the garden.

In the garden, there was a dance party. On the branches of the trees swayed paper lanterns scattering a colorful glow on hundreds of vacationers dancing in pairs. They were having fun outdoors to the lively sound of a jazz orchestra.

"Look at that beautiful car!" exclaimed a young person, interrupting the dance.

"And at that space rocket behind it! What is that monstrosity?"

"There is a trend for unusual cars," said a man knowingly. And another girl said:

"They are foreigners!"

We pushed through the crowd of dancers, looking for the bandit. Where had he gone? Maybe he disappeared at the other end of the garden?

First, we aroused general interest and then amazement. Just think: a man jumped out of a beautiful car and ran, pushing his way in between the dancing couples. Then a really odd car pulled up, and a beautiful girl jumped out of it, followed by a man. And they also pushed through the dancing floor.

The orchestra broke off in the middle of a tune.

"They are chasing each other!" shouted a female voice.

"Maybe they are gangsters?" cried a lady with a huge cleavage.

We did not hear any more voices. We jumped over the wooden fence surrounding the garden and over the hedge that grew along the ridge of the steep hill. We scanned the surface of the lake.

"He got away," Karen said. "We won't be able to find him now. He's holed up in some house along on the shore."

Lake Hajikovski (Polish: Charzykowskie)
The town on the far side is the location of the dancing party.
Love Island is on the left.

In pursuit of the motorboat. On the island of love. Mr Hamster again. Back to the fifty-kilometer mark. We can go slow now. Anka's disappearance.

Karen and I stood at the top of the high ridge, over a slope falling steeply to Lake Hajikovski. To our left and right, all along the top of the ridge, stood rows and rows of holiday homes. At our feet lay a sheet of water glistening in the starlight and stretching off into the impenetrable horizon. There seemed to be no end to the lake, but since I had been there before, I knew that the opposite shore was not far and that there were two wooded islands in the middle of the lake.

The skies were clear, and in the starlight, we saw the motionless shapes of yachts and motorboats moored at wooden piers running out into the lake.

"Let's go down," I said.

We skipped down the stone steps of a narrow street to the waterfront. In the café garden, the orchestra took up some dance theme again. It was pleasant to walk in the warm night, listening to the music coming from far away.

"It's very nice here," said Karen. "I wish we were sightseeing. And in general, I very much regret that we have become adversaries."

"That's all your doing," I said.

"Mine? I have offered you cooperation several times!"

"But that's just it! You wanted to have me as a hired collaborator. But I am a free man and don't need a job."

We passed the entrance to the quays. In front of us, wooden piers stretched out onto the water, some illuminated by lanterns. Suddenly, Karen clutched my hand.

"Oh, there, look! There, at the end of the platform. Isn't that Malinovski?"

In the dim light of a street lamp, we saw a figure jump into a motorboat. Then we heard him try to start the engine. The whirr of the motor, which didn't immediately catch on, echoed loudly in the quiet of the night.

"It's him! For sure! I recognize him!" cried Karen.

The engine caught on. Slowly, the boat slid away from the pier, reversed, and turned towards the lake.

"Quick! Back to the car. We'll catch him on the water!" I said to Karen.

We ran back up the same stone steps. Again, like a speeding missile, we barged on through the dancing couples and ran to my car. I jumped into my vehicle.

"Wait!" cried Karen, lifting the hood of the Lincoln. Then she lowered the hood and took the keys left in the ignition by Malinovski. With one leap, she was in my vehicle, in the shotgun seat.

"I immobilized the car," she explained. "Under the hood, there is a lever that disconnects the electrical system. Now, no one will be able to steal it."

Some holidaymakers stopped dancing and, curious about the goings on, went out into the street. I swung my car 180 degrees in front of the cafe and, a few houses down the street, I jumped onto a steep street running down to the waterfront. As we trundled on the stone steps, we had a view of the lake in front of us. Malinovski's motorboat was a tiny speck, but it drew a huge wake on the surface, and we heard the whirr of its engine.

We arrived at the shore. There were coupes on the beach. As I now dashed along the beach, looking for a convenient place to jump into the water, I heard people yelling:

"Don't you have some other place to go?"

"Hey, Mr. Crazy, watch out, or you will fall into the water!"

And:

"Hope you can swim, moron!"

Soon, I saw an approach to the lake—I had remembered there was one. I accelerated the vehicle, and we jumped into the lake like a galloping warhorse, throwing up a huge splash of water.

"Oh my God!" shouted a girl's voice on the beach.

But we were already floating ahead on the water, carried by our momentum. The dark spot that had been Malinovski's motorboat disappeared from our sight. We heard only the quiet whirr of his engine, and it pointed to the bandit's location.

I switched gears to activate the turbine and put the pedal to the metal. The front of the vehicle rose above the surface of the water, and the propeller bit into the wave. The surface of the water boiled behind us, and we left a triangular streak of white foam behind us. I turned on the windshield wipers to clear the windshield of the water that constantly splashed on it and obstructed our view.

"He's fleeing toward Love Island," I said to Karen, listening to the growl of the speedboat coming from the distance.

"Love Island?"

"People call it that because it is the favorite hangout of young couples."

"Have you been there?" she asked.

"Yes. I have been there once, looking for a certain scholar who might explain to me the mystery of a lost collection of old coins. He was spending his honeymoon on Love Island and I ended up interrupting his idyll."

"I can imagine what he thought of that," Karen laughed. "And did you find the collection?"

"Oh, yes. Although that was one of my most dangerous adventures."

"But you will not find the Templar treasure," Karen said firmly. "Get that out of your head."

"There you go again. Hasn't the story with Malinovski taught you anything?"

"Oh, yes, I will be more careful in the future. But that doesn't mean I'm giving up the treasure hunt. I will beat you to it."

"That remains to be seen, Ma'am" I smiled.

I have to say: I was impressed. After all she'd been through, I assumed she would give up the fight for the treasure. But she was tenacious, stubborn, and ambitious. I liked that.

"Quiet!" hissed Karen suddenly. "Can you hear?"

"Ah. Precisely. I can't hear anything.... The whirr of the motorboat stopped."

"That's what I meant," said Karen. "He probably brought the speedboat ashore and turned off the engine. Why did he choose Love

Island? He is not in love, is he?" she giggled.

"He must have been here before and knows the area. When he realized that he would soon run out of gasoline, he remembered Hajikoveh and the many nooks one can hide here. He wants to get away from us and cover his tracks."

And now, suddenly, right before our faces, a tall, black mass of an island emerged from the dark. It looked menacing and mysterious. All the more menacing because we knew that a bandit was watching our approach from the shore.

"Is the island inhabited?" Karen asked.

"No. Only tourists camp here sometimes. They come by kayak."

Now that we were near the island, I turned on my floodlights and rotated them to sweep the coast.

Immediately, we saw a motorboat stuck on the shore, nose first, at the foot of a steep bank. The boat looked abandoned. The man who had steered it had disappeared in the coastal bush.

We pulled up next to the motorboat. I stopped my engine, grabbed a universal wrench from under my seat, and jumped across.

"What are you doing?" Karen shouted at me. "He's not there!"

"I am going to take the sparkplugs out. He won't get away from us again."

I threw the sparkplugs in my pocket, jumped back into my vehicle, and motored along the shore, looking for a convenient place to ride up. I didn't worry about the fact that Malinovski might be watching us. Looking for him in this darkness was pointless anyway. We had to wait until daybreak.

I found a breach in the steep bank, a ravine through which rainwater cleared from the island. I climbed into the ravine and then to an extensive forest clearing on the high shore.

"We'll wait here until daybreak," I said to Karen.

We decided to stay in the car. It was warm and cozy, and we could see all around.

The stars shone overhead, shiny beads of mercury and silver.

"The Templar treasure," whispered Karen, "probably contains as many jewels as there are stars in the sky. I like gems very much," she explained. "When you look at them, when you hold them in your hand, it is difficult not to believe that some mysterious power is contained in them. They are such a rare phenomenon in this world. They were created as a result of such unusual and complex processes of nature. Sometimes, they seem to me nothing but miracles."

"I guess I am not the only one. People tell all kinds of stories about precious stones. They say that because of its bright red color, the ruby inspires joy and motivates us to take action. It is a stone that should be worn by people who want to act or persevere in pursuit of a goal. And besides," she laughed, "red is also the color of love. I also like emeralds, but I would be afraid to wear them. They are said to make one clairvoyant. But the person wearing an emerald should have great qualities of spirit: be modest and temperate, poised and full of kindness. I'm afraid I'm not like that. But you, Mr. Wheels, should wear a ring with an emerald on your finger."

"Oh?" I was surprised. "Have you discovered a positive quality in me?"

"Oh, come on. I recognized your noble qualities during our first meeting. Of course, now I hate you a lot more because I know what a dangerous opponent you are. Still, I will never forget what you did for me tonight."

And then she leaned over and—pecked me on the cheek.

And then, as if ashamed of this gesture, which she probably considered an expression of weakness, she got out of the car and said:

"Look, the day is breaking."

Indeed, the day was breaking. The forest was turning gray. The stars in the sky had dimmed.

I got out of the vehicle and stretched. It was chilly. I felt ravenously hungry. Hunger always puts me in a contrary mood.

"Well, Mr. Malinovski," I muttered. "Wouldn't you know it! Here we are, you and I, with a rendezvous on the Island of Love. I am very curious to see your face."

I took the flare gun out of the car.

"Do you plan to kill him?" Karen jumped up.

"Well, this gun will probably not anybody. But the rogue might be scared of it. Thugs like him are usually only brave when they think they have the upper hand. I suspect that Mr. Malinovski will turn out to be a chicken."

I locked and secured my vehicle, and we set off.

We walked along the high shore of the island to the place where the motorboat stood. We found it in its place, meaning that my idea of taking out the sparkplugs had worked: Malinovski had not managed to restart the motorboat.

Now, we plunged into the forest, looking all around carefully, even though we realized perfectly well that Malinovski, hidden in some hole, could easily avoid detection. The forest was overgrown with lots of undergrowth, and there were many hollows in the ground. Eventually, we emerged into a large clearing stretching all the way to the other side of the island. The terrain here was flat, the grass was too short to hide a man, even one lying really flat on the ground. Only at the shore were there some bushes. We tore through them, marching right into the biggest thicket. But we didn't see Malinovski anywhere.

Meanwhile, the day had risen, filled with the sun, which shone bright and strong but was not yet hot. The other shore of the lake looked· beautiful. It was low-lying and covered with lush green meadows. Further away, the ground rose steeply up to a wall of a huge, ancient forest. Just to the left, along the shore, the brick walls of a lone homestead shone red among the meadows. A pair of storks was nesting on a weeping willow tree.

Looking back in the direction of Hajikoveh, we saw the expanse of the lake stretching for a good mile and a half, while on this side, the distance from the mainland was very short, a quarter of a mile at most.

"Look!" cried Karen. "Someone's clothes are lying in the bush!"

We ran up and leaned over a bundle of clothes.

Damn! I thought.

"I have feared this. Malinovski stripped and swam across the lake at night. He stripped because clothes restrain your movements in the water."

"Look. It's a biker's outfit," Karen said.

And she was right. It was the same clothes Mr. Hamster had worn. Or ones a lot like them.

"Is this Malinovski?"

"Ha, have you noticed this biker fellow, Mr. Hamster, who hung about Milkokuk and later came to Malbork? We have seen him in both places. Could he be Malinovski? Is that his outfit?"

I searched the pockets but did not find even the smallest trinket. Reckoning on the possibility of us finding his clothes, the bandit had carefully emptied them all.

"He won't get far. He is as naked as a newborn. That's pretty noticeable," laughed Karen.

But I shook my head.

"No. I don't think so. First, he is not naked at all. He is probably wearing swim trunks. We are on a lake, in a resort town. Here, a man dressed from head to toe is an oddity, not someone in swim trunks. And, he has the twelve thousand you have given him. He will simply buy clothes, if only from that farmer across the lake."

"Let's go there. Maybe he was there," Karen suggested.

Suddenly, a realization hit me. I slapped my forehead in awe.

"Oh God, but we are fools! Idiots of the first degree!"

"What happened?" asked Karen, taken aback.

"We got taken for a ride!" I said. "Literally! Malinovski had set your meeting at the fifty-kilometer mark because *he has a vehicle*. He would not have walked thirty miles on foot. Thanks to this outfit, we know he has a motorcycle. When I arrived at the fiftieth kilometer, he jumped into your Lincoln and drove away. Why did he flee in your car?"

"He wanted to steal it?"

"Nonsense! He would have never been able to fence it. He fled in your car *in order to draw us away* from the place where he had left his vehicle. He didn't want to run away on his bike because we would have immediately recognized him as that acquaintance of Miss Anka.

Now do you understand?"

"Oh my God," whispered Karen. "Now what do we do?"

"Malinovski swam across the lake at night. From the farmer on the other side, he acquired some clothes. Then he stepped out on the Bittov-Hoynitse highway to hail a ride that might take him back to the fifty-kilometer mark. And you know what this means? This means that if we hurry, we might arrive there before him."

We ran to the vehicle and drove it into the lake. We attached the motorboat to the car and towed it to the marina in Hajikoveh. There, we parked it in the same place from which Malinovski had stolen it. I screwed the plugs back into the engine, and we drove up to the top of the ridge. Using a rubber tube, I transferred some gasoline from my vehicle into the Lincoln's tank. Karen jumped into her car, and we set off at high speed for the fifty-kilometer mark.

Already from very far away, I could see a motorcycle standing by the road, and next to it a man repairing something. My heart skipped a beat. "I've got you, Malinovski," I muttered and sped up to block his escape.

But it wasn't Malinovski. It was a local teenager was repairing the chain of his SHL.

"Hello, young man! Hello! Hello?" I called out, jumping out of the car. "Have you seen a man on a *Yunak*?"

"Have I seen him? Why, I brought him here from Hajikoveh. He had a *Yunak* hidden in the woods. Is he a friend of yours?"

"My friend, indeed!" I became indignant. "He is a bandit. A robber! A thief! A dangerous and wanted criminal!"

"Oh, boy!" the teenager was aghast. "He showed up at our farm at daybreak wearing only swimming briefs. He said he had been kayaking across Lake Hajikovski, but his kayak overturned and sank, and he swam ashore. He bought clothes from my father and then saw that I had a motorcycle. He offered me five hundred zloty if I took him to Malbork. And he paid it, too. Only instead of Malbork, he told me to stop here. This surprised me, and I was even more surprised when he entered the forest and then came out riding a *Yunak*. A bandit, you say? A dangerous criminal?"

SHL

A brand of Polish motorcycles produced from 1938 until 1970

"When did he leave?" I interrupted him.

"About half an hour ago."

I explained to Karen what had happened. We set off again, but this time without haste. Further pursuit no longer made the slightest sense. Soon, we found ourselves at the Malbork campground. Captain Petersen jumped out of the camper and, at the sight of his daughter whole and healthy, waved his hands with joy.

And then the scouts came running from the river. I had them fix breakfast because I was starving. Of course, I had to tell them about our night adventure immediately.

"And now," having finished the story, I turned to Tell. "Run to the block of flats where Mrs. Anka is staying and try to bring her to us. Say breakfast, news, and stuff like that, but do not tell her about my adventure last night. When she shows up here, then we'll question her. I think she is friends with this Malinovski—after all, he brought her here. Maybe this is no accidental acquaintance? Maybe they are a team?"

To be entirely honest, I didn't believe it, but Tell took off like a rocket.

"The worst thing is that we didn't record the number of the *Yunak*," said Hawkeye. "In the future, I will try to remember the registration plate number of every vehicle whose owner seems suspicious."

"I once saw a movie," nodded Squirrel, "in which the English police managed to capture dangerous criminals thanks to Boy Scouts writing down car numbers.”

“And Malinovski is a dangerous criminal,” said Hawkeye. Like a Chicago gangster. He extorts ransom. He robs diamond brooches.”

Soon, William Tell came back running. He yelled from far away:

“Miss Anka is not there! She’s left for Warsaw!”

“What? When?” I was so surprised by this news that I interrupted my breakfast.

“She left at midnight. She told the gentleman from whom she rented her room that she had to leave for Warsaw suddenly. She took her things and left.”

“She left!” I whispered. “Isn’t this curious?”

I finished my breakfast and ordered the boys to roll up camp.

“We are leaving for Kortumovo. Go get Eve. We leave at two sharp.”

But again, we were not given the opportunity to leave on schedule. I was invited to the Petersen’s camper, where another meeting took place. This time, despite Karen’s reluctance and Kozlovski’s advice not to give publicity to the story with the bandit, Captain Petersen was determined to turn the case over to the militia.

“We are all accessories to the crime, to some extent,” Kozlovski said. “On several occasions, we entered into shady arrangements with the bandit. That’s illegal. Plus, you paid for a stolen document.”

Captain Petersen spread his hands with a gesture of helplessness.

“Fine. I am ready to pay for my crime. If it comes to that, I will go behind bars. But I want satisfaction: let them lock Malinovski in the same cell with me.”

We went to the militia station in Malbork, where we wasted a lot of time because—since the crime involved a foreigner—an investigator from Gdansk had to be summoned. During the interrogation, a little fraud of Kozlovski came to light. It wasn’t a very big deal, and the officer who interrogated us had his tiny mustache twitching with laughter, but it undermined any sense of trust the Petersens had placed in the man. It turned out that the Petersens had no contract with the Polish state for their search for the Templar treasure. The document they held was an agreement concluded with... Kozlovski. It was signed on the one hand by the Petersens and on the other by—Kozlovski. Kozlovski explained himself:

"I did this for patriotic reasons. I wanted to make sure that these foreigners should not give up their search but stay in Poland and leave more foreign currency in our country. And obviously, to do that, they would need to be able to search legally and have an agreement with the authorities. I first went to the Ministry of Culture to get them to sign an agreement with the Petersens. They refused. They simply laughed at me. They said: "Look, you don't know if these treasures are works of art, and we are only interested in such objects. When you find them, you come to us." So I went to the Ministry of Finance. There, too, they laughed at me: "First, find the treasure, and then we can sign a contract. Our Ministry is a serious institution, and you are making some kind of a joke about it." So what was I supposed to do? I drafted a contract and signed it. In this way, I thought I accomplished the needful: the Petersens had a treasure-hunting contract, and the state was assured of its share in case they actually found anything."

The militia officer instructed Kozlovski very sternly that he had been wrong to do so, then explained to the Petersens that their agreement had no legal basis. He then added that he was not competent to comment on whether they did or did not have the right to look for the Templar treasure. And in case, he added, he was not a treasure specialist and was only interested in catching thieves.

"My business is catching this Malinovski," he said, scratching his head. "And as for the treasure... I think we will worry about it when you find it. OK?"

The Petersens agreed—what else could they do? We left the militia station late in the evening. The boys and Eve had been waiting for me in the vehicle. We said goodbye to the Petersens, and they shouted, "See you later!"

And we left Malbork and took the highway for Kvidzin.

CHAPTER SIXTEEN: IN KORTUMOVO

In Kortumovo. Eve's morning discipline. Does the church have a dungeon? "An underground vault." What is in the garden cellar? The theory of stray currents. Ruins in the forest. Prelude to a jam.

Kortumovo is a small village stretching along the shore of a lake of the same name. At the southern end of the village is a wide, blunt-ended peninsula, and at its base stands a church. On the peninsula behind the church is a white-washed, red-tiled rectory, a few buildings belonging to it, an orchard, and a garden. All around the village stretch coniferous forests, full of picturesque hillocks and ravines. The lake—a fairly large lake—is overgrown in places with tall reeds; it is a nature reserve of wild swans. The area is quite nice, suitable for summer recreation, but not visited by tourists, as it lies far from the main traffic routes.

We arrived there at night and camped just beyond the church and the peninsula, in between the lake and the forest. The following day, we found out that we had chosen the best place: we were outside the village but, at the same time, close to it. Plus, it seemed that the old church was to be the main object of our interest, for there were no other old buildings in the village.

I ceded my tent to Eve and slept in the vehicle.

Neither the boys nor I were morning birds. Anyone who has ever spent any time camping knows how unpleasant it is to wake up on a cold morning, wash in a cold lake, and then, teeth chattering, try to fix a meal. But Eve gave us a seven o'clock wake-up: she slipped her hand through the half-opened car window and pressed the car horn several times. We jumped up, terrified, but having realized that this was just Eve having fun at our expense, we dove back into our sleeping bags.

Then Eve resorted to more radical measures: she brought a cup of cold water from the lake, and, having made a sprinkler out of a pine branch, she began to "bless" us. I rolled up the windows and the boys laced up their tent and did not react even when she loosened the pins of their tent, and the whole thing collapsed on them.

Only Eve's last resort proved effective: she made breakfast. She boiled a pot of coffee, and its smell lured us out like the smell of honey lures bears out of the forest. The boys yawned and groaned. Hawkeye stuck his nose into the pot of coffee and got a whack of the spoon from Eve.

"First, you wash up," she ordered him. "I'm not going to eat with dirty people."

We stood in a row one step away from the cold lake. We looked at each other. No one wanted to be the first to make contact with the water. Finally, William Tell dipped both hands in.

"Cold, huh?" asked Squirrel, and his teeth started chattering in expectation. Hawkeye said:

"Are you familiar with this old folk proverb: 'He who washes himself frequently lives but a short while?' We will be better off not to wash."

"Oh, you hooligan! There is no such proverb. You made it up!" exclaimed Eve. Tell withdrew his hands from the water and wiped them with a towel.

"There. I have washed," he declared proudly.

"And your face? And your teeth?" Eve asked.

"Sir," Hawkeye turned to me. "You always set a good example. You do it first."

"Personally, I think bringing her here was the dumbest idea we had all summer," declared Squirrel suddenly. "To bring Eve here with us! Why on earth have we done it? Were we missing anything? We have ever only washed at noon, or better yet, in the afternoon, in the greatest heat."

"Or not at all," Tell observed matter-of-factly.

"What?" I became indignant. "This is the first time I hear that we have such improper customs. It's terrible. I have never heard of it."

"You have probably never paid attention to such a mundane activity as washing in the morning," Eve noted. "You were probably all busy thinking from morning till dusk about finding the Templar treasure, no?"

"I think this washing-up-in-the-morning business will prejudice our treasure hunt," Squirrel was getting worked up. "It takes away all joy of life. When I get into a bad mood like this first thing the morning, no good idea ever comes to me the whole day."

"Keep calm and wash up," said Eve. "There are enough ideas for everyone. Besides, I already know where the treasure is."

"Oh?" we all stared at her.

"I'll tell you after you wash up," she said.

With this, we were finally won over. We took off our shirts, and the splashing began.

Washed and refreshed, we sat around the spirit stove.

"Now tell us," said Tell, grabbing a thick slab of bread generously smeared with lard.

"The treasure is hidden... is hidden..." Eve began in a mysterious voice. "It is hidden... hidden..."

"Well, I think we all know it is hidden!" interrupted Hawkeye impatiently.

"It is hidden... hidden..." Eve continued.

"Please. I can't stand the suspense," complained Hawkeye. "Eve, are you making this stuff up? You just wanted us to bathe, but you really don't have a clue, do you?"

"Oh, don't be such a smart aleck," Eve pouted. "I am certain that Knights Templar washed up first thing in the morning."

"Gad. What is the matter with this girl?" sighed Squirrel.

"Well, nothing's wrong with me!" burbled Eve. "I know where the treasure is, but I won't tell you because you're blabbermouth.".

"You won't say because you don't know," said Squirrel with an air of fundamental finality.

"Ha!" pshawed Eve. "I know exactly where the treasure is! It is hidden in the dungeons under the church!"

We all turned to look at the nearby church. It was small, built of red brick, with a slender Gothic steeple. It didn't stand out in any special way. It seemed like an ordinary village church.

"In this church?" Hawkeye shook his head skeptically. "It does not look like it has any dungeons."

"I doubt it," said William Tell. "We seem to have come to the wrong place."

"And what do you think about it?" Squirrel turned to me.

I wondered aloud:

"I can't tell—I just got up! But honestly, if you ask me, the church looks quite modest. And I suppose it does seem hard to believe that the treasures of a powerful monastic order, which had owned scores of mighty castles, were brought from distant France to be buried here. But, as you know, the situation was strange, for all those mighty castles in France proved no defense against King Philip; while this humble church, on the other hand... Who would have ever suspected, you see? And if the original name of Kortumovo really was *Your Heart*... Who knows?"

Teutonic Church in Unislav
Built in early 14th century and located in the Helmno county,
it is probably the model for the Church in Kortumowo

Tell objected:

"I see no trace of mighty buildings nor anything to indicate that this once was *Cor tuum*."

I said:

"True. But, we are looking at this place through the prism of our visit to Malbork. We have just arrived from a huge castle rising all the way to the sky. Have we expected to see something similar here? For all we know, Peter of Avignon worked at *Cor tuum* for only a short while. He was probably engaged in planning the future capital: measuring the land, testing the soil, making drawings, and perhaps laying some markers in the ground. Perhaps he never managed to build anything before he was recalled to France.

"We will have to ask the locals if they have noticed any remains of old buildings anywhere. Keep in mind that the future capital must have been planned on a large scale. If work had started, perhaps it started in several places at once, and we don't know if any of those parts advanced enough to bury the treasure. The smallest clue can prove extremely valuable. Do not disregard any information, even information that may seem insignificant and improbable."

We finished our meal and, having left Squirrel to wash the dishes, we walked toward the church. It was open, still smelling of the candles that had burned during the morning service. With beating hearts, we stepped into its cool interior.

There was no doubt that the church had been built by the Teutonic Knights. We could see that from the outside: it had been built with the "fingerprint" red Teutonic brick—a sort of brick marked with slight groves made by the fingers of the brick makers. Inside, the church was very white. The church had been whitewashed, and its furnishings looked extremely modest. The interior decoration was much later than its shell. We saw a Baroque altar with gilded chubby angels and a raised pulpit decorated with the same. Along the church walls hung paintings of the Passion of Christ, and wooden pews for the faithful stood in the center.

At the entrance to the church, we noticed a large baptismal font carved in sandstone. And that was it, no stone carvings on the walls, no frescoes, no tombstones, no doors or stairs leading into the crypt. In a word, we didn't see anything that would give us any reason to suppose that the church was more than met the eye.

We went outside to the small cemetery surrounding the church. Several old poplars grew here, on which a flock of crows had made their nests. Their cawing reverberated in the air.

Slowly, inspecting carefully the old walls, we walked around the church. My gaze slid down the smooth brown walls and came to rest at something like a semicircular annex or apse with an iron door. This was probably the entrance to the sacristy. Above the door was a large stone panel with a cross.

We kept walking. And then suddenly, something occurred to me. I stopped, my heart at my throat, my head in chaos. It seemed to me that I had just realized something extremely important, but the thought escaped me. I could not understand it.

"What happened to you?" asked Eve, who noticed my strange state.

Easy, easy, I whispered to myself.

I walked back a dozen steps, and the kids followed me.

"Look at the cross," I said.

They looked at it for a long time. Finally, Hawkeye said:

"It's a cross."

"Anything special about it?"

"What do you want? It's a church. In a church, a cross over the entrance—it's the most ordinary thing on earth."

I reached into my pocket and pulled out the notebook in which Miss Petersen had drawn mason's marks.

"Take a look," I pointed to one of the signs.

"Well, I never!" they shouted in a chorus so loudly that the crows flew up from their nests and began to circle over the church, cawing like mad.

"This sign says *an underground vault*," I whispered.

But after a second, my joy gave way to doubt.

Perhaps it's just a coincidence? Did stone masons always think very deeply about these things? To mark *an underground vault*, they adopted the sign of a cross on a double-stepped base. Someone else may have carved the same sign without ever realizing it meant anything special.

On the path leading from the rectory appeared the black figure of a priest in a cassock. We waited until he approached us, then greeted him. He greeted us warmly. It probably pleased him to see us studying his church with such great interest.

The priest was no longer young, with a bald head and rosy

cheeks. He smiled at us with great kindness.

"Our church is small and impoverished, but it is very ancient. It dates from the beginning of the 14th century," he said, raising his index finger to the sky as if to emphasize the importance of his words. "For most tourists, it is not an attraction at all, which is why we rarely get visitors here. Although the area is very beautiful, forests, a lake with wild swans..."

"We like it here very much. We want to stay a little longer," I said. "We have pitched out tents just behind the church, over there."

"Tents? Very healthy for young people," nodded the priest. "Just be careful swimming because the lake is very deep. And if you want fresh apples, or gooseberries, or currants, feel free to come into my orchard. There is no fence. Anyone can go in. And don't be afraid of my housekeeper—she sometimes can be a little harsh. If she comes at you, say that I invited you."

He smiled and winked at us facetiously, which probably meant that he knew his housekeeper's character well but didn't take her moods seriously.

Meanwhile, Squirrel caught up with us.

"Oh! Another one!" the priest seemed genuinely pleased.

And Squirrel—the Blabbermouth—immediately asked the priest:

"Is there a dungeon under this church?"

"A dungeon?" frowned the priest. "And why, my child? Why would there be a dungeon under the church? There is no underground here. It's a tiny, simple church!"

I tried to change the subject so awkwardly started by Squirrel. I said diplomatically:

"The church, we heard, dates back to the 14th century. So presumably, the whole village is historical as well."

"And yes, yes, right," agreed the priest. "Admittedly, I have not read anything about our village in history books, but it must be historical because many signs point to it."

"*Signs*?" I asked, and the boys pricked their ears. But the priest meant completely different "signs." He said:

"Where my orchard and outbuildings are, some kind of an old

building must have once stood because if you dig three feet underground, you hit stonework. Something like foundations or remnants of old walls. Apparently, there used to be various pits there, too, but my predecessor had the area leveled, new soil brought in and then planted the orchard. The whole peninsula you see behind the church must have been a city, or a fortress, or something like that. But now, only one large cellar remains, and it contains a deep well. My housekeeper has arranged a storage room for vegetables and potatoes in the basement. She lowers a bucket with milk and butter into the well because even in the worst heat such cold blows from the well that it makes your teeth chatter."

"She has made herself a nice refrigerator," I chuckled

And the boys' eyes opened wide with curiosity.

"Oh, if it were possible to see that well!" sighed Hawkeye.

"Oh, no!" the priest threatened him with his finger. "My housekeeper keeps the basement strictly off-limits! She doesn't let anyone in, and the place isn't just under lock and key, it is under five locks and seven keys! And do you know why?" he laughed again. "Because there are not only vegetables and potatoes in there, but also... jams, pickled mushrooms, and... home-made wine!"

A bulky woman in a white apron and a red kerchief on her head appeared in the doorway of the rectory. She folded her hands about her lips to make the sound carry and called out toward us in a surprisingly deep voice:

"Please, father! Your elevenses are on the table! Where are you?"

The parish priest smiled at us once again:

"Do you hear? I have to go now because the housekeeper really doesn't like it when her food gets cold. But do look into my orchard. You have my permission!"

And he wandered off down the path to the rectory, where his housekeeper still stood in the doorway, eyeing us sternly as if we were trying to starve the priest.

"We are going to have a hard time with this person," Eve sighed.

But the boys did not want to think about the difficulties that awaited us. For them, the most important thing was that Kortumovo seemed to be the village we had been looking for.

"So there are the foundations of old buildings here," said Tell. "Was this Peter of Avignon's work? Was this going to be *Your Heart*? And above the side entrance to the church, there is a mason's sign: *an underground vault.*"

"All very well, but how do we find the cache?" Squirrel asked. "There used to be some ditches on the peninsula, but they were filled in, and now trees grow there. We aren't going to dig up the orchard, are we? And no door leading underground can be seen in the church because—you heard the priest—there is no underground at all."

"Our only hope is that cellar in the garden... I'm just thinking about it," muttered Eve. "We have found a dungeon, but how do we get into it? The housekeeper won't give us the key."

"First, let's inspect the area," I said.

We walked onto the peninsula. There were large plum trees, gnarly apple trees, cherry trees, gooseberry bushes, and currants. The land had been leveled and sown with grass. In places, there were flower beds. No one would ever guess that this orchard had been planted on the foundations of a Teutonic building. The only trace of construction was the cellar located in the middle of the orchard. At the back, there was a rather wide hillock planted with gooseberry bushes, but in the front, in the slope, there was a section of Teutonic brick wall, an iron door, and a tiny window with an iron grille. The size of the hill and the wall indicated that the cellar was quite large. The entrance to it was guarded not by five, as the parish priest joked, but by a single but very massive iron padlock.

"It will take a very skillful conversation with the housekeeper," Tell said. "How do we beg her to show us the inside of the cellar?"

"No good if she *shows* it to you," Hawkeye shrugged. "You don't want to inspect it in her company, and she will not leave us alone with her jars of jams and pickles. And it will take time to inspect the basement thoroughly because *if* there is an entrance to the underground in it, it has to be well hidden, or the housekeeper would have found it a long time ago."

"We need some kind of subterfuge," I reflected. "Only a subterfuge can save us. Do not get into any negotiations with the housekeeper because you will only make her suspicious, and the whole thing will be off."

"So what do you propose? A break-in?" asked Squirrel in a whisper.

"No, no," I laughed. "Let's see if we can come up with some idea. At the moment, I can't think of anything sensible, but give it time."

"Ha! Well! I have an idea," Eve assured us. "Just give me some time to work it out."

"Fine. We'll give you until evening," Tell said smugly.

"Now let's get out of here," I said, "or the housekeeper will start to worry that we are hanging around her kingdom too much."

We walked over to our camp. The boys left us to—as they said—"explore the village properly." I guessed that they simply wanted to get more information about Kortumovo and the old Teutonic foundations.

And the two of us—Eve and I—sat down in front of her tent. She was pondering something, and time and again, she plucked a blade of grass from the ground and chewed on it.

"Do you maybe have thirty feet of thin electric wire?" she asked unexpectedly.

"Yes. Every car owner carries some wire with him in case he burns out some electrical wire."

"Then lend it to me," she said. "And do you have batteries?"

"I have batteries, but they are in my flashlight. I will need them."

"There is a store in this village, right? I'll go get batteries there," said Eve.

I gave her my coil of copper wire. She accepted it with a mysterious look on her face, packed it in her bag, and slung the bag over her shoulder. Nodding goodbye to me, she marched off into the village.

I was left alone. I sunbathed on the shore of the lake for half an hour, but after a while, I started to feel bad: I was the most lazy member of our expedition. Eve went to run some mysterious errands, the boys were looking for information about old foundations, and I was lying in the sun!

I decided to inspect the forest surrounding the village. I set off along the edge of the wood, intending to walk all around the village. I covered at most a quarter of a mile when I saw a tree-growing in the middle of a debris of bricks. The debris stretched over a large area and formed a clear square. It looked as if the bricks were the remains of a large building, perhaps a tower, that had once stood there. I recognized the red brick "fingerprint," similar to the bricks used to build the church. And, as I thought about the location of the site, its relation to the village, the church, and the peninsula, it occurred to me that this had probably been part of outside fortifications—perhaps of an entrance gate.

Of course, if this site had been planned for a tower, perhaps an entrance gate, it was difficult to suppose that the foundations concealed an underground vault. But how could I be sure that this had indeed been a watchtower? To make sure, I would have to excavate somewhere on the side of the debris and see how deep the foundations went. This was a job requiring a great deal of effort and time.

I went further into the forest, but I didn't find anything of interest anymore. The forest was varied, in places coniferous and in places oak. Around the oak trees, the ground had been plowed by boars looking for acorns, and I saw lots of blackberries.

I returned to our camp in the afternoon. Eve and the boys were preparing lunch. My young friends looked very mysterious and very pleased with themselves.

"Well?" Eve asked me. "Did you find anything interesting?"

"Not much," I replied modestly.

"And I learned from an old farmer in the village," said Squirrel proudly, "that very long ago, before the First World War, there lived a peasant in Kortumovo who found an entrance to the underworld. Only that no one knows where this entrance is. This peasant went in, and all trace of him was lost. He never returned. And for many weeks, people heard satanic noises in the church, like the moaning of the damned in hell."

"Why—the damned?"

"I don't know. It's just a local legend. Maybe people assumed that the secret entrance he took led to hell?" said Squirrel.

Eve spoke up:

"Mr. Wheels... could you lend us the battery from your car? What is the voltage in it?"

"Twelve volts."

"Perfect. That's exactly what we need."

"I can't lend you the battery. You will discharge it, then we won't be able to go anywhere."

"We will not discharge it," Eve assured me.

"Wait. You want me to take the battery out of the car and give it to you to play with?" I was astonished.

"We don't need your battery to play with," Eve said with all seriousness. "And no, we will not discharge it. And, for the moment, it's all very quiet, and there's no sign of any upcoming car chase. Malinovski hasn't shown up yet. So, it should be OK to take out the batter for a short while."

"Eve knows electricity," Tell said. "She said that she plans to go to the polytechnic to study electrical engineering."

"A girl who knows electricity," shook his head Hawkeye with disbelief. "So far, I've only met girls who were afraid of electricity."

"Could I ask what you need the battery for?" I asked.

"Oh, no! This is our secret!" they shouted in a chorus.

"I have had enough of all these mysteries," I grumbled. "The mystery of the Templar treasure, the mysterious Mr. Malinovski, and now finally: the mystery of the car battery."

Squirrel interjected:

"Have you heard of the theory of stray currents?"

"Blabbermouth!" shouted the other boys immediately.

"Well, I didn't say anything," said Squirrel indignantly. I simply asked if Mr. Wheels has heard anything about the theory of stray currents."

"I have heard something like that," I scratched my head. "But I confess that I know nothing about electricity."

"Well, ha. But *we* know the theory," laughed Hawkeye. "The battery is needed in connection with this theory."

"We will not discharge your battery. I promise. Word of honor," Eve raised her hand in a vow.

What was I supposed to do? They made a sympathetic gang,

and it seemed they were having fun with what seemed like a coming prank.

"Fine. But, I beg you, do not try the theory of stray currents on me. I am very afraid of electricity."

"Don't you worry," said Eve. "Nothing untoward will happen to you. I am the queen of electricity, and I wield lightning. That's right, guys," she turned to the scouts. "You are to title me Your Majesty from now on. And now, please, the battery."

I lifted the hood of the vehicle and unscrewed the battery. I handed it to the boys, and they immediately carried it off to their tent. Eve also went in with her bag, in which I noticed a dozen electric batteries.

What the heck? I thought.

I sat on the shore of the lake, a little sad that I had been excluded from the mysterious activity. Behind my back, I heard voices from the tent:

"I *told* you, moron, you must connect them in a series... Not so, silly you. In a row. God, what a bunch of airheads. Well, hold the end of the wire..."

"I'm afraid... I'm afraid," wheezed Squirrel.

"Don't be afraid!" Eve upbraided him sharply. "What a coward! Why don't you just run away, huh? Here, I will show you how to hold it."

Hawkeye stuck his head out of the tent.

"Mr. Wheels!" he called out. "Why don't you fix yourself a fishing rod and go fishing? Or try taking a walk around the neighborhood and investigate the village?"

I got up.

"You want me to go away? OK, I'll go," I muttered. "How lucky I am that I don't carry dynamite with me. You would probably have demanded that from me as well."

Hawkeye giggled, and a triple giggle from the depths of the tent answered him. Goaded by the boys' laughter, I walked toward the old church.

In the back of my mind, I felt that Hawkeye was right. I had no idea how to go about looking for the entrance to the underground—if there was one at all.

Once again, I walked around the entire church, meditating at length on the cross visible above the door to the sacristy. Again, I compared it with the drawing left in my notebook by Karen. But instead of thinking about the Templar treasure, I began to wonder what Karen was doing. Was she still in Malbork, or had she gone somewhere further afield? I was sure that sooner or later, she, too, would come up with the idea of looking up the Latin name *Cor Tuum* in a geographical dictionary of Polish localities. It was to be expected that she would soon come here in her Lincoln. Therefore, I was even more angered by the thought that I could not figure out how to use the present moment to find the entrance to the underground.

And Anka? What's going on with her? I wondered. *Why did she leave so suddenly? Could it be that she has really lost all interest in treasure hunters?*

When I returned to camp, dinner was ready. Eve and two of the boys were bustling around the spirit stove. Only Tell was missing.

"Where is Old William?" I asked.

"On the lookout," replied Eve curtly.

I didn't ask anymore because I understood that "on the lookout" was supposed to sound mysterious. I sat down to dinner in silence. Eve poured soup into my aluminum bowl, and I started eating.

Suddenly, a quiet whistling sound came from the bushes lining the edge of the priestly orchard. Eve immediately rushed into the boys' tent while Squirrel and Hawkeye waited for something, with great tension evident on their expressive faces.

A few minutes passed, and from the depths of the garden sounded first a woman's squeal, then a scream, then some unintelligible shouts. The bowl fell out of my hands and rolled on the grass. I jumped to my feet and rushed into the garden, with Hawkeye and Squirrel running after me.

At the cellar door, we saw the priest's housekeeper. She was trying to touch the padlock, then jumping away from it, screeching and yelling.

"What happened?" I asked, breathless from running.

"I don't know. The padlock is hot. Touch it, it burns," saying this, she gingerly touched the padlock and again jumped away from it as if scalded.

I remembered the borrowed battery.

I said judiciously:

"This is some very mysterious story, ma'am."

"Yes, yes," said the housekeeper, resting her hands on her large belly. "In the morning, I took a pot of milk from here, and the lock was normal, but now it burns. It's strange—the sun doesn't shine on it at all!"

Hawkeye approached us with a very serious expression.

In his hand, Hawkeye held a light bulb from an electric flashlight. He touched the bulb to the padlock, and the bulb lit up.

"Holy Jesus!" screamed the housekeeper. "There is electricity here! But we don't have electricity in the village! My God, how come there is electricity in the cellar door?"

And such astonishment appeared on her puckish face that I nearly burst into laughter.

"Holy Mother of God! I have to run and tell the priest! Imagine this! Electricity in the basement door?"

"There is probably some underground current flowing through here," Hawkeye said gravely. "Have you heard of stray currents?"

"My child! What are stray currents?" the housekeeper was astonished. "You think a stray current has strayed into my cellar? And where did it come from?"

"No one knows," said Hawkeye grimly. "I am guessing that somewhere far away, could be a hundred miles, a high-voltage line broke. And the current, instead of flowing along the wires like it normally does, escaped into the ground. And it wandered, wandered.... wandered... wandered...." recounted Hawkeye with a voice full of suspense. "And it emerged here. The door is iron, the padlock is iron. These are good conductors of electricity."

The housekeeper turned to me:

"Older sir! Is this true what this young man says?"

"I am not that old at all," I objected.

"Oh, I didn't mean to upset you," stammered the housekeeper. "I meant to say: you are the senior person among all these young people.

I thought you were their teacher."

"Well, I am responsible for them, it is true," I said. But just in case, I added: "But I don't know anything about electricity. These boys know something about it, though. The younger generation is far more familiar with modern technology than we."

The housekeeper wrung her hands:

"And is there nothing we can do about this stray current to make it go away?"

"Actually, yes, there is," Hawkeye said. "The basement should be insulated."

"What's that?" the housekeeper was astonished again.

"*In-su-la-ted,*" he repeated emphatically.

"And what is that now? Is it expensive? Will it take a long time to make such *insultation*?"

Hawkeye looked at the sky, looked at the ground, looked around the lake. Then he scratched his head for a long time.

"You know what? We will do it for you. You look after the parish priest and he is a nice person and allowed us to take apples from the garden. It won't take long to insulate the basement, a day at most. You must give me the key to the basement tomorrow, and we will take care of the insulation. We will prepare the materials tonight and get to work first thing in the morning."

"And is it necessary to go into the basement?"

I thought I detected a note of suspicion in her voice.

"Well, how else can we insulate it?" asked Hawkeye. "We have to go into the basement. If you have any valuable things in there, take them out today. Although, when it comes to confitures, you don't have to worry about us. We don't like confiture."

"How will you enter the basement if the padlock is burning?"

"I will insulate the padlock immediately," said Hawkeye. "It will not be permanent insulation, but I think it will last for a while."

Hawkeye took a spool of electric tape from his pocket. He tore off a piece and wrapped it around the hook of the padlock. As he worked, he whistled some melody. I guessed that he was communicating with Eve, who was probably operating the battery.

"I think you can open the padlock now," said Hawkeye

triumphantly. The housekeeper put out her hand and touched the padlock with her fingertips.

"Why!" he exclaimed joyfully. "It's not hot. Not even a little!"

Acting now with more confidence, she put the key in the padlock and turned it.

"What smart, helpful boys you have," she said to me, looking gratefully at Hawkeye. "Who would have imagined those stray currents? I have never felt one before. Yes, yes, you have to *insultate* the basement. You say you don't like jam?"

"I hate it," deadpanned Hawkeye. "We all hate jam. We like only mutton chop and pig trotter."

"And meatballs?" she asked.

"Depends on what kind," said Squirrel cautiously.

"In this case, I invite you to dinner. There will be meatballs of my making. You boys in your tent are probably cold and hungry, so treat yourselves at my place."

"Well, if you've made the meatballs, we'll certainly enjoy them," said Hawkeye.

In this way, a friendship was established between the stern housekeeper and the three Boy Scouts.

Back at the camp, I said to the kids:

"I am neither thrilled with your theory of stray currents nor do I approve of the electroshock method you used on the elderly lady."

"But we will have the key to the basement!" cried Eve with triumph.

"That's right, Queen of Electricity!" shouted the boys.

CHAPTER SEVENTEEN: THE CELLAR

Nocturnal visitors. A meeting on the road. We visit the cellar. What is in the well? The decisive moment.

Evening came, and then night. Dinner at the rectory—which I, uninformed as I was about stray currents, did not attend—was much to the liking of my friends. They dwelt for a long time on the superlative properties of the meatballs. Finally, silence fell in our camp, and all we could hear was the quiet murmur of the waves on the lake and the occasional bird bustling in the reeds.

Before going to sleep, I went for a walk in the woods—back to the place where I had seen the rectangular outline of old foundations. It wasn't far, but there was a dense copse of trees between our campsite and the place. Only at the last moment did I realize that someone was already there—indeed, had set up camp. I nearly banged my nose on— the Petersen's camper.

I retreated into the grove and carefully walked around the ruins, hiding behind the trees. I thought there was ample time to greet Karen and her father, but in the meantime, I would try to learn something by observing them.

They must have come by a road through the forest, bypassing the village. And they must have arrived recently since Kozlovski was just finishing setting up his tent. The captain was sitting on a tree stump, smoking his pipe, while Karen—despite the night gloom—was walking around the ruins, shining an electric flashlight here and there. I was glad that this was where she wanted to look for the treasure. She must have asked about old ruins in the village and was told about the remains of a foundation in the forest. She probably had no idea that there were old foundations under the priest's garden, too.

Or maybe she is right? I asked myself. *Maybe the Templar cache is located here, not there?*

"Tomorrow, we will use our detectors," Karen called out to her father. "It's not much for a future Teutonic capital, don't you think?" she asked.

"Well, you said that it was unfinished," the captain said.

"A construction project on such a large scale probably started in several places at once. It is not at all certain that this is the place where we should start," she said.

Clever girl. I thought angrily.

Kozlovski spoke up:

"I wonder what Mr. Wheels and his gang are doing now."

"Probably, same as us: looking for treasure," Petersen said.

Kozlovski laughed:

"I do wonder if they guessed that *Cor tuum* is Kortumovo."

"You didn't think of that, either, Mr. Kozlovski. I came up with it. I really have no use for you," said Karen. "And as for Mr. Wheels, it remains to be seen whether he won't show up here tomorrow in his satanic vehicle. He is a clever man."

Tomorrow? I thought. *I've been here since yesterday.*

"I wonder where they went?" wondered Karen aloud.

"Who?" Kozlovski asked her.

"Mr. Wheels and his boys. Who else?"

"Oh, you are still on about him," Kozlovski said angrily. "I say his fame is a little exaggerated."

"But he has saved my daughter from danger twice," said Captain Petersen.

"Well, I, too, advised Miss Karen against going out alone to meet that bandit at the fifty-kilometer mark," Kozlovski reminded them. "It was different at Milkokuk. It's OK to pay ransom, but going alone to the fifty-kilometer mark? That was insane."

"I wonder if he's gone looking for Malinovski?" said Karen. "If so, then we can expect to see him here any minute. Because Malinovski is probably still following us and waiting for more opportunities to fleece us again."

"I'll skin him!" Petersen yelled.

"Who?" Kozlovski jumped up, astonished.

"Don't you know whom I'm going to skin?" roared outraged Petersen. "Malinovski, sir. *Ma-li-nov-ski!* I don't think Mr. Wheels will do me the injury to capture this Malinovski without my help. We promised each other that we would catch him and skin him together."

"Malinovski has got enough out of you. He's probably very far away enjoying his loot," Kozlovski said. "He would be very foolish to hang around still."

Petersen cleaned his pipe by knocking it on the stump.

"I'm tired, and I'm going to bed. As for Mr. Wheels, I will tell you that you underestimate him. Perhaps, even at this very moment, he is standing somewhere nearby listening to your stupid chatter."

I froze. Had the captain spotted me among the trees? No, no. Impossible. He just thought I was a clever man. As a precaution, I retreated deeper into the forest. But I did not return to our camp. I recalled Karen's words that Malinovski was perhaps on their trail and decided to walk around the area some more.

It took half an hour before I reached the main road of Kortumovo.

The night walk yielded no results. I saw nothing suspicious. I sat down by the roadside to take a breather. And then I heard the creak of badly greased axles of a peasant wagon and the clopping of horse hooves.

"*Viooooo, hey-ta*!" the driver was talking to his horse.

There was nothing unusual or peculiar about the scene: a peasant returning to the village from the city. The wagon was getting closer and closer, the creaking of the axles became louder and louder. I raised my eyes to see the coachman, and I saw—Anka!

She was sitting next to the coachman and swaying sleepily.

Well, wouldn't you know it! I thought, jumping to my feet. *Whenever I look for Malinovski, Anka turns up.*

"My respects to the young lady!" I called out. She jumped up, surprised by my voice coming out of the roadside ditch.

"Oh, it is you?" she said with relief. And she immediately fell into her ironic tone: "Mr. Wheels on the lookout? And where are your young heroes?"

"Please don't call me Mr. Wheels," I growled. She asked the coachman to stop the horse.

"I've arrived!" she said, handing the man a bill. "This is the person I was looking for!" And then, turning to me, she said: "How nice of you to wait for me!"

She jumped down from the cart. She had a tiny suitcase in her hand.

"I was not waiting for you at all," I said.

"Oh? That's unfortunate," she sighed. "Nevertheless, I am very happy to have found you. I was worried that I might not find your campsite in the dark."

"You are—coming to see us?" I was aghast.

"Of course! Hadn't we agreed that I would share the tent with Eve?"

"Well, yes. But then you disappeared mysteriously."

"There was nothing mysterious about it. I simply went to Warsaw on business. But here I am."

"Miss Anka," I said with great seriousness. "Please be honest with me. Are you in cahoots with Malinovski?"

She burst out laughing.

"You've become like Mr. Petersen! *Are you Malinovski?*" Naturally, I am Malinovski. I have a mustache and a beard!"

"Don't laugh this off. I guess you already know what happened to Karen when she went the fiftieth kilometer?"

"How should I know? I'm coming from Warsaw. But I hope you're going to tell me that Miss Petersen eloped with Malinovski and is never coming back."

"How can you say that," I became indignant. "Malinovski took Karen's gold watch and diamond brooch. He wanted to take the ring off her hand, too, but luckily, I got there just in time."

"As was to be expected. A noble knight rescued a damsel in distress! Again."

"And do you know who this Malinovski is?" I said, looking into her face and hoping to see some sign of confusion.

"Who? I'm very curious to know."

"Your friend. The motorcyclist. Mr. Hamster."

She took my words with total calm. She shrugged her shoulders.

"He is not my friend, but only a young fellow who took me by motorcycle from Ghiby to Malbork. He tried to flirt with me, yes, but that's all. And besides, you are wrong. He is not Malinovski."

"No. How can you be so sure?"

"Because I know who Malinovski is," she said. "Or, more precisely, I think I can *prove* who the real Malinovsky is. No. I will not tell you," she anticipated my question. "I leave you the mystery of the treasure while I unmask the villain. As for Mr. Hamster, remember an essential detail: Malinovski was in Paris and tricked Petersen there. And the young man with a *Yunak* has never been to Paris, indeed, has never traveled abroad at all. Anyway, why am I explaining all these details to you? I'm sleepy and tired. Now, please take me to your camp."

What was I supposed to do? I took her to the lake and woke up Eve, who took her into her tent.

My head was in chaos. At night, I dreamt of Malinovski, who had the face of the priest from Kortumovo and wore a cassock.

"Yes, yes, Mr. Wheels," said Father Malinovski. "I took the Templar treasure from the dungeon yesterday, and for you, I have left only empty chests."

In the morning, I was awakened by the booming voice of Captain Petersen. He and his daughter had come to wash up at the lake and discovered our camp.

"Mr. Wheels!" cried Karen angrily, looking inside the vehicle, where I was still lying in the embrace of sleep. "Will I never be free of your company again?"

I got out of the car.

"I'm very sorry," I said, shaking her hand. "But I was here first. It rather seems to me that it is I who can not free myself from your company."

Petersen patted me on the back.

"It's great to see you. Let's get Malinovski."

Kozlovski arrived with a pail in hand.

The boys, Eve and Anka, emerged from their tents.

"There is nothing left for you to do here," said Tell to Karen. "Mr. Wheels found the Templar treasure yesterday, and though we begged him, he left nothing for you. Not one scrap."

When Kozlovski translated Tell's words for Karen, she burst out laughing:

"You terrible, terrible boys! Mr. Wheels is a very bad influence on you. And you are not surprised by our arrival?" she turned to me.

"No. Not at all. I have known since yesterday that you were here. But I'm well-mannered and don't pay nocturnal visits."

"Do you hear, Karen?" triumphed Petersen. "I told you that Mr. Wheels has been here for a while."

Miss Karen didn't say anything—she just got busy washing up. We, too, saw to our morning toilet. And any stranger watching us from outside would have thought that we were a company of friends.

"We will drop in on you after breakfast," I said, wiping my face, "because we intend to investigate the ruins in the forest today."

"No way. You have no right to those ruins," Karen said sharply. "They belong to me. I live there."

"But I was there first."

"So what? Did you stake out a claim? No, you camped *here*. You camped here, so you search here," she said mischievously, waving with her hand in the direction of the lake, the church, and the rectory. "And our camp is *there*, and we will search *there*. I think it best if everybody sticks to their area."

I pretended to be thinking of a reply. In truth, this was the deal I had been aiming for, but I didn't want to make it obvious.

Before I could reply, Anka interjected:

"Mr. Thomas, are you going to let her trick you again?"

Petersen said:

"I think you, Mr. Wheels, and I should really be looking for Malinovski."

I pointed to Anka.

"Malinovski is an area of search reserved for this lady. You must work with her."

"Oh, yes?" beamed the captain. "Have you also been duped by this scoundrel?"

"Yes," I said. "He promised to marry her and did not keep his word."

Anka scooped up water in a bowl and splashed it on me.

"What a loser! I would have never walked out on such a beautiful lady," Kozlovski said politely.

"Thank you, sir," Anka smiled at him. "I am glad someone here has refined manners."

"However, let me express my astonishment," said Kozlovski, "that Mr. Wheels has assigned the most dangerous area of investigation to you."

"Oh, but with an opponent like Miss Karen, treasure hunting can be very dangerous, too," I replied.

"Oh, don't make such a monster of me," chuckled Karen. "I appreciate your virtues, and I even like you a little."

Captain Petersen turned to Anka.

"I am very pleased to have such a charming partner. Can I really count on your help?" he asked.

"Absolutely," Anka said. "You can count on my wit. I, on the other hand, hope to count on your strong shoulder."

"Oh, yes, I still have a little strength left in me," boasted the captain, showing off his biceps.

"All brains and brawn, aren't we? But so far, it is Malinovski who is on top," Kozlovski deadpanned.

"It won't be long now. Very soon," said Anka. "I am much closer to the truth about him than it may seem."

I said:

"Then we have sorted out our areas of research. Mr. Petersen and Miss Anka will take care of Malinovski. Miss Karen and Mr. Kozlovski will search for treasures in the ruins in the forest. And me, the boys, and Eve will take care of the area by the lake and the church."

"There you go! You fell for Miss Karen's tricks again!" cried Anka.

"Are you perhaps jealous?" Miss Petersen asked. And she nodded at Kozlovski, signaling to him that it was time to go to work. As they walked away, they spoke amongst themselves. A scrap of a sentence reached my ears.

"He agreed to my proposal too easily. This is suspicious. What's with the church?"

We ate breakfast in a hurry. It was obvious to us that from now on, every hour would count. If the Templar treasure was located in Kortumovo, it would belong to whoever found it first. Immediately after breakfast, the kids and I went to the rectory. Anka, on the other hand, went to the Petersens' camp to—as she said—hold a council of war with the captain.

We met the housekeeper in the garden. She was hanging altar boys' pinafores on a clothesline.

"We decided to get down to insulating the basement," said Hawkeye, saluting her in a scouting manner.

"Will it take a very long time?" she worried.

"We will finish by the end of the day for sure," William Tell stated categorically.

We saw Mr. Kozlovski coming from the church towards us.

"Oh, Mr. Kozlovski!" exclaimed Hawkeye joyfully. "Mr. Konfiturski!"

"What? Who is Mr. Konfiturski? That's not a name, is it?" the housekeeper asked, surprised.

"Naturally, that is not a name. This gentleman is an acquaintance of ours from Malbork. We nicknamed him "Mr. Konfiturski" because he is terribly fond of jams and preserves. When he sees a jar of jam, he begins to shake all over with gluttony. Completely unlike us, ma'am. We get nauseous at the sight of jam."

"I understand," nodded the hostess. "There are some people who do not like sweets. And there are those who are fond of sweets. For example, our priest is very fond of tea with jam. That's why every year I prepare a lot of jam for him. I have all those jars, all lined up in the cellar—you will see. I did not take them out because why should I? You boys don't like sweets."

"No. We are totally nauseated by sweets," the boys confirmed in a chorus.

"And you?" she suspiciously glanced at me.

"I hate jam," I said, putting my hand on my heart.

And then, the housekeeper took the key to the cellar out of her apron pocket and handed it to Hawkeye.

"And there will be no more stray currents?" she made sure.

"Not even one," promised Hawkeye. "Neither wandering nor standing. Because you should know that there are also standing currents. Besides, you know, there are also sea currents and air currents."

She raised her hands in protest.

"Oh, don't even tell me! You go to it. Insultate as soon as possible. And don't let me burn my hand on the padlock again!"

We nodded politely and walked into the garden. When we were obscured by the currant bushes, we stopped and cautiously looked out from behind the thicket. We saw Mr. Kozlovski approaching the housekeeper.

He bowed politely and asked:

"Would you be so kind as to inform me to whom the cellar in the garden belongs?"

The housekeeper put her hands on her hips and barked out:

"It belongs to me!"

"To you?" Kozlovski was visibly pleased. "I am very interested in the architecture of this basement. It seems to me extremely ancient. Would you be kind enough to lend me the key? I would like to take a peek."

"What?" the housekeeper was profoundly upset. "You want what? The key? To my cellar?!"

"Oh, don't get me wrong, I very much want to learn about its architecture."

"Architecture? Or *confitecture*?" shouted the housekeeper, now seriously angry. "Oh, I know you, sir! I have been warned about you and my jams! Oh, I have heard about you, Mr. Konfiturski!"

"But my name is Kozlovski, not Konfiturski!" Mr Kozlovski tried to explain. But the housekeeper was now past all argument:

"I know that Konfiturski is not your name. You are only called that because you are very fond of jam and confiture."

"But no, you are wrong! I'm all about architecture. I will gladly pay to see your basement!"

"You are not fooling me, Mr. Konfiturski," said the housekeeper.

Finally, Kozlovski also became angry.

"Ma'am! Have you lost your mind?" he shouted. "I offer you money to see your basement, and you carry on about some confiture!"

"Mind? Have I lost my mind? Goodness gracious! Some

nutcase shows up here and insults an honest woman!"

She was so furious now that Kozlovski decided to make a strategic retreat. But the housekeeper remained on the battlefield for a while, cursing and shaking her fist.

"Well, at last, we got rid of Konfiturski for a while," I said, choking with laughter. We stood in front of the iron door of the basement. Hawkeye took command:

"Squirrel will stay here, keeping an eye on things. He can play spit-and-catch or pretend he's preparing the insulation material. And we will prowl among the jams and confitures."

He put the key in the padlock and turned it. We entered the basement.

At first, we were overwhelmed by darkness, but after a while, our eyes got used to the dim light. Some daylight came in through a narrow window, and it became quite bright once we turned on our electric flashlights. We saw a low, vaulted ceiling supported by two thick stone pillars.

"Guys, this place was not built as a basement," I said. "I think it was supposed to be some kind of a meeting hall."

We saw smooth walls of brown brick, here and there recesses of some kind, and shelves and shelves of jars of jam, preserves, and confitures, and rows and rows of dusty wine bottles. In the corners of the cellar stood crumbling crates and decaying barrels. And in the left back corner was a wellhead covered with wooden planks.

Carefully, lest one of us slip and fall into the well, we took off the planks, board by board. A cool, moist, musty smell hit our nostrils. The beams of light from our flashlights reflected on the surface of the water down below, some good thirty feet away. A pebble thrown into the depths made a loud splash.

I don't know why we were overwhelmed by an unpleasant feeling of foreboding, as if we were looking not into a well but into a bottomless abyss, yawning with cold and horror. Leaning over the well, the boys abruptly straightened up and moved away.

"The most ordinary musty well," stated Hawkeye. "And in general, I see nothing interesting in this cellar except jam."

We put the boards back into their former place. Eve swept her torchlight over the large cobweb hanging over the well.

The dungeons of the Teutonic Castle in Brodnitsa (Polish: Brodnica)
were probably the inspiration for the housekeeper's cellar.

"My goodness!" she exclaimed. "That's a serious spider-web! And, oh,
what is that? Look! There is a sign on the wall!"

Tell ran out to the garden and brought a broken branch. He
used it to wipe the spider web away.

"This is not a sign. It's just a line," Eve was disappointed.

"But at the end of the line, a litle to the left, is a tiny rectangle.
Moment... moment..." I reached into my pocket for my notebook.

"Ha! There it is! Do you know what a dash with a rectangle
means? According to Miss Karen, it says *nine yards*. Do you remember
what Karen told us at the Goat Market? She'd seen the sign in some
French castle."

"I see the line, yes. But I don't see any rectangle," said Eve.

"There it is! Take a close look!" exclaimed Hawkeye. "There is
the rectangle! Right there!"

The lights of our flashlights began to wander along the walls. It
turned out that the walls were not as smooth as they had seemed. Here
and there, under a layer of dust, we could see cracks and crevices, which,
to our excited imagination, suddenly became Templar signs.

And then, on one of the stone pillars supporting the vault,

236

Hawkeye saw... a triangle.

"Is this the triangle of Peter of Avignon?" he asked quietly.

And we all gave a joyful shriek, so loud that Squirrel, busy outside "preparing insulation materials," ran into the basement alarmed.

"Calm down, calm down!" I admonished them. "The most important thing is the sign above the well. Nine yards. What do you think that means?"

The housekeeper arrived, probably concerned about her jams.

"I heard a scream, so I thought something happened here," she explained. Hawkeye's reaction was lightning-fast:

"We discovered the main vein of the stray current. It runs from the well. This will be more difficult than we thought," he shook his head with great concern,

"But can you manage?" she worried. "How about calling someone from the city? Some specialist engineer?"

"A specialist?" squawked Hawkeye contemptuously. "Do you think they know about stray currents? These specialists do not believe in the existence of such currents at all!"

"Well, well," she nodded appreciatively. "Our parish priest will be very surprised when I tell him about this."

"It would be better if you don't tell him," I became worried.

"And why? Do you think he won't believe you? He is a wise and honorable man."

"Not every wise and noble person believes in stay currents," I said. "I know a lot of learned people who think it's all nonsense."

"Yes, you are right," admitted the housekeeper. "Well, I'm off to the rectory. I have to cook lunch."

She left. I said to Hawkeye:

"If you don't stop clowning around, I'm going to get mad. I don't see any reason to keep on fooling this good-hearted woman."

"It's just for now," the boy defended himself. "It's all about finding the treasure, yes? I promise that once we find it, I will confess and explain everything to the housekeeper. And I will apologize. I give you my word."

William Tell prudently diverted the conversation to another

topic.

"Nine yards, you say? I measured it. It is exactly nine yards from the well to the opposite corner of the basement. So that's where we need to start looking."

"You go right ahead," I said, rolling my eyes. "Haven't you noticed that this dash is pointing *downward*?"

"Actually, yes, you are right. It is pointing down," said Tell.

"Down," I stressed. "And the sign is right above the well. So, presumably, the idea would be to look nine yards *down the well*."

"In the water?" asked astonished Hawkeye. "Do you suppose the treasure is in the water?"

"The sign says *nine yards*, and it looks like the water table is lower than that."

"So what do we do?" asked Tell.

"I will use a rope and descend into the well."

I gave him no time to cool down from his astonishment. I started giving orders:

"Hawkeye! You run to the car to get the rope. There is a coil of rope in the trunk. Tell will stand lookout because it is time to relieve Squirrel—he really does talk too much."

I noticed Tell's silent protest. I put my hand on his shoulder.

"It is quite possible that we stand before the most important moment of our expedition. The success of it will depend on two people. On the one who lowers himself down the rope into the depths of the well and on the one who stands watch. You are going to lock us up inside."

"What do you mean: lock you up?"

"I mean, you will padlock the place and hide the key deep in your pocket. You'll sit in the garden and keep a watchful eye on what's going on in the neighborhood. We must have absolute freedom of action in the basement for a few hours. I will go down into the well, and Hawkeye, Squirrel, and Eve will remain on top to support me if necessary. Do you understand? Kozlovski has already sniffed something out. He asked for the key, but he didn't achieve his goal, so he probably went back to Karen and informed her about it. What do you think she will do now?"

"She will try to get into the cellar," Tell said.

"That's right. You must not let them cotton on that you have the key. If they ask about us, tell them we went to the forest because we discovered some interesting ruins there."

"I get it. Well, Mr. Wheels, you can rest assured that Karen will not get into the cellar," vowed Tell. Just at that moment, Hawkeye ran in carrying a thick coil of rope.

"Lock us up!" I ordered Tell.

We heard the bang of the iron door. Then, there was the clatter of a key being turned in the padlock.

CHAPTER EIGHTEEN: TRAPPED

I descend into the depths of the well. In the trap of the Knights Templar. The mystery of the old baptismal font. Nine yards down.

From the circular opening of the well wafted darkness and a cool, musty smell. I laid the thickest of the wooden planks across the opening. I made a dozen or so knots on the rope, tied it to the plank, and prepared to climb down.

"You will stay here and wait for my instructions," I said.

Hanging an electric flashlight around my neck, I grabbed the rope and hovered in the well.

Even though I am not particularly athletic, going down was not difficult. Time and again, I found indentations in the brickwork—as if specially prepared for my feet. From time to time, I turned around and studied the walls of the well. The well had been built in the same way as the rest of the basement—of thick medieval "fingerprint" brick.

"What do you see? What do you see?" the kids' impatient questions came from above.

Their voices rang out in the well as if someone somewhere nearby pounded a piece of iron with a hammer.

"So far, nothing!" I reported.

I had probably four meters of embrasure overhead when I noticed that the walls around me began to widen. I hung onto the rope, supporting myself with my back against the damp wall, while I searched for another depression with my feet. Another thick knot slipped through my fingers. I sank one yard more into the dark funnel of the well.

Suddenly, I wobbled on the rope. My feet, with which I had been bracing myself against the wall, found no support. My hands were numb from exertion—I now hung on them with all my weight. I could hear my accelerated breathing. I was soon wheezing with fatigue. I pinched the rope between my knees and slowly slid down, feeling the rough fibers abrade the skin of my hands.

Another thick knot slipped between my fingers. Suddenly, my

feet found support. In the dark, right in front of me, I saw a narrow opening. My feet were resting on a ledge in front of it.

"Yoohoo, kiddoes!" my voice boomed and echoed up the well. "I found a landing! There is a passage here just big enough for a man. You wait upstairs until I return. Wait for two hours if it comes to that."

"What if you do not return after two hours?" Eve asked sensibly.

"Ok. Let's say this: you wait ten hours. And if I am still not back, you run to the militia," I shouted.

I stepped onto the ledge before me and saw an underground passage disappearing into the wall. Its entrance was so low and narrow that even on all fours, I struggled to squeeze in. The passage did not continue straight, but turned now left now right, now descended a little, now rose again. I quickly lost all sense of direction.

Then, there was a ramp leading up again. And another one going down. Then, a turn and the passage widened into a semicircular cavern. Like the basement and the well, it was made of fingerprint brick. In the beam of my flashlight, I saw a door in the wall ahead. Heavy, iron, with a tarnish of rust.

It was a strange door. It was hung at an angle, more like a sloping trapdoor than a door. Next to it was an iron wheel. I grabbed it and tried to turn it with all my might. But either the flap was too heavy, or maybe the hinges got rusty: it took a lot of struggle to lift the flap an inch. With a great effort, I managed to open it just wide enough to slide my hands in. Only now was I able to lift it to the accompaniment of unpleasant rasping and squeaking. Interestingly, this rasping did not come from the hinges—it came from the wall. It seemed as if the opening of the door activated some mechanism hidden inside.

Only after I opened the flap did I realize that there was no way to block it open. The moment I let go, it would fall with a tremendous bang and slam the opening shut. By design, it could not be tilted at an angle greater than forty-five degrees, and by the sheer force of its weight, it fell back into its former position. But behind it, I could see stairs leading down and disappearing behind a bend in the wall.

I held up the flap with my hands and slipped, feet first, into the narrow gap. My eyes and nose were irritated by the dust that lay thick everywhere here. Standing at the top of the stairs and holding the flap up with my hands, I found myself wishing I had something with me that I could put under the trap door to hold it ajar. But nothing came to mind. The moment I let go, the trap door would close. For a moment, I thought about going back to the well and asking the kids to pass me some object with which to block the flap, but I was very eager to advance and decided that when I wanted to get out, I should be able to just lift the flap with my arms again.

I lowered the flap. It slammed with a loud clatter. Slowly, in the light of my flashlight, I began to descend down the stairs. I counted eight steps, then there was a bend, the staircase narrowed, and the steps began to ascend. I began to climb up. One step... two steps... eight steps... ten steps, and I found myself in a narrow cell, something like the penitential cell I had seen in Malbork Castle.

I swept its walls with my flashlight and—almost screamed in shock. There was a skeleton sitting across from me! Good grief! Leaning against the wall sat the remains of a man with shreds of decayed clothing on his limbs and the remnants of hair still on his skull.

But what I found most terrifying was not the skeleton itself but the position in which it lay. It was curled up in a ball, bizarrely contorted as if the man had died in great agony. I suddenly remembered the legend of the peasant who had entered the underworld and never returned. He probably found his way down the stairwell, like me, and ended up here. But why didn't he go back the way he had come out?

I broke out in a cold sweat. Only now did I realize that the cell was blind. It had no other opening.

Why didn't this man go back the way he came? the thought came back to me.

I was overwhelmed by increasing anxiety. I almost ran back down then up the steps and reached for the iron flap. I propped it up with all my strength. It didn't even budge. I leaned my back against it, set my feet against the wall, and pushed like the devil. My heart was pounding, and sweat started running down my forehead.

But the flap remained unmoved.

I now remembered the strange rasping that accompanied the opening of the flap. Some kind of mechanism was activated in the wall when one used the wheel. It allowed the flap to be unbolted from that side but prevented it from being lifted from underneath. The iron door was—a trap.

I became breathless and hot with terror.

Now I understood why the skeleton in the cell was lying in such a horrifying position. The man had died of hunger and thirst. He entered but never managed to leave. *No one gets out of here alive*, I thought with fear. *Me, neither.*

Once again, I tried to lift the iron lid. I was drenched with sweat again and had to rest for a long time before the pounding in my ears caused by excessive effort finally stopped. I did not manage to lift the lid even a millimeter.

I returned to the cell where the skeleton lay. Various pieces of information I had read about the Templars, about the secret passageways they built, the trapdoors, the hiding places, the traps prepared for those who tried to penetrate the secrets of the order were flying through my head like a murder of angry crows.

Why didn't it occur to me that the treasure would be protected by a trap? I should have been more careful! I was furious with myself. And at the same time, I tried to console myself: the Knights Templar were masters at building secret passages. There has to be an exit from this cell. Hidden. Only for those who know. This fellow didn't find it, and that's why he died of hunger and thirst. But I will find my way out. And, at any rate, after ten hours have passed, the kids would notify the militia. And the militia would lower themselves on a rope to the porch, unhook the iron trapdoor, and free me from the underground.

And then, suddenly...

Tap... Tap... Tap...

I heard slow tapping on the ceiling.

No. It wasn't tapping. Someone was *walking* overhead. Someone in high heels. The vaulted ceiling, unlike the smooth walls made of brown brick, was made of sandstone slabs and resounded with a loud echo of the footsteps. Also made of sandstone was a smooth pilaster half buried into the wall in the left corner. It had a large, round capital, which supported the vault.

I now seemed to hear the murmur of a conversation. I shouted loudly once and twice. But the strange acoustics of the room transformed my voice into an indistinct, pitiful moan. It was a sound so awful that I did not try to call for help again.

I understood. The story that Squirrel had reported was true. The man whose skeleton lay at my feet had heard human voices above him and cried out for help. His were the groans of the "damned souls." And they were heard in the church, which meant... which meant that my cell lay under the floor of the church! After all, the floor in the church was made of sandstone slabs!

Peter of Avignon had constructed the trap in such a way that whoever found himself in it could hear human voices coming in through some hidden openings in the ceiling, but his own voice came out in the form of an indistinct murmur. This increased the torment of the trapped: they could hear but could not be heard.

I studied the walls of the room in the light of my flashlight. In vein. Nowhere did I see any sign, indentation, or protrusion that might offer hope that it concealed a trap-opening mechanism. The walls were smooth, built of tightly fit bricks. None of the bricks wobbled or could be moved. The floor was the same: a smooth surface made of bricks. Only the ceiling was made of sandstone slabs, but I could not reach the ceiling, it was too high. Efforts to climb the wall proved futile.

One hour passed, then another. From time to time, I turned off the flashlight so that the battery would not die. The darkness that fell then had a very depressing effect on me. The proximity of the crumbling skeleton was deeply unpleasant. For although I was aware that after ten hours, my friends would begin a rescue operation, in the dark, I gave in to the feeling that I would never get out and would die in here agony.

Again, I heard the clatter of women's shoes overhead. This was followed by heavy, rumbling footsteps. The murmur of voices intensified, and I began to distinguish individual words and even whole sentences. The conversation took place in English, probably right near one of the openings in my trap.

"Why are you so anxious?" I heard Karen's voice.

"We left the camper and the tent unattended in the woods. I am worried about them. And the captain and this journalist have just left with the car," Kozlovski said. "Do you know where they went?"

"They are looking for Malinovski."

"What? Is there a plan?"

"They didn't tell me about it. Stop bothering me about that business. Did you see the sign on the church wall? It is the work of the Templars. It means *an underground vault.*"

"Well, if that is a sign of Knights Templar, then these signs are everywhere. Hundreds of churches, chapels, even private houses bear the same sign in this country. I think we should hire twenty workers and dig up the ruins in the woods."

"And I think the treasure is here," Karen stomped her foot above me. "Take a good look around the church. It is from the early 14th century. But all its furnishings were done in much later times, in the Baroque era. Only the walls, the floor, and this sandstone baptismal font are from the time of Peter of Avignon. Do you see the ornament circling the baptismal font?"

"Looks to me like ordinary cross-hatching."

"Well, yes. That's what it was all about, to make such things seem unremarkable, unnoticeable to ordinary mortals. But this hatching forms a sign: *be vigilant.*

"You have a very fertile imagination! Meanwhile, Malinovski will rob our camp," grumbled Kozlovski. "What do you want to do? This baptismal font is embedded in the floor."

"Please look down here!" exclaimed Karen. "There is an opening in the base of the baptismal font. What was it made for? What do you think?"

"I am sure I have no idea."

"Bring me a rod."

"Huh?"

"Yes. A rod. I want a metal rod to put into this hole and try to turn the font."

"Are you planning to demolish the church? This font must weigh a ton!"

"I ask you to do what I told you to do."

Stomping footsteps marched off into the distance. Kozlovski had gone off to look for a suitable rod.

I sat on the hard floor of the dark cell and thought:

Karen is the smartest, cleverest girl I have met in my life. If she frees me from this trap, I will agree to cooperate with her. All she had to do was walk into this church and—presto!—see how many details she noticed immediately. And I'd been there so many times and only noticed the sign for an underground vault.

As I pondered in this way, Kozlovski returned. He must have brought a suitable rod because Karen immediately set to work.

"Please look about to make sure no one is around," Karen said. "Stangrers might think we are vandalizing the church."

"No, there is no one. It's noon, the men are working in the field, and the women are cooking.

"And Mr. Wheels?" she asked.

"I have not seen him all morning. Neither him nor the scouts. Only one of them sitting near that cellar in the orchard playing a game of knives."[8]

"Playing a game by himself? That's is very suspicious. I wonder where they all disappeared to? Anyway, let's get on with this."

Now, I heard a crunching sound. It came from above, from the left corner of the room, where a sandstone column stood embedded in the wall.

Dear God! I thought. *The capital of that column is the base of the baptismal font!*

"Come on, Mr Kozlovski, press harder. Haven't you had breakfast today?" Karen commented angrily.

It heard that whirr again. The pilaster in the corner slowly turned, and a beam of light shone into my room from above. Another moment, another shove, and the beam expanded. A large triangular opening appeared in the corner. Interestingly, as the pilaster turned, it revealed a dozen recesses. One could climb it like a ladder.

"So here it is! We found the hidden entrance to the underworld!" whispered Karen.

I retreated deeper into the cell as Karen shone the light of her

---

[8] A game of skill using a knife, which involves sticking the knife into the ground after performing a specific trick.

electric flashlight through the opening.

"Well, go on. Climb down," Karen said to Kozlovski.

"Me? Why should I go down first? I'm not looking for treasures. You are."

"What a coward you are," laughed the girl, and she boldly slid down the steps on the column. She stood on the floor, turned, and pointed her flashlight at me.

"Oh my God! Someone is here!" she screamed.

I bowed politely:

"My respects to young Miss!"

"Mr.—Mr. Wheels!" she gasped with a mixture of surprise and anger.

"In the flesh," I said.

"How on earth...?" She was lost for words. "How did you get here? And have you found anything? Where is the treasure?"

I shrugged.

"So far, I have only found a dead man," I said, and I pointed to the skeleton.

"That's right!" she whispered in horror, studying the skeleton in the light of her flashlight.

But she quickly overcame her initial shock. She noticed the opening in the wall through which I had come and boldly plunged into it. I took the opportunity to scamper up the column and out into the church.

"Well, well! And how is your day going, Mr. Wheels?" Kozlovski asked. "And what is down below?"

"Why don't you go down and see for yourself?" I said.

"Is there treasure?"

"Nope."

"Then why should I get dirty crawling in there? I'm wearing the wrong clothes for this."

We waited for a while before Karen's fair-haired head appeared in the opening of the underground.

"There is an iron trap door further on, but there is no way to open it," she said with disappointment in her voice.

"That door slammed shut behind me as I came this way."

"You came this way? You mean you did not get there by the baptismal font? How did you get there?"

I said solemnly:

"Miss Karen. I am grateful to you for freeing me from the trap. I have great admiration for you. And that is why I have decided to accept your proposal and work with you. We will search for the Templar treasure together."

I caught a momentary glint of satisfaction in Karen's eyes. But after a moment, distrust appeared on her face.

"What happened, Mr. Wheels? Have you suddenly come to distrust your abilities?" she mocked. "You have rejected my proposals to cooperate so many times, and now suddenly there is a change? Now you offer me cooperation? When I am one step away from the treasure? Oh, no, Mr. Wheels. Now, I will do without your help."

"Well, I decided to offer you my cooperation because you freed me from this trap. I owe you a debt of gratitude," I explained.

"Is that so? Then all the more reason for me not to accept your help. You have rescued me from trouble twice: at the Goat Market and at the fiftieth kilometer. At last, I have repaid my debt of gratitude. We are even, Mr. Wheels. And now, help me slide this font back."

I helped. But I did not say another word, deeply affected by the affront she had done to me. We parted in front of the church. I went to the garden crypt, and Karen and Kozlovski to their camp in the woods.

"Is that you, Mr. Wheels?" whispered Tell fearfully. "Haven't I just locked you up in the basement?"

"Yes, you have! But it seems that I have learned to penetrate walls since then!"

I greeted the kids sitting at the wellhead. They grumbled when I told them how my adventure had ended. But they were very impressed by the story of the skeleton.

"Will we be able to see it?" they asked with great excitement.

"Of course! But we will enter by way of the baptismal font. Not now, though. I've had enough of the underworld for one day," I said. "You can take the key back to the housekeeper. We won't need it anymore."

I felt tired. The hours spent in the dark, searching in great suspense for a way out of the trap, have taken their toll. All I dreamed of now was to spread out on the grass on the shore of the lake, rest, and breathe in the fresh air.

The boys prepared dinner, but I was not hungry. I soon fell asleep and woke up some hours later. Meanwhile, it became hot and stuffy—another summer storm was brewing. In the evening, torrents of water poured from the sky, and the kids took shelter in their tent. Darkness fell faster than usual, and the sound of rain encouraged sleep. Our camp plunged into silence and only I kept vigil in my car, refreshed and rested after my afternoon nap.

At eleven o'clock, a figure wrapped in a huge raincoat appeared next to my car. It was very dark and pouring rain, so only when she knocked on the window of the vehicle did I recognize Anka.

"Have you seen Karen or Kozlovski?" she asked. "We have just returned from Gdansk, but we found neither Karen nor Kozlovski at the camp. The trailer is locked up, Kozlovski's tent is laced up. Captain Petersen is very worried about his daughter."

"She is looking for treasure," I yawned.

"And you?"

"I am listening to the rain and meditating."

She shrugged, indignant at my sloth, and went to tell Petersen that Karen was not with us.

The rain rattled monotonously on the roof of my car. In my mind, I relived the breakneck trek down the rope into the depths of the well and then through the underground corridor. I kept thinking that I must have made a mistake during my trek. I missed some detail somewhere, which is how I ended up in a trap.

"And yet I did as the sign said," I contemplated. "Nine yards into the well..."

I suddenly sat up. I tossed the blanket off. I hastily pulled on my pants and, disregarding the rain, jumped out of the vehicle.

Nine yards? I certainly had not lowered myself nine yards. I had gone six yards at most!

I grabbed a few things and dashed off. I ran through the priests' garden, rain pouring on my head. I reached the cellar soaked to my underwear and suddenly realized that it was padlocked: I had told the boys to return the key to the rectory. Further exploration had to wait until the following day.

Troubled by an indefinable feeling of unease, I glared at the basement door. The padlock hung loose, the lock had been broken, probably with the crowbar that lay at my feet. Someone had broken into the basement.

Who?

I had no doubt. It was the work of Karen and Kozlovski. They failed to get the key from the housekeeper and decided to break in. And now they were probably wandering through the underground corridor, and in a moment, Karen would find herself trapped, just as had happened to me.

"Miss Karen!" I called out, entering the cellar. I was hoping she had not yet lowered herself into the well.

But a deafening silence answered me. I had come too late. A thick rope hung dangling from a plank thrown across the mouth of the well. Karen and Kozlovski were probably in the underground corridor or had been trapped already. My first thought was that they could be freed by turning the baptismal font. But then I realized that the church was locked at night.

I will go through the underground corridor, open the trapdoor, and call Karen. That way, I can free them, I justified my action to myself as I grabbed the rope and slid down it into the well.

This time, I did it much faster and much more skillfully than in the morning. In a few moments I found myself near the opening to the underground passage.

Suddenly, the rope began to vibrate alarmingly. I looked up, and seeing nothing, I shone my flashlight. And... I was stunned.

In the opening of the well, high above my head, I saw a pair of human hands. The light of the flashlight reflected on the blade of a knife.

"Stop! What are you doing!" I shouted.

But the person, whoever it was, cut the rope.

Screaming, I plunged into the depths.

CHAPTER NINETEEN: ALL MYSTERIES SOLVED

A murderer. Where does this secret corridor lead? The trapdoor. One step away from the treasure. Where is Karen? All mysteries solved. The militia.

I hit the water with a huge splash. For a moment, the cold depths swallowed me, but I quickly regained the surface. I found myself in a spotlight: someone was shining a flashlight from above. Whoever was there, was checking was checking what had happened to me.

But—as I said—the well had been shaped like a funnel opening wide towards the bottom. I swam to the wall and disappeared from the field of vision of whoever was on top. And not a moment too soon: a huge splash blew up right next to me: whoever was at the top, a man or a woman, had just dropped a huge boulder into the well. It hit the surface exactly where my head had been just seconds ago. It could have shattered my skull. Whoever that was—the person at the mouth of the well, was—a murderer.

I pressed flush against the wall, trying to keep out of sight. Meanwhile, he (or she?) brought another stone and threw it into the well again. Then, he (or she) shone his (or her) flashlight for a long time, looking for me in the water. Not seeing me, the killer must have assumed that I had gone to the bottom with my head crashed into a pulp because there were no more boulders.

I was a good swimmer, and I kept myself afloat with small movements of my arms and legs, hoping not to disturb the surface of the water. But the water in the well was very cold.

How long can I stay afloat?

In the dark, I tried to feel along the walls of the well with my hands, looking for some protrusion or indentation that I could cling onto.

"Nine yards," I repeated to myself. "It was supposed to be nine yards. And here I am, I think, at the nine-yard level."

And then, my outstretched hand came upon the edge of a large opening. I grabbed onto the ledge and drove my fingers into the hard surface of the bricks. They were slimy, covered with damp residue. My hands kept slipping. Each time I tried to pull myself up, I slid back into the water.

My fingers were numb, I broke my nails. One more effort, one more attempt to lift myself into the hole, and again—I slid back into the water, this time with a loud splash. I waited anxiously to see if any more rocks would fall from above, but all was quiet. Perhaps the murderer had already left the cellar?

I waited a little. I managed to slip off my shoes—shoes really suck you under. But this was not an easy operation and time and again, I dipped under the water and took a drink. I threw my shoes into the hole I intended to climb into. Only now did I renew my attempt to climb up. And this time, it turned out easier than I had thought. My toes found support in the little spaces between the bricks. All I had to do was push off with one leg, and this greatly relieved my hands.

I was short of breath, blood throbbed in my temples, but here I was, in the opening of an underground passage very similar to the one three yards higher. That one had led to a trap. And this one?

I must be very careful, I admonished myself. *If any trap door slams shut behind me now, no one will ever see me again. No one will ever suspect that there were two underground corridors here, one on top of another. And no one knows that I am here except the killer overhead.*

I crawled a few steps on the slimy, wet floor. I put my shoes back on and tried to see if my flashlight worked. Surprisingly, the bath hadn't hurt it: after I gave it a shake, it gave the same powerful light as always.

Another moment of rest. I could not predict what adventures awaited me ahead. It seemed necessary to gather strength.

I thought of the person at the top of the well. Who was he? Or she? Why did he (or she) try to kill me?

A moment of rest passed. I rose from the damp floor and moved deeper into the corridor. Just like the passage higher up, this one, too, had several turns. And again, there were steps going up and up. I counted twenty-five.

The corridor narrowed, then widened; its ceiling lowered and rose; and suddenly—a surprise: the passage forked. One branch ran to the left and the other to the right. Both looked the same. So which one to choose?

I went to the right.

The corridor continued for about thirty paces and ended in... a blind wall. When I put my ear to it, I seemed to hear a quiet hum, as if I were inside a huge sea shell. Fresh, moist air was seeping through the cracks between the bricks. I poked about what seemed to me a loose brick and—surprise, surprise—managed... to take it out!

Putting my eye to the opening, I saw the rain-whipped expanse of the lake. It was agitated by the wind, and waves were crashing against the steep shore. The passage reached all the way to the lake!

This could only mean one thing: whatever the builders of this complex had had in mind, their plan had been to build like Malbork: all the way to the water. And the corridor was meant to lead out of the complex. Many medieval castles had such secret passages to ensure a way for messengers to get in and out of the fortress in the event of a siege.

I retraced my path back to the fork and, this time took the passage to the left.

If that passage led to the lake, this one has to lead to the church, I thought.

I came upon a few steep steps up. Trying to orient myself, I studied the walls and saw a sign: a sort of "2" with two tails. I remember that sign from Karen's notes: it was a warning: *danger.*

I stopped to look about carefully. And not a moment too soon: ten feet ahead, there was an opening in the floor. Once, it had probably been covered by wooden planks, which collapsed when stepped upon by an uninitiated person, but over the centuries, the wood had rotted away, and I could see the rust-eaten remains of the sinkhole mechanism.

I gathered strength and jumped over the well, and continued my advance. Again, a few steep steps down and... I found my path blocked by an iron door framed by an ornate, carved portal. The iron was thick and solid. Rust had failed to take hold of it. It sat firmly in its stone frame. I saw neither a handle nor a keyhole nor any other opening device: it was a smooth plate set in a stone frame.

I studied the portal. It had been decorated with branches of vine as if growing out of the two columns. In the center of the ornament, there were two diagonally intersecting lines and one longer line crossing them horizontally.

I recognized the sign.

Ground level, it said.

I knelt down and examined the floor. It was made of brown bricks, as were the walls and ceiling. None of the bricks moved. But at the bottom of each column I found an opening the width of two fingers.

I remembered the mechanism of the baptismal font. The people who designed this underworld reckoned with many eventualities, above all, the fact that iron mechanisms rust and become difficult to manipulate. Templar mechanisms were based on the rather simple principle of a turnstile: a rod had to be inserted into a hollow, and then the column had to be turned using the rod as a lever. This had been the case with the baptismal font, the extension of which was the pilaster in the room below it.

I took out my knife, inserted its handle into the opening at the bottom of the right column, and tried to turn it first to the left and then to the right. As I pressed right with a great effort, the column began to budge. Inch by inch, it made a quarter turn to the right. As it turned, a stone making up a part of the bottom frame of the door slid aside.

I now did the same with the left column—I inserted my knife, but this time, I turned the column a quarter turn to the left. The remaining stone in the bottom section frame slid aside. The door was now free to open.

I pushed at the door, but it did not give way. I stopped to think for a moment and then remembered the trapdoor I had dealt with that morning. Did this door hang on hinges, too? If so, then, presumably, all I had to do was push it *at the bottom,* and it would swing open like a pendulum?

I did. It did.

I pushed, and it gave way.

But the pendulum has the property that, once moved away from the level, it immediately returns to it. What if I swung it open, pushed past this door, and it closed behind me like the trapdoor on the floor above had done that morning? I had to prevent the door from closing shut. It had to remain ajar so that I could get out again. All I had to do was leave a small gap, enough to slide in my hand.

I didn't have any item in my pocket that was suitable for this purpose. But apart from the electric flashlight, I only had my knife. I turned around and went back to the fork in the passage, took the right-hand passage to the end, and picked up the brick I had loosened from the wall. The whole operation took quite a long time, but now I had something to stop the door with.

I looked at my watch. It was almost three in the morning. I had been in the underground for almost four hours. How true was the old saying: time flies when you're having fun! I started worrying that the battery in my flashlight might give out. The light had gone from bright yellow to dull reddish.

At half past three in the morning, I swung the door open and blocked it with the brick. Sliding through, I found myself in a spacious square cell with a sandstone slab ceiling. Of course. This cell had to be under the old church in Kortumovo.

Straight ahead, I saw narrow stairs leading up and ending in—the wall. Literally, the stairs led into a solid brick wall.

How odd, I thought and climbed them. When I did, I found that my head reached the ceiling. Right next to my face, on the sandstone slab overhead, was an iron handle. Could the slab be raised?

Looking about in the dimming light of my dying flashlight, I discovered a mason's sign: a square divided by a vertical line. *Two treasures*, I whispered under my breath.

The mortar between the bricks surrounding the sign appeared to me to be slightly lighter in color than the mortar elsewhere in the room. Had someone smashed the wall and then patched the hole with new brick?

I took a deep breath.

I understood.

Behind this wall lay the Templar treasure.

It would take an iron crowbar—or a jackhammer—to get at it.

Carefully, using my handkerchief, I wiped the dust off the wall and wrote on the brick with a pencil:

THE TREASURE HIDDEN BEHIND THIS WALL WAS DISCOVERED BY MR. WHEELS AT FIVE IN THE MORNING ON 17 JULY 1962.

Now, all that was left to do was to get out of the underground. But do you realize how much effort it takes to lift a sandstone slab?

My pants and shirt had already dried on me during the several hours of wandering in the underground corridors. But by the time I finally managed to lift the slab with my shoulder and swing it aside, my shirt was once again wet with sweat, and red circles were spinning in my eyes. With what felt like the last reserve of my strength, I raised myself through the opening and found myself on the stone floor of the old church. I stretched on the cold floor and lay motionless, trying to catch my breath. Eventually, the cool of the floor seemed to revive me. I realized that I was lying behind the altar, with the pink light of the morning already seeping in through the high windows.

I slid the slab back into its place. It was no different from the others of which the floor was made. I made a tiny cross on it with my pencil to be able to identify it in the future. Then, tottering on bendy legs, I walked out from behind the altar.

A tiny, gray-haired old man, probably the sexton, was sweeping the floor between the pews. He saw me, dropped the broom, shouted "The Devil!" and ran out. I have to say, for an old man, he moved extraordinarily fast.

I went out. The gray-haired old man was running toward the rectory. I was still tottering on my feet, but the fresh air of the morning was restoring my strength with each passing moment. I marched to the lake, and the mirror surface of the water told me that my face, hands, shirt, and pants were as black as the devil's. I wore upon me the centuries-old dust of the underworld, where the treasures of the Templar order lay.

I threw off my clothes and jumped into the lake. While

swimming, I watched the shore with our tents and my trusty vehicle.

And then I remembered Karen. What happened to her? Had she fallen into the Templar trap, or was she back in her caravan?

With a few strong strokes, I reached the shore. I got out of the water and ran to my vehicle. Quietly, so as not to wake the boys and Eve and Anka, I changed into clean clothes. Then, I headed to the Petersen encampment.

As I approached, I slowed down and took cover among the trees: if the person who had cut my rope was here, it was necessary to make him think that he had killed me. Perhaps then, my sudden reappearance might shake him into betraying himself?

As I approached the edge of the forest, I saw a table set before the camper and Petersen, Kozlovski, and Anka sitting around it.

Petersen was very agitated.

"Mr. Kozlovski! I ask you again, where is my daughter? Where is Karen, Mr. Kozlovski?"

Kozlovski shrugged his shoulders:

"You can rest assured, Mr. Petersen. I told you: she is in a safe place. I will release her if you write a statement that you make no claims against me."

Petersen extended his large paws toward Kozlovski but did not grab him. He helplessly spread them out on the table and groaned with anger:

"Malinovski, Malinovski! It never crossed my mind that you are Malinovski! Only this young lady managed to unmask you!"

"Look, you can't touch me," laughed Kozlovski. "If anything happens to me, your daughter will die of starvation underground. Do you know how terrible death from starvation is? So, Mr. Petersen, not only will you not do me any harm, but you will, out of your own free will, write a statement about how delighted you were to cooperate with me. Yes? I, Mr. Petersen, have always considered you and your daughter to be a loonies. Treasure hunting is silly business. Was I not to accept the four hundred dollars that you so readily offered to me in Paris? I took them as Malinovski and quickly left. We should always take money when it is being offered, no? I thought it would all end there, and you would be discouraged from looking for your treasure. But no, you came to Poland and just *happened* to come across me again. I thought, hello, here is the opportunity to pluck you again. So, I volunteered as your translator. My buddy, Valery, followed us on his motorcycle. He beat us all to the teacher's house and secured the document. It seemed obvious you would be prepared to pay for it. The story with the shrine was pretty cool, too, no? To this day, you don't know how that letter ended up there. It seemed to you that Malinovski wore the cap of invisibility."

"Your buddy, Valery, is already in custody," Anka said. "We spoke to him yesterday in Gdansk."

"He will never rat me out," Kozlovski shrugged. "He got caught, but he knows that if I get caught, too, he will not get out of prison for years. And if he can hold his tongue, I'll try to get him a good lawyer. Besides, I didn't tell him to assault Miss Karen at the fiftieth kilometer. He did it on his own initiative, out of stupid greed. He improvised. And that lost him."

"No. That's not what lost him," said Anka. "I had guessed from the beginning who this Malinovski was. I deciphered you back in Milkokuk when, in a conversation with Mr. Wheels, you laid out your philosophy on robbing foreigners of their money. I immediately thought: this Kozlovski is a crook. But then doubts crept in—nobody could not be in several places at once. And only much later did I realize that Malinovski was not one, but two people. But once I realized that everything became clear.

"Now, I never fell for the cap of invisibility business. It was obvious all along that no one could have gotten close to the shrine when all three of you were watching it. And then, guess what, I learned that the first person to approach the shrine in the morning, impatient with the all-night vigil, was—you. Of course, you *knew* there had been no money in the shrine—you had known it even before you all went there. You had prepared the second letter in advance. And all you had to do was walk up to the shrine and call out: "Look! There is a new letter here!" And hand it over to the captain.

"Yet, it was obvious that the letter was not written by your hand. Therefore, I kept my suspicions to myself, deluding myself that perhaps you were innocent. And then, I met a young man on a motorcycle who agreed to take me to Malbork. We arrived there before Mr. Wheels, so this young man had the time to observe the couple in the blue Skoda. He started following them. He caught up with them in the underground and took their letter from France from them.

"Of this, of course, I had no idea. But this young man, this Valery—as you call him—wanted to flirt with me. He arranged a date with me at the restaurant by the Nogat, but then he was told out of the blue that he was to show up at the fifty-kilometer marker. So, he left me a polite note of apology at the restaurant. One look at the handwriting told me that he was Malinovski. I took that and one of the Malinovski notes from the Captain and went to see a graphologist in Warsaw. The graphologist agreed with me that both Malinovski's and my suitor's notes were written by one and the same hand. And then I rejoined you in Kortumovo.

"By that time, the militia was already searching for a young man on a *Yunak*. I gave them the license plate number of the motorcycle. And thus, our friend Valery found himself in custody in Gdansk, and the militia recovered Miss Karen's brooch, watch, and money.

"And now, Mr Kozlovski, they will come here to reclaim you."

"Well, well," said Kozlovski. "They are welcome to it! Captain Petersen is about to write me a letter that he has no claim against me whatsoever."

"Malinovski! Malinovski!" repeated Petersen in helpless rage.

"But even before all this happened," continued Anka, "I thought to myself that an employee of a state travel agency with an excellent knowledge of languages certainly travels abroad quite often. And it turns out that when Malinovski defrauded Mr. Petersen in Paris, you, Mr. Kozlovski, were there with a tour. But that's where your career ended. You were fired by the travel agency on some grounds. And then you attached yourself to Petersen."

"Well, so what?" grumbled Kozlovski. "Since the captain does not make any claims against me, no one will be able to do anything to me. Well, sir, go ahead and write that statement of yours and we will part in harmony. You will get your daughter back, and I will go home peacefully. I don't suppose you want your daughter to starve to death in the cold underground?"

"Perhaps the captain will write such a statement," said Anka. "But how will you escape Mr. Wheels?"

Kozlovski laughed quietly:

"Oh. Don't worry about Mr. Wheels! He is cooling his heels in hell."

"Oh, no!" shouted Anka and rose from the table. "You are not serious!"

Kozlovski shrugged his shoulders:

"I think he fell into some pothole and broke his neck. He's just as loopy as Miss Karen."

Hearing this, I decided to emerge out of my hiding.

"Actually, Mr Malinovski, I am in the best of health," I said.

At this, Kozlovski jumped up from the table. He made to run away, but the captain grabbed him in his paws and held him in place.

"How did you get out?" mumbled Kozlovski, terrified.

"Rope! Rope!" I called out to Anka. "Let's tie him up! He has tried to kill me!"

Anka ran into the camper and fetched a piece of rope. We tied Kozlovski to his chair.

"He knows where my daughter is," the captain said to me. "We can't do him any harm, or she will starve to death."

"I know where your daughter is. I will free her from the underground immediately," I said.

"And then we will skin him!" shouted Petersen.

Kozlovski struggled in his bonds and growled:

"He is lying! He doesn't know where Karen is! Only I can point out her hiding place! Besides, you can't prove anything! I haven't done a thing!"

Petersen and I left Anka to guard Kozlovski and went to the church. We slid the font aside and opened the dungeon. As I had suspected, Karen was in the Templar trap. She had ignored my advice, entered the underground corridor through the well, and the iron trapdoor cut off her escape.

When we rotated the baptismal font, Karen—dusty, dirty, and terrified for having spent several hours underground—emerged.

She was quiet, shaken; a different girl from the Karen I had known. She had spent a terrible night in the underworld, at times losing hope that she would ever be freed. The proximity of the skeleton of a man who had starved to death and the thought that—perhaps—the same fate awaited her unsettled her nerves. Crying, she threw herself into the captain's arms.

"Let's go away from here! Right away! I think I am done looking for this treasure," she said. Captain Petersen stroked her head and muttered:

"Well, well, my child. I've always told you that treasure hunting is not an occupation for girls. We'll leave immediately. I'll only skin Malinovski first."

And he told Karen about the unmasking of Kozlovski, and the demand he had made as a price of her release.

I kept quiet about Kozlovski's attempt to murder me in the well. After all, I would have had to explain how I got out of there, and that would have meant revealing the secret of the second corridor. I preferred to keep quiet about it. Karen was an ambitious girl, and she had wanted so badly to find the Templar cache. She would have been completely heartbroken to learn that it was me—not her—who had found the treasure.

Her story was just as I had assumed. Together with Kozlovski, she broke into the cellar and lowered herself down the well. She then swung open the iron trapdoor, and it closed behind her. For a while, she deluded herself into thinking that Kozlovski would guess that she had fallen into the trap and would come to free her. However, as hours passed, she heard the clatter of footsteps overhead, but release did not come. She came to the conclusion that perhaps something bad had happened to Kozlovski as well, and then she lost all hope of getting out of the underground. From then on, she was overwhelmed by the terrifying thought of dying of starvation. She vowed to herself that if, by some miracle, she found herself at large again, she would abandon the treasure-hunting business.

"It brings bad luck," she said to me. "This treasure brought down the Templar Order. It will bring joy to no one. I advise you to abandon the search, too."

Petersen winked at me and, rubbing his hands, said:

"And now, Mr. Wheels, let's go torture Malinovski. How do you feel about skinning him alive?"

I liked this project very much. I summoned the boys and Eve—they had already woken up and even eaten breakfast. We gathered at the Petersen camp, where Kozlovski still sat tied to his chair.

The captain stripped to the waist because—he told Kozlovski—"skinning was a messy business." Squirrel climbed a tree to hang an intricate tangle of ropes from the branch, as the captain had instructed him. Kozlovski was to hang because, the captain explained, "it is easiest to skin in the hanging position."

At first, Kozlovski followed our actions with rather indifferent expression. But when Petersen ordered his daughter to boil a bucket of water, he regained his voice and asked:

"Why do you need hot water?"

"Oh, you see, the skin needs to be scalded with boiling water first. Then it comes off easier," Petersen said.

"What? You are joking! You are not going to skin me, are you?" yelled Kozlovski. The captain shrugged his shoulders:

"Until now, you had the upper hand. Now, I do."

And, with a serious look on his face, he began sharpening a long-bladed knife on a whetstone.

And suddenly, Kozlovski became panicky.

"Milita! Help!" he yelled.

But we were pretty far out of the village and the only person to hear us was the priest's housekeeper, who now came into the encampment. Her face was red with anger.

"Someone broke into my cellar!" she declared, measuring us with a suspicious gaze. And then, seeing Kozlovski tied up in a chair, she yelled:

"Why, if this is not Mr. Konfiturski! It must be him! He kept prowling about my cellar all day yesterday! But why is he tied up? Has he done some mischief to you?"

"I do not know if it can be called mischief," I replied. "This gentleman is a robber, a thief, and an attempted murderer. We are going to skin him alive."

"What?" cried out the astonished housekeeper. "You will what?

You will *skin* him? But why?"

"Because these are Danish customs, Ma'am," I replied.

The hostess felt sorry for Kozlovski. She folded her arms and began to plead:

"Well, that's not very nice. Yes, he did break into my cellar, but he didn't take any jam. Go easy on him."

The imploring voice of the housekeeper irritated Kozlovski even more. He jerked in his bonds and hissed angrily:

"Will you stop with your stupid jam already? Do you think the whole world thinks of nothing but your stupid jam?"

"Oh?" the housekeeper got angry. "You sit here tied up like a hog but hiss like a viper. I plead with these people to take pity on you, and you call me stupid?"

She untied her apron and proceeded to slap Kozlovski across the head and back with it.

"There, take this! You burglar! You thief!"

And just at that moment, a militia car pulled into the clearing. A mustachioed officer jumped out of it—the same one who had interrogated us in Malbork.

"Good citizens!" he cried out with disapproval. "Yes, Mr. Kozlovski is facing serious charges, but is it fair to whip him with an old rag?"

"This is not a rag! This is an apron," the housekeeper explained.

"Very well, an apron, then. Still, you shouldn't be doing this."

He untangled the knots of Kozlovski's bonds and replaced them with shiny new handcuffs.

"Your friend Valery has told us very many interesting things about you. They require some explanation. So you understand that I have to take you with me."

Kozlovski did not resist when the militiamen showed him to a seat in their car. He got in docilely without casting a single glance at us.

"And you," the officer turned to us, "will receive a special summons to give testimony concerning the charges against Mr. Kozlovski. As for the gold watch and the diamond brooch, Miss Petersen must collect them in person at the Provincial Headquarters in Gdansk. She will receive them against a receipt."

They drove off.

Captain Petersen jumped into his trailer and brought out a bottle of cognac.

"Let's celebrate! We are about to leave. First to Gdansk, and then to Warsaw. From there to Paris, and then on to Matanzas Bay. Recovering gold from old galleons is a far better business than searching for Templar treasure."

Karen didn't say anything, but she seemed to share her father's opinion.

"And we?" William Tell asked.

"We, too, will break camp," I said. "We will go with the Petersens as far as the road to Gdansk."

At noon, a small cavalcade left the village of Kortumovo. In front went the Lincoln pulling the caravan, and behind came my vehicle with my friends.

The boys and Eve consoled themselves as best they could.

"It's OK that we did not find the treasure," said Hawkeye. "The most important thing is that we had some wonderful adventures. It isn't about finding. It's about searching, isn't it, Mr. Thomas?"

"That's right," I nodded.

"We also learned a lot about the military orders and about the Yotvingians," Tell said. "And when we study the Teutonic Knights in school, we will remember the night we spent in Malbork Castle!"

"And I," said Anka, who was sitting next to me, "I have enough material for several articles about loonie treasure hunters. And about a swindler who fooled them all. The concluding article will end with the scene of the swindler's arrest, and the final sentence will be: 'Your treasure is where your heart is.' And, I wonder, Mr. Thomas. Where is your heart? Maybe in the car in front of us?"

I replied:

"If I were you, Miss Anka, I would wait a little with writing the ending of your article."

"Oh?" she asked and blushed a little.

But I didn't have time to explain. Before us, we saw the wide-spreading Vistula and a huge bridge over it, and to our left, the picturesque town of Helmno shining on a hill.

Here, we said goodbye. The Petersens went to Gdansk. And I, the boys, Eva, and Anka, went to Helmno.

I parked in the center, left my friends to explore, and went into the post office to place a call to a certain high-ranking official at the National Museum in Warsaw. Our conversation lasted quite a long time. Finally, I left the post office and got behind the wheel of the vehicle.

"Now, where to?" Anka asked.

"Why, back to Kortumovo, of course," I replied.

"What for?" exclaimed the astonished boys.

"What do you mean: for what? To collect the treasure!" I grinned.

Anka shrugged.

"You are a bigger nut than I had imagined!"

By evening we pulled up in Kortumovo, a small village on a large lake. Murders of black crows cawed in the huge poplars next to the old church. The parish priest walked slowly along the path to the rectory, and in the priest's garden, on a line hung up between two apple trees, his housekeeper hung out to dry white altar cloths.

A quiet, picturesque corner, a large sheet of lake with flocks of wild swans, and all around, the green of rushes, and meadows, and of the dark forest. And yet it was here, to this tiny village, that the threads of our plot had brought us, threads tangled centuries ago by the tragic fate of Jacob de Molay, the ambitions of Grand Master Siegfried von Feuchtwangen, who wanted to erect the capital of *Cor Tuum* here, and the fate of Werner von Orseln, murdered in the doorway of the church in Malbork. 'Your treasure is where your heart is' was inscribed by Feuchtwangen on an iron crucifix given to de Molay. And I thought:

But my heart is always where adventures lie.

CODA: HOTEL EUROPE

Hotel Europe (Europejski), now the Raffles Hotel in Warsaw.
A Warsaw landmark built between 1855-1877.

It was a warm, sunny morning. Karen and I were sitting in the café-garden of Hotel Europe in Warsaw. We were drinking coffee. On her wrist, I saw her gold watch, and on her blouse, her brooch with diamonds.

"My father wants me to take part in his new expedition," she said. "But extracting gold from sunken ships is not an occupation for me. Diving for old galleons is boring. It requires great physical stamina and lots of patience. Machines blow the silt away, and then you have to go underwater and enter the decaying hulls. It's hard physical labor. But I am interested in what puzzles the intellect."

She noticed that I was looking at her brooch.

"Yes," she nodded at my thoughts. "I made a deposition in connection with the arrest of Kozlovski and his accomplice. Oh God, how naive I was to listen to his advice. My only consolation is that you also fell for his deceptions."

"Probably because I disliked him," I said. "From the very beginning, he seemed really unsympathetic to me. I pushed my suspicions away because I felt that they stemmed from my dislike for him. He had an important advantage over us because he participated in all our meetings and knew our every move in advance. And yet, we had clues if we only cared to look. For example, I saw Kozlovski kayaking near that island in the reeds on Lake Milkokuk. But neither then nor later was I prepared to connect the dots that Kozlovski was in cahoots with the burglar. Do you know that he tried to kill me?"

"Who? The burglar?"

"No. Kozlovski. I think that what happened at the fifty-kilometer mark convinced Kozlovski that I was more dangerous than he had thought. On a couple of occasions, I nearly thwarted his plans. Both times, they worked out only because of your distrust of me. So he decided to neutralize me."

"*Neutralize* you? How? When?"

"That night, when you went down the well, I hurried into the cellar after you because I was afraid you would fall into the Templar trap. I saw the rope hanging in the well and assumed that both of you had gone down and decided to follow you. But I was wrong. Only you had gone down. Kozlovski had stayed behind. In the darkness of the cellar, I did not see him. But when I lowered myself into the well, he cut the rope. I fell into the water, and then—then he threw huge rocks down the shaft in order to kill me."

Karen squinted as she usually did when she suspected that I was fooling her.

"Mr. Wheels," she said. "That's quite a story. And how did you get out of the well?"

I shrugged.

"The scouts found me and pulled me out."

She shook her head:

"You don't know how to lie, Mr. Wheels. You are hiding something. Tell me the truth: you have found the treasure. You know where it is, don't you? But you do not want to tell me about it because you want to spare me the disappointment. Because I have so much wanted to find it."

I felt sorry for Karen.

"No, no, that's not true. I don't know anything about the treasure," I wriggled.

"Please be honest," she said, taking my hand in hers. "I want to know everything. Was there another corridor? Lower down?"

"Yes."

"You see, it just occurred to me this morning. And on my way here to meet you, I planned to suggest to you that we go back to Kortumovo together. But you have already been there, haven't you?"

"You are right. There is a second passage, lower down, just above the water table. I saw it when I fell into the well. I climbed in and found a different room with its own exit to the church. That exist is just behind the altar."

"And the treasure?"

"In that second room, on one of the walls, I found a sign indicating *two treasures*. We removed the bricks and found a box with liturgical vessels. Ten gold chalices set with precious stones, mostly rubies and emeralds. And a chest of five hundred French florins of Philip the Fair."

French golden florin, showing Philip the Fair seated frontally, crowned, holding a scepter in his right hand and a lily in his left, between two French dynastic lillies. This 4.7-gram coin was issued in 1305.

"And—that's it?" said Karen with disbelief. "That was the legendary

Templar treasure? Ten chalices and five hundred coins? I expected urns and urns filled with jewels and pearls and golden rings.”

“Perhaps the Templars weren’t as rich as Philip the Fair had imagined?” I said. “Maybe the immeasurable wealth of the Order is just a tall tale? Anyway, the Templars were bankers, so most of ther assets were loans and promissory notes, not cash.”

“Or maybe this isn’t *the* Templar treasure at all.”

“*Your treasure is where your heart is,*” I said. “I keep thinking about those words. Who knows if they don’t hide another meaning? The trick with two corridors sheds some useful light on how the Templars hid their secrets. The first corridor was a trap into which we all fell. We both knew to lower ourselves to a depth of nine yards and yet when we spotted the first opening, we forgot the information contained in the sign and entered that corridor. So, I am thinking that perhaps this humble treasure we found is a trick? Perhaps it is meant to satisfy the person who finds it, to feed his greed and pride, and to make him think that he has found *the* legendary Templar treasure? While the real treasure continues to lie in peace, waiting for the one who will be guided by his heart?”

“What an extraordinary idea,” whispered Karen.

Among the tables of the café, we saw Captain Petersen walking towards us. He beamed at the sight of me and patted me on the back.

“Tomorrow, we’re off,” he declared cheerfully. “Let’s drink to that. By this time tomorrow, we will be very far away. And in a week, I will be at sea. I have received confidential information about a sunken Nazi submarine off the coast of Argentina. It fled Germany in the closing weeks of the war with a cargo of valuables looted in Europe. I guess it will be worth looking into?”

“Of course, Father,” said Karen. “But next summer, let’s come here again. Let’s continue to explore the mysteries of the Templars. Only, this time, I don’t think Mr. Thomas will refuse to cooperate with us?” she turned to me.

“It’s a deal,” I said, and I extended my hand to her. “Next year, we will go on a new expedition. And in the same company, it seems,” I added at the sight of Anka entering the cafe.

She was beaming, too.

"My editor approved my treasure hunt articles for publication. He liked them very much," she said, sitting down with us, and I raised my hands to my head in a gesture of grief.

"Dear God! And I hoped that your articles would be rejected. I can just imagine what you wrote about us."

"Oh, don't worry. Only Kozlovski and his accomplice will have a reason to be dissatisfied," she laughed.

At this, we all laughed with relief. And then, we laughed again because we realized that we had become good friends.

**HERE ENDS BOOK 1
OF THE ADVENTURES OF
THE LEGENDARY POLISH DETECTIVE
MR. WHEELS**

I hope you enjoyed this wonderful book. It has been a great pleasure to translate and publish it for you. If you like my taste in books and the way I publish them, you may be interested in other books I have published.

Joe Alex
The Ships of Minos

This five-volume series tells the tale of a 1600 B.C. journey of exploration: Minoan adventurers sailing up the river systems of Eastern Europe in search of the sources of amber. The book, stylized after the *Odyssey* and the *Aeneid*, imagines the world of Eastern and Northern Europe as it must have been three and a half thousand years ago. This epic tale, written by a great translator of English literature and the only man in the world to have translated all of Shakespeare, was first published in 1975. It has since acquired in Eastern Europe a fan following a little akin to that of Tolkien's cycle in English.

Arkady Fiedler
The White Jaguar

In 1726, a Polish-Virginian renegade fleeing the law joined a Stone Age tribe on the Orinoco. This tale of pirates, castaways, runaway slaves, and a European man becoming a full-fledged member of a Latin American Indian tribe is based on a few mentions in old Spanish chronicles and oral traditions preserved among the Arawak of Guyana and Venezuela.

Its author, Arkady Fiedler, was a traveler and a best-selling writer with special love and experience of the Amazon region.

Witold Makowiecki
Fleeing Carthage

Written during the dark days of German occupation, the two volumes of tales about the adventures of Greek youths set in Greece, Italy, Asia Minor, Carthage, and Egypt in the middle of the fifth century B.C. draw a wonderful, entertaining, and humorous picture of the Mediterranean world in the Classical Age. Their literary accomplishment and historical accuracy have made them part of the school curriculum. Pick up your copy today and enjoy the nefarious political plots, mysterious Oriental priests, Olympic games, runaway slaves, garrulous merchants, chases at sea, and the heroism of war.

Jacek Bocheński
The Notorious Roman Trilogy

Jacek Bocheński's great trilogy, set in the waning decades of the Roman Republic and the first decades of the Roman Empire, is arguably the most important literary work to emerge out of Eastern Europe since

World War Two. Written in a beautiful experimental style reminiscent of Kazuo Ishiguro and Orhan Pamuk, the books have not merely served to delight. Its first volume--on the career of Julius Caesar--was taken by the communist authorities as a criticism of the system and banned, causing a furor and turning the book into highly sought-after contraband; it also set its author on the unintended career of a political dissident which was to make him one of the leading figures of the Solidarity movement.

Aleksander Krawczuk
Aleksander's Antiquities

Aleksander Krawczuk (1922-2023) was an institution: a scholar, professor at the Jagiellonian University in Krakow, minister of culture of Poland (1986-1989), and author of over 30 immensely popular books on Graeco-Roman antiquity. His delightful, accessible, conversational, highly readable style, addressing complex topics in an approachable manner without ever dumbing them down, made antiquity come alive to both professionals and fans but also to ordinary readers who normally take no interest in the period. International best-sellers in Eastern Europe, his books have shaped three generations of antique lovers, but, as a consequence of Soviet cultural policies, they appear in English only now.

Maria Rodziewiczówna
The Wonderful World of Maria Ro

Maria Rodziewiczówna (1864-1944) was a daughter of Polish gentry in today's Belarus, then Russian Empire. Dispossessed by Russians and exiled with her family to Siberia as a child, she was entirely self-taught. Orphaned, she returned to Poland aged 18, where she inherited a badly mismanaged estate of over 6,000 acres, cut her hair off, donned man's clothing, and took over the management of the property. She proved an excellent farm manager and tough but fair leader of men. She paid off debt, introduced modern agricultural techniques, built roads, hospitals, and churches, led the Boy Scout movement, propagated Theosophy, and wrote over forty books. She was one of the most successful authors of her time and most of her books remain in print today. Hated by the right for her unconventional lifestyle (she was a lesbian and lived in a menage a trois with two other women) and by the left for her staunch anti-communism and her commitment to traditional forms of religious piety, she remains one of the best known and widest-read Polish writers forty years after her death.

www.ingramcontent.com/pod-product-compliance
Lightning Source LLC
LaVergne TN
LVHW010317200726
843507LV00010B/1256